"Do you still want to go for a drive?" Tyler asked.

"Not tonight."

"Then how about me coming over tomorrow or the next day and looking at those blueprints?"

"Sure." Sarah walked him to the door and was almost afraid to look out in case another gift bag had been left, which was absurd because the police had only departed a few minutes earlier. "Good night, Tyler."

He hesitated, staring at her mouth.

Sarah gave it a brief moment of thought before rising on her toes and planting a thorough kiss on his lips. After all, there was no point in being coy, and it would be a much better ending to the evening than a creepy gift.

His arms went around her and he deepened the kiss. Every inch of her skin burned and the response from his body was unmistakable.

Dear Reader,

It probably isn't a surprise that I enjoy writing about large families. (Was that a big "duh" I just heard?) Sarah Fullerton enjoys her many relatives in my third Poppy Gold story. She is open and loving, despite a bad marriage, and very busy running her dream business. I've paired Sarah with Tyler Prentiss, a man who struggles to be close to anyone, much less his own small family. Tyler has several concerns, including a grieving mother and a brother recovering from serious military-related injuries, but he can't restrain his protective instincts when Sarah is threatened.

I hope to write more Poppy Gold stories in the future, as well as revisit the Hollister family from my series Those Hollister Boys. Lots of stories, just never enough time to tell them all!

Classic Movie Alert: share a smile with me by watching *Bringing Up Baby*, starring Katharine Hepburn and Cary Grant. Cary is a paleontologist whose life is turned upside down by a madcap heiress and a leopard.

Please check out my Facebook page at Facebook.com/julianna.morris.author. Readers can also contact me at c/o Harlequin Books, 225 Duncan Mill Road, Don Mills, ON M3B 3K9, Canada.

Julianna Morris

JULIANNA MORRIS

Bachelor Protector

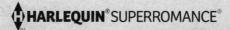
HARLEQUIN® SUPERROMANCE®

Recycling programs
for this product may
not exist in your area.

ISBN-13: 978-0-373-64034-8

Bachelor Protector

Copyright © 2017 by Julianna Morris

Printed in U.S.A.

www.Harlequin.com

Julianna Morris isn't crazy about housework, but she enjoys home canning because it connects her to the farming and pioneering roots of her ancestors. Of course, this conflicts with everything else she enjoys, including hiking, traveling, reading, painting and photography. But the way Julianna sees it, she'd rather have too much to do than too little. One thing is sure—she'll never be bored!

Books by Julianna Morris

HARLEQUIN SUPERROMANCE

The Ranch Solution
Honor Bound

Those Hollister Boys

Jake's Biggest Risk
Challenging Matt
Winning Over Skylar

Poppy Gold Stories

Christmas with Carlie
Undercover in Glimmer Creek

Other titles by this author available in ebook format.

In loving memory of Burt and Emily

PROLOGUE

SARAH FULLERTON PRESSED a finger to her forehead, trying to concentrate.

In the past four years, she'd gone from running a small sweet shop with two employees to overseeing a bakery and catering business with more than twenty employees. The front of the shop looked the same as before, but the operation behind it had become a monster.

A loud clatter out in the main kitchen made her jump.

"Sorry about that," called Gabby Michaelson, one of the shift supervisors. "Just dropped some pans. No harm done."

Except to my nerves, Sarah thought, pushing the order forms away. She'd hoped to finish her office work during regular hours, but it would have to wait.

Lately she'd begun to daydream about getting a full night's sleep. While the business was booming, it was partly due to nepotism. The nearby Poppy Gold Bed and Breakfast Inns was owned by relatives, and they'd contracted with her to provide all the food needed at the facility. Now their kitchens were quiet most of the time and hers were insane.

Granted, things were crazier than normal right now because her aunt, who'd been helping to manage the shop, had recently broken her leg. It would get better when Aunt Babs came back. *If* she came back. She'd asked Sarah to look for a permanent replacement for her, but it wasn't easy finding an experienced office manager in Glimmer Creek.

"Sarah, can you help Aurelia?" Gabby called. "With David out, she's swamped. A bunch of customers just came in, and we're filling éclairs for that special order."

With a tired sigh, Sarah got up and went out front, a babble of voices greeting her from the waiting area.

Sarah's Sweet Treats was on the edge of the Glimmer Creek historic district and the tour buses parked nearby, so they got groups coming and going. She usually had two employees at the counter, but David had called in sick and Aurelia was trying to handle everything herself.

"I'm sure you'll love the fudge," said a familiar voice. Sarah's eyes widened—it was Rosemary Prentiss, a Poppy Gold Inns guest she'd talked with several times. "The cappuccino flavor is my favorite," Rosemary continued. "I also love the banana muffins. They're wonderfully moist and have chunks of dried apricot."

"Those sound delicious, too. I'll take four."

Rosemary had been visiting the sweet shop for the past several days, sitting and drinking tea for extended periods. Now she was behind the display counters, boxing a selection of fudge and muffins. She handed the containers to Aurelia to ring up at the cash register and cheerfully greeted the next customers in line.

Once again she efficiently filled the order, her enticing descriptions of the baked goods convincing the older couple to order a dozen peanut butter cookies, a caramel apple pie and a pan of bread pudding.

Sarah shook off her surprise and stepped forward. "I can take over, Rosemary, but thanks for helping," she said. "It's awfully nice of you."

Rosemary smiled. "I don't mind staying. We're doing fine. Aurelia is handling the cash register, and I can manage the rest. I'm sure you have other work to do."

Aurelia Fullerton, one of Sarah's many cousins, nodded fervently. "She's a whiz, Sarah. I hope you don't mind."

"Uh, okay."

Nonplussed, Sarah watched for another minute. Rosemary had explained she was staying at Poppy Gold with her youngest son, an Army captain who was recovering from a bomb blast in the Middle East. To give him time alone, she'd been exploring Glimmer Creek.

"Shoo, we've got everything under control," Rosemary ordered, looking happier than Sarah had yet seen her. She'd seemed sad and lonely sitting at a corner table for hours, reading and drinking tea. When Sarah had said hello the first time, Rosemary had even anxiously asked if she was in the way.

Sarah gratefully retreated, thinking she would give Rosemary a gift certificate or selection of baked goods as a thank-you.

Sarah's Sweet Treats had been a lot more fun before it expanded; Sarah wanted to be a baker, not a businesswoman, but she couldn't let her cousin down—Tessa was the owner-manager of Poppy Gold Inns and had wanted to outsource their food needs. And the contract had helped pay off the debts from opening the shop.

Sarah was even starting to save for a rainy day. Sooner or later her frantic schedule would sort itself out, and she'd have more time for the things she loved.

In the smaller secondary kitchen, she began a batch of fudge. She had a swing-shift employee who made candy, but the fudge was a huge seller and they could always use more. Once she got a few of the standard batches made, she might experiment with a new flavor—chocolate, cinnamon and cayenne. Unique recipes were her specialty.

The familiar task was more soothing than office work, and soon she had several pans cooling on the candy rack, including her latest experiment. The challenge was making it zippy enough to wake up the taste buds but not too spicy.

Periodically she went out to check on Rosemary and Aurelia. Sales had remained brisk and she expected to find empty spaces in the display cases, but Rosemary had found time to restock them from the supplies in the back.

"Maybe I should put you on the payroll," Sarah joked in a rare lull between customers.

"I've noticed your Help Wanted sign in the window. How about hiring me?" Rosemary asked, surprising Sarah. Rosemary dressed chicly and wore expensive jewelry. On top of that, Poppy Gold wasn't cheap; this couldn't be a woman who needed a job.

"What about your son?"

"He says he mostly needs peace and quiet and that I drive him crazy when I hover. So I could work afternoons to start and add mornings when he's better."

"I…sure," Sarah said. "If you're serious, I'll get an application."

Rosemary suddenly looked uneasy. "I'm quite

serious. But I've never had a job, so I don't have any references. I've managed numerous fund-raisers though, and I can give you names of people involved with them. I'm sure they'd vouch for me."

"That's fine. I mostly need to do a standard background check."

Sarah went to get the application, unsure if she was batty or desperate. But Rosemary had already shown she was capable, and Sarah believed in listening to her instincts. The one time she hadn't, she'd ended up married to a guy with the conscience of a snake.

As a matter of fact, her ex made snakes look good.

CHAPTER ONE

Tyler Prentiss was frustrated and worried.

His red-eye flight had been delayed coming into the Sacramento International Airport, and then the car rental company had lost his reservation. It took an hour before he was finally able to get a vehicle and head for the small town of Glimmer Creek.

He'd never visited California's Gold Country and wouldn't be going now if his mom and brother hadn't lost their minds. The thought made Tyler wince. It was closer to the truth than he liked.

Rosemary Prentiss had almost suffered a breakdown after his father's death a few months earlier, and now Tyler's younger brother, Nathan, was struggling to recover from post-traumatic stress and injuries received while serving overseas.

The employee at the Poppy Gold Inns reservation desk directed him to the John Muir Cottage where his family was staying in the Yosemite suite. Nathan was sitting in a comfortable chair in the back garden, and Tyler's gut tightened. It had been a month since they'd seen each other, but his brother's face seemed as gaunt as before.

"Hey."

"Hey," Nathan returned tonelessly.

"I was able to come home a few days early and went to the rehab center for a visit, only to learn you'd checked out. You didn't mention it when I called."

"I knew you'd do the big brother thing and try to stop me."

"Yes, if you weren't ready," Tyler couldn't keep from retorting. "I happen to know your doctor didn't want you to leave. One of the patients at the center told me."

Nathan made a rude gesture, which was completely out of character for him. "Screw doctors, I'm sick of 'em. When I said I was checking out of rehab no matter what, Mom got a referral or something to come here."

Tyler looked around. "Where *is* Mom?"

"At a shop called Sarah's Sweet Treats. I didn't like her hanging over me, so she got a job there. Now she's gone most of the day, except when she brings something for lunch and checks in on her breaks. It's much calmer this way."

A job?

Tyler stared. His mother had never worked in her life, and it seemed unlikely she was in any condition to start now considering how shaky she'd been when he'd left for Italy just a few weeks earlier. Lately she'd seemed a little better when he'd phoned, but still anxious and uncertain.

The guilt he felt for even going on the business trip returned full force, but what else could he have done after postponing it twice? He'd designed a private museum in Rome, and his contract required him to spend a certain amount of time on-site. While the clients were sympathetic and had agreed to a shorter period, they'd run out of patience when he'd tried to delay his visit another time. Then he'd needed to leave for a few days in the middle to fly to Illinois for an emergency.

"All day?" Tyler repeated. "As in full time?"

"I guess. The first day she was just gone in the afternoon, and then she asked if I minded her staying away longer. I was all for it. I'm sick of people fussing at me."

It was hard for Tyler to picture their mother being able to focus on anything, much less stick to an eight-hour workday. Rosemary Prentiss was a Washington, DC, socialite—a sweet woman with a short attention span, flitting from one cause to the next. She'd never even balanced her own checkbook or paid a bill, leaving everything to her husband.

When Tyler's father had died, Rosemary had fallen apart. She'd been so unstable, her doctor had considered hospitalization. Then Nathan had gotten injured in Iraq. Needing to concentrate on her son's recuperation had forced her to set aside her grief for a while, but it didn't mean she'd fully recovered, any more than Nathan had.

"I'll go check on her," Tyler said.

Nathan shrugged. "Are you staying?"

"If I can get a room."

"No problem. There are two extra bedrooms in the suite. Mom asked for the largest space available, thinking it would be quieter. That's one of the problems with the hospital and rehab center—it's never really quiet." Nathan put his head back and closed his eyes.

More concerned and frustrated than ever, Tyler looked up Sarah's Sweet Treats on his phone and followed the directions. It occurred to him that he ought to think it through first, but instead he marched inside.

"I need to speak with Rosemary Prentiss," he told the woman at the counter.

"Rosemary isn't available right now."

"She works here, doesn't she?" The question came out harsher than he'd intended.

"Uh, yeah. Let me get the owner."

She hurried into the back, and a minute later another woman appeared. There was a smudge of white on her right temple, and she was wiping her hands on a towel.

Tyler assessed her quickly. Young, probably no more than thirty. Beautiful. Pale blond hair in a French braid. Striking green eyes. She also had an enticing figure, discernible despite the spotless chef's apron wrapped around her.

"Hello, I'm Sarah Fullerton. I own Sarah's Sweet Treats. Can I help you?"

Tyler pushed his physical response to her aside.

"My name is Tyler Prentiss. I want to know what you were thinking, hiring a woman as fragile as my mother to work for you?"

SARAH BLINKED.

Rosemary...*fragile*?

Were they talking about the same person?

Over the past two weeks, Rosemary had saved her sanity. The woman was an organizational marvel, with a quiet way of stepping in wherever needed. While she hadn't been paid to work before, she'd spent most of her adult life running massive charity events, blood donor drives and church bazaars. Apparently marshaling volunteers into line was excellent training for managing the chaos of a bakery-restaurant and catering business.

"I'm sorry, but my employees aren't your concern," Sarah replied carefully.

"They are if my mother is one of them. There are safety issues to consider, along with everything else. I don't want her exhausting herself in a hot, crowded kitchen."

Sarah glanced at Aurelia who was watching wide-eyed. Other customers also appeared to be watching with varying levels of interest.

"Let's step outside," Sarah said in a tight tone. She didn't appreciate scenes, particularly in front of her patrons.

"Just tell me where my mother is and we'll *both* get out of here."

His arrogance took Sara's breath away. "What are you going to do, issue an order and expect Rosemary to follow it?"

"I'm going to reason with her. You can't possibly understand the situation."

"I understand you're a chauvinistic jackass— how's *that* for a start?" she shot back, quickly losing the battle to control her temper. Rosemary had talked often about her son the architect, but she hadn't mentioned he was utterly impossible.

"Sarah certainly has figured you out, my darling," said Rosemary. She'd returned from a visit to the office supply store and was glaring at her son. Sarah was reminded of her iron-willed grandmother who'd helped raise her. Yet Rosemary's expression softened when she gestured to the red scar at her son's hairline.

"What happened? You didn't tell me you'd had an accident."

He snorted. "You didn't say anything about coming to California, either. We've talked every day since I left, and the subject never came up?"

Rosemary turned pink. "I knew you were busy and didn't want to distract you. How did you get hurt?"

"It isn't important. I'm fine." He lowered his voice. "Look, you *have* to realize your doctor wouldn't approve of you working. And I know that Nathan checked out of rehab against medical advice. So let's go back to the suite and pack your things. We can leave in the morning."

Rosemary shook her head. "I'm *not* going anywhere, and I'm sure Nathan wants to stay, too. Besides, I have a job now. Responsibilities."

"You aren't strong enough to hold any sort of job, much less do the kind of labor this place must require."

"What do you think I'm doing here, scrubbing floors with a rag and toting hundred-pound sacks of flour?"

"It doesn't matter. Nathan needs to go back in rehab. That's where he belongs, and I'm sure you want to be near him."

"He wasn't getting better in that place and wanted to leave."

Sarah bit the inside of her cheek to keep from

laughing. The men in her family could be opinionated and old-fashioned, but Rosemary's son made them look like models of modern thinking by comparison. Of course…Tyler Prentiss might have a point if his brother wasn't following medical orders, but he wasn't going to fix the situation by acting this way.

"Nathan needs professional care," Tyler said. "I've got plane tickets for tomorrow. We're going back to DC."

Rosemary crossed her arms over her stomach. "Enjoy your flight."

"I have tickets for *all* of us."

Whoa.

Sarah had never seen someone actually talk between clenched teeth before, but Tyler Prentiss was doing a credible job of being rock-jawed and speaking at the same time. It was too bad to see so much striking masculine appeal wasted on a guy like him.

When she'd first seen him—before he'd opened his big mouth—she'd actually felt a flash of awareness. Tyler was tall and classically handsome, with a strong bone structure. Paired with his dark hair and cool brown eyes, she'd found him quite compelling…until he'd started talking.

Tyler turned and focused on her again. "Please understand, Ms. Fullerton, my mother's doctor told her to avoid stress. She's had a difficult time since my fath—"

"Richard Tyler Prentiss," Rosemary interrupted. "This is my place of employment, so unless you're going to buy some of the delicious goods we sell here, please leave."

"Fine. We'll talk later." He stomped out the door with a grim expression.

As soon as he was gone, Rosemary began to deflate. "I'm sorry my son made a scene, Sarah. Tyler means well, and I'm sure he'll regret this when he calms down. Please don't fire me."

"I don't fire employees because their sons behave badly," Sarah assured. "In fact, I'm promoting you to assistant manager. My aunt won't mind. She's been hoping I'd hire someone in her place. You can focus on the office, supplies and coordination the way you've been doing, and I'll manage the kitchen."

Rosemary beamed. "In that case, I'd better get busy."

She hurried away and Sarah rolled her shoulders to relax them, but before she could return to her baking, Great-Uncle Milt arrived.

"I heard you had a disruptive customer and came to help," he announced.

"Thanks, but everything has been resolved." Sarah had to rise on her tiptoes to give him a kiss. He was extremely tall, with a shock of thick white hair and a pair of youthful blue eyes. Folks in Glimmer Creek referred to him as the Big Kid, though as Glimmer Creek's recently retired police chief, he could be stern about the law. Not that he was *completely* retired. The town had given Great-Uncle Milt the title of Police Chief Emeritus at his retirement ceremony.

"What happened?"

She tugged him out to the front sidewalk and explained, not wanting Rosemary to hear the comments being made about her eldest son.

"I'll check into this fellow," Great-Uncle Milt declared when she finished, his eyebrows drawn together.

"It's fine. I'm sure he won't be a problem," Sarah said, though she was still annoyed that Tyler Prentiss had tried to interfere. She'd like to give him a sharp kick in the rear.

"Nevertheless, I'll talk to the new police chief about it," Great-Uncle Milt insisted. "I won't have some stranger upsetting things around here."

"If it makes you feel better," Sarah said, yet the corners of her mouth twitched. The "new" police chief was Zach Williams…Great-Uncle Milt's grandson. Zach was her second cousin, though in Glimmer Creek family was family. Period. And in-laws were relatives the same as anybody else. Great-Uncle Milt just didn't like emphasizing the connection in case folks thought his grandson had gotten the job because of the relationship.

Yet Sarah's humor faded as she thought about her cousin's wife. Gina had died from a ruptured ectopic pregnancy. Zach had never been the same.

It was worse to bury a spouse than get divorced, but at least he remembered his wife with love, instead of the loathing Sarah felt for Douglas.

TYLER PACED THE GARDEN around the John Muir Cottage until his brother barked at him to go away. Inside the large Victorian farmhouse, he couldn't find an informational booklet, so he called the Poppy Gold registration desk to get the Wi-Fi password. He had to do *something* while waiting for his mother to return.

Did she really think sunshine and fresh air would be enough to help Nathan?

Tyler frowned as he worked at the table in the suite's kitchen. When Nathan had been in the military hospital, he and his mother had taken shifts so someone would be with him around the clock. She stayed days, while Tyler had stayed nights.

He'd never forget the first time he'd seen Nathan in the throes of a violent nightmare…groaning, thrashing, striking out violently. Sometimes yelling, revealing hints of the horrors he'd lived through. Even his less-intense nightmares had been disturbing to witness.

After that, Tyler had done research on PTSD. Nightmares occurred in a fairly large percentage of cases, and since Nathan was an expert in hand-to-hand combat, it wasn't safe to get near him while he was experiencing one.

The minutes passed slowly, and finally the side door off the utility room opened. His mother walked in, bright and chipper, though her cheery expression faltered when she looked at him.

"You owe Sarah an apology," she said flatly. "And you owe me one, too. I can't believe you'd embarrass me like that."

"I can't believe you and Nathan would fly to California without a word," Tyler retorted. "Three months ago you were still so distraught about Dad that you asked me to postpone going to Rome a second time. You didn't want me out of the area for even a few weeks."

Rosemary raised her chin. "I just felt it was too soon after Nathan had gone into rehab and that you should be there. But yes, I was also still upset about your father. I'd lost my best friend and the love of my life. Can you blame me for not being able to handle it right away?"

Tyler frowned.

While he'd respected his father, the idea of his parents enjoying such a close relationship was a challenge. When would they have found time? Richard Prentiss had often worked ninety hours a week, though admittedly, some of his work had included schmoozing with clients, his wife at his side. He'd been a lawyer, greatly in demand. More than anything he'd wanted his sons to go into practice with him, but Tyler had wanted to be an architect and Nathan a soldier.

Still, Tyler was willing to believe his parents had been closer than he'd realized. It would certainly explain why his mom had fallen apart so badly.

"I'm not blaming you," Tyler said carefully. "On the other hand, I don't think getting a job on a whim is the answer. What are you planning to do, move here?"

"Perhaps. Glimmer Creek is a nice town."

"I don't think you'd like it for long. The nearest place to buy designer accessories has to be fifty miles away."

"Is that what you really think of me?" Rosemary asked sadly. "I needed to dress a certain way because it was important to your father that I looked like a successful attorney's wife, but I've never cared that much about stylish clothes and jewelry. I thought you understood."

Tyler didn't know what he understood. At the moment he was exhausted, jet-lagged and his career was on shaky ground. He supposed there was a certain truth to his mother's claim, though. His parents' social circle would have expected them to be perfectly dressed.

"In case you haven't noticed, I'm wearing sensible shoes." Rosemary lifted a foot. "Kurt got them for me when he went shopping in Stockton."

The comment went over Tyler's head for an instant then he frowned. "Who's Kurt?"

"Sarah's father, Kurt Fullerton. He manages the Poppy Gold greenhouses and working gardens, but he also helps the bakery by shopping down in Stockton for specialty items. He's a lovely man."

The warmth in her voice made Tyler pause. "Are you dating him?"

It might explain a lot.

The disappointment in his mother's eyes deepened. "Your father has only been gone for eight months. While some people are ready to move on that quickly, I'm not one of them. Kurt and I met two weeks ago at the bakery. Hard as it may be for you to understand, men and women can just be friends."

Tyler worked with both men and women, but he couldn't claim any of them as friends. He didn't *have* that many friends, even from college. After he'd rejected law school, his father had refused to pay for his education. So Tyler had worked and borrowed his way through college, which hadn't left time for socializing.

"I still don't see why it's so important for you to work," he said. "If you want to get involved with something again, what about your causes back home? Surely they need you."

"I'm needed here." Rosemary's face lit up. "I hear Nathan outside with Kurt. They often spend time together in the afternoon."

"Maybe I should meet him."

"Fine, but mind your manners. I'll freshen up and be out in a minute." She hurried upstairs.

Tyler's head ached worse as he stepped into the garden and saw a burly fellow talking to his brother. *This* was the guy his mom called "a lovely man"? He certainly didn't resemble the petite blonde at the sweet shop. Sarah Fullerton was slender with an elfin face, while her muscular father would look right at home in a Hells Angels jacket and straddling a Harley-Davidson.

Kurt and Nathan were deep in a debate about the merits of Humvees versus the earlier jeeps used by the military, and for the first time in months, Tyler saw animation in his brother's face.

Fullerton looked up. "I'm guessing you're the brother."

Since he hadn't said "chauvinistic jackass,"

Kurt probably didn't know what had happened at Sarah's Sweet Treats.

"Tyler Prentiss." He put his hand out, and Kurt shook it with the strangling grip of a wrestler. "It sounds as if you've been in the service."

"I'm retired army."

"Kurt was in Kosovo and did a couple of tours in the Middle East," Nathan interjected. "He saw more than his share of action."

The older man sighed heavily. "We've all seen too much." He stood as Tyler's mother came through the door. "Good afternoon, Rosemary."

"Good afternoon." She smiled and pointed to her feet. "The shoes you picked out are wonderful."

Kurt Fullerton looked abashed. "I just got what Sarah told me was comfortable."

Tyler stepped back and watched his mom chat with Kurt, trying to decide if there was an underlying thread of flirtation. Friendship was one thing, but he wanted to know a whole lot more about Fullerton if something serious was going on. After all, his mother was a financially comfortable widow who was shockingly naive for a woman her age.

Nathan had become quiet again, the hollow expression creeping back into his eyes.

Hellfire. Why had he become a soldier instead of something safer? Yet even as the thought crossed Tyler's mind, an uneasy sensation followed. He'd defended Nathan's decision to enlist, saying it had to be his choice.

"Sarah mentioned that you've been promoted," Kurt said to Rosemary. "Assistant manager, no less. Not bad."

Rosemary sent a smug look in her eldest son's direction. "That's right. I love working for your daughter."

"She's a good kid, all right."

A promotion?

Pain pounded in Tyler's head. This would make it even harder to convince his mother to leave. She might be doing all right at the moment, but her moods had been wildly erratic since being widowed. For a while she'd be like her old self, then something would happen and she'd fall apart. It seemed unlikely that she'd drastically improved in the few weeks he'd been gone.

Perhaps he should try enlisting Sarah Fullerton's help rather than antagonizing her, though he wasn't sure what she could do. But at least if she fully understood the situation, she might be more supportive.

Of course, first he'd have to convince her that he wasn't the chauvinistic jackass she'd accused him of being. And since he'd not only stuck his foot in his mouth but jammed it all the way down his throat, it might take some doing.

SARAH SLID INTO her bathtub that evening, feeling utterly decadent. She hadn't enjoyed a long soak since her business had gone crazy, but thanks to Rosemary Prentiss, she might be getting her life back.

Imagine, she'd actually gotten six hours of sleep the night before. *Six.* She might have gotten seven if her cat hadn't demanded treats at 2:00 a.m.

She looked over and saw Theo's whiskered face gazing at her from the basket of clean laundry she'd brought upstairs.

"Thanks, Theo, I really wanted to wash that stuff again."

He yawned, stretched out his front legs and rested his chin on them, a vision of smug contentment.

Sarah smiled and closed her eyes, reveling in the warm water and silence. She loved her business, but it was no longer quiet there, day or night. The shop was open for customers nine to five thirty, but the kitchen operated twenty-four hours a day.

The phone rang abruptly, and Theo lifted his head with a reproachful meow.

She considered not answering since she'd been

getting numerous calls from an "unavailable" number—mostly silent messages on her voice mail—and figured they were telemarketing robo-calls. Then she realized it was almost nine, which was a little late.

"Sorry, toots." She scrambled out of the tub and grabbed the receiver, shrugging into her robe. "Hello?"

Silence.

Irritation filled her. It probably *was* a robo-caller, checking to see when she was home so a "live" telemarketer would know when to reach her. Still, silent calls made her uneasy. Her ex-husband had used them to check on her a dozen times a day, paranoid that she might be cheating.

What a joke. *He'd* been the one cheating. He'd also used other tricks to frighten and control her. It had taken a long time after the divorce to stop being afraid of every odd occurrence.

Sarah looked at the caller ID log and saw the number was shown as unavailable, just like all the other calls. With an effort, she pushed the thought away and looked at Theo.

"Come to bed," she told him.

As a male companion, he lacked certain qualities, but he slept next to her every night instead of tomcatting around like her ex. Not that she'd *stayed* married after learning about Doug's infidelity.

And Theo's feline smugness was a whole lot more appealing than Tyler Prentiss's arrogance.

Sarah got into her nightshirt and lay down, thinking about Rosemary's eldest son. He might be sexy and gorgeous, but she'd learned all too well what a handsome face could hide. She hadn't left her marriage hating men; she knew her ex was a selfish, narcissistic creep who didn't represent men in general. But when she was ready for another relationship, it wouldn't be with an uptight guy like Tyler Prentiss. When the time was right, she wanted to be with someone who was easygoing and open, with no hidden dark side.

After a long time, she finally drifted into sleep, only to be jerked awake when the phone rang again.

Heart pounding, Sarah glanced at the clock. It was after midnight. She then checked the display and saw the number was unavailable. It couldn't be anybody from her family, so they couldn't be phoning with an emergency.

Her finger hovered over the talk button. She really didn't want to know if silence would greet her if she answered.

After the last ring, she pushed the phone under a pillow.

With an anxious cry, Theo cuddled up to her again, his velvety black fur making him virtually invisible in the darkness. He put his paws around her neck and licked her cheek.

"Hey, buddy," she murmured, grateful for his comforting warmth. It seemed to take forever to calm down, no matter how firmly she told herself to not overreact.

But it was hard, and the minutes ticked by.

Finally she got up to dress and head for the shop. If she couldn't sleep, she might as well bake.

CHAPTER TWO

TYLER WOKE TO the chirp of birds outside his window. His family's suite was in a sprawling Victorian farmhouse surrounded by gardens, a far cry from the modern monstrosity his father had built in DC.

Okay, that wasn't fair.

The architect had probably hoped to create something different, but Richard Prentiss would have demanded a house designed for society entertaining, rather than comfortable living. Something that fit their affluent Foxhall Crescent neighborhood.

Tyler tucked his arm under his neck and wished the birds would go somewhere else. Ordinarily he adapted well to time changes, but sleep was difficult these days between concern for Nathan and his mother.

And then there was the other thing...

Pain shot through his head, though he didn't know if it was from the injuries he'd gotten two weeks earlier or from memories that were too fresh and unresolved to let go.

He resolutely turned his thoughts back to his family. In DC, his mother had a social circle and familiar surroundings. For Nathan, there were therapists and doctors experienced at treating military-related injuries and PTSD. Even if Nathan didn't return to rehab, home seemed better than a tiny tourist town on the opposite side of the country.

But when they'd talked the previous evening, Nathan had refused to leave Glimmer Creek. Maybe it was the lack of experienced doctors that he liked, because he wouldn't have to answer uncomfortable questions.

But if both Nathan and Mom insisted on staying, Tyler would have to stay, as well. Among his other concerns, he didn't think his mother should be alone with Nathan at night. She'd been warned by the doctors not to interfere if he was having a nightmare, but it was still a concern. Tyler also wanted to be there in case she had another emotional crisis.

At any rate, the last time he'd left, his family had traveled across the country, defying medical orders. Maybe he *was* a chauvinist, but this time he was staying put and keeping an eye on things. The plane tickets he'd bought would have to wait.

A light knock sounded, then Rosemary called, "I'm leaving for work. Breakfast is in the refrigerator—Poppy Gold has it delivered every morning. Be sure to eat something."

He got up and opened the door. "I don't need to be told to eat, Mom. I'm not a child."

"You're treating *me* like one. The way you acted yesterday was outrageous."

Plainly, she hadn't forgiven him. But he hadn't forgiven himself, either, so it was understandable.

"I was tired and not thinking straight. I apologize."

Rosemary looked him up and down. "I accept your apology, but it's Sarah I'm thinking about. She works horribly long hours and doesn't need that kind of trouble."

Tyler let out a heavy breath. It felt as if his mother was more concerned about a stranger than her own son. "I'll apologize to her, too, but right now we need to discuss going home."

Rosemary checked her watch. "I told you there's nothing to discuss, and I'm out of time. I don't believe in being late for work."

Tyler scowled as she left. Rosemary Prentiss had been raised in a comfortable, old-fashioned Boston household, the only child of older parents. They'd expected her to simply marry well and raise a family, so it was difficult to see her having any preconceived notions about employment.

Yawning, he trotted downstairs and found Nathan on the couch in the living room.

"Did you spend the night there?"

"Yeah."

"I see. Have you had any nightmares since you got here?" Tyler asked, deciding he couldn't pretend everything was normal. It wasn't and might never be again.

"Most days, but not a bad one until the night before last. I get claustrophobic in my bedroom, so I'm going to start sleeping out here."

Tyler doubted claustrophobia was responsible, but he didn't say so. "The bedrooms upstairs are spacious."

Nathan angrily slapped his injured leg. "Maybe, but it's hard to get there. Besides, there's less chance I'll wake Mom if we're on different floors. Not that I'm sleeping much at night."

Tyler didn't know if Nathan's anger was a good sign or a problem. Surely it was healthier for Nathan to be outwardly angry than tearing himself up inside. Still, sleeping on the couch and wearing clothes that couldn't have been changed in two days sounded like more than anger. Nathan had always dressed sharply, even when off duty.

"You're analyzing, big brother," Nathan said softly. "Stop or your head may explode."

The comment made Tyler feel better. It was an old joke between them. Nathan always went with his gut. He was instinctive, popular with his peers, the life of every party. Tyler wasn't. He thought everything out. Analyzed. One girlfriend had called him an ice man when they broke up—it was his only serious relationship, and it had affirmed he wasn't cut out for commitment.

All of which made his behavior at Sarah's Sweet Treats even more bizarre. He should have reasoned the situation through and chosen a more effective strategy instead of charging in the way he had. Some ice man.

He looked at Nathan. "My head is fine."

"And you had to analyze your answer before giving it to me. Eat breakfast—you need brain food."

Tyler went into the kitchen and helped himself from the containers in the refrigerator. He reheated the meal in the microwave, then sat down and ate a bite of the potato casserole. It was delicious, though he nearly choked when he realized the decorative logo on the containers was the same one he'd seen on the sign at Sarah's Sweet Treats.

So the bakery was more than a bakery, fed hundreds of people each morning. His knowledge of restaurant operations was limited, but he knew it was a high-stress, competitive business.

How long could his mother handle it? The term

"nervous breakdown" wasn't used much anymore, but whatever it was called now, she'd come close to one after his father's funeral. On top of everything else, she'd panicked at the thought of dealing with her finances. So Tyler had spent months sorting the tangle his father had left.

Fortunately there was more than enough money, despite his father's unexpected taste for risky speculations. Now he mostly needed to review her accounts each month to be sure everything was in order and that the automated bill payments had gone through.

Back in the living room, Tyler found his brother staring at the ceiling again. It didn't look as if he'd moved an inch.

"Do you want to eat, or should I get rid of the leftovers?"

"Get rid of them."

Tyler tidied the kitchen before heading upstairs to shower and dress. In the bathroom, he took out his electric shaver and began running it over his jaw.

Perhaps he could invite Sarah Fullerton to lunch as an apology—be tactful and treat her the way he would a difficult client. If she understood how important it was, she might even encourage his mother to quit and return home with Nathan.

Tyler nodded at his reflection in the mirror. It wasn't much of a plan, but at least it was something.

SARAH STARTED A batch of bread while the rest of her employees finished clearing up from the breakfast sprint. Preparing and delivering breakfast to Poppy Gold was always a tight operation. She was exhausted from lack of sleep and lingering tension but refused to slow down.

She'd just put eight pans of Nebraska oatmeal bread into the oven when Aurelia came in. "Uh, Sarah, that guy from yesterday is back," she said in a low tone. "He wants to talk to you."

Why couldn't he leave her alone?

"All right, I'll be there in a minute."

Gabby took over while Sarah removed her apron. Tyler Prentiss was on the sidewalk, so she stepped outside. "Yes, Mr. Prentiss?"

He gave her a deliberate smile he probably thought was charming. "Please, it's Tyler. I came to apologize. I'm sorry for the way I behaved yesterday. It was inappropriate. Normally I'm quite calm and controlled."

"Okay," she said cautiously.

"Please let me take you to lunch so that I can explain. I checked on restaurants in the area. The steakhouse sounds good."

Sarah blinked. Why did he think she'd want

to eat with him? "Uh…sorry, I don't take long lunches." Perhaps he didn't understand the demands of her business. She might be the owner, but that meant she had even less free time than anyone else.

"Maybe we could discuss it now."

She let out a breath. "I've accepted your apology, so there's nothing to discuss."

A hint of unidentifiable emotion flickered in his eyes. Today, at least, Tyler Prentiss was projecting the dark, brooding thing perfectly, giving the impression that something more intense was going on.

"That isn't entirely the case," he said politely. "You heard me talking with my mother yesterday, so you're aware that my brother should still be in rehab. I was hoping that if you knew more about the situation, you'd help."

Sarah cocked her head. "I don't see how. Rosemary told me about Nathan's injuries, but I've never met him. Oh, unless you're thinking my dad could do something… I know he's been spending time with your brother."

"Actually, I hoped you'd urge Mom to go home. Then Nathan would go, as well."

Sarah released an exasperated breath. "Doing that would make Rosemary believe I'm unhappy with her work, which isn't the case."

"Maybe, but why did you hire her in the first

place?" Tyler asked. "Mom doesn't have any experience. And promoting her so quickly?"

Sarah could barely control her irritation. Her ex-husband had made her feel as if she was incapable of making her own decisions, and she refused to let that happen again.

"I'm not going to justify myself. This is *my* shop. Your mom says you're an architect. How would you like me to ask why you chose to put skylights or recycle chutes into one of your building designs?"

"It isn't the same," he returned in a clipped tone. She might have hit a nerve, though it was hard to tell with Tyler. He seemed to have no problem revealing anger, but his other emotions were much less clear.

"It's exactly the same. That's your business— this is mine," she retorted.

Tyler's brown eyes focused intensely on her, but she could tell little from his expression. "Fair enough. Look, I know my mother. She's a lovely woman with good intentions, but she isn't the nine-to-five type."

"She's working eight-to-four, though that's beside the point. It's up to Rosemary if she wants to return to the East Coast with your brother— I'm not going to manipulate her. And for your information, *she* asked for the job—I didn't twist her arm to take it."

"I'm sure you didn't since she doesn't have any qualifications," he snapped.

No matter what Tyler seemed to think, Sarah wondered how well he actually knew his mother. Experience could be gained without a paycheck. From what Rosemary had said about her volunteer work, she had a huge amount of management experience.

Yet in a way, Tyler had a point. Rosemary was a visitor to Glimmer Creek, staying at Poppy Gold temporarily. She'd said nothing about moving permanently to California or whether she would leave when Nathan was ready.

Tyler cleared his throat. "Sorry. That was uncalled for. It's just that I don't know what to do. Nathan isn't getting the care he needs and Mom is so annoyed with me, I doubt she'll listen to anything I have to say for a while."

Sarah suppressed a smile. The way he'd made the stiff, embarrassed admission was almost endearing; plainly he wasn't comfortable relying on anyone else.

"You may be right," she acknowledged. "But can I ask you something?"

"Of course," Tyler said, seeming wary.

"Well, I get why Nathan might be better off in rehab, but what will you do if he keeps refusing?"

IT WAS A valid question, and Tyler wished he had an answer. Confiding in anyone was miles outside his comfort zone, but he might be forced into it. His mother and Nathan's welfare were too important, and right now Sarah Fullerton seemed the most likely person who could help.

Yet before he could say anything else, Sarah stirred restlessly. "Sorry, but morning is my busiest period. I need to get back to my kitchen."

Tyler let out a sigh of his own as she turned and disappeared into the bakery. He'd been right about her figure—without the chef's apron, her body was a delectable balance of slim lines and curves.

He shook his head to clear it. Getting distracted by a beautiful woman was the last thing he needed.

Officially he was under investigation for a recent building collapse in the greater Chicago area, an incident that had injured five men. Prior to the start of construction, Milo Corbin, the owner, had demanded unsafe modifications to the plans. He'd grown so unreasonable that Tyler had resigned from the project. Changes had subsequently been made to his original design, but

Corbin and the second architect were still trying to shift the blame to Tyler.

They wouldn't be successful.

Tyler had gone over his original blueprints and knew they were sound. He'd also kept careful documentation about the alterations Corbin had wanted. Nonetheless, Tyler *felt* responsible. He should have done more to prevent construction from moving ahead.

Ironically, Corbin had promptly screamed for Tyler's help after the collapse, so he'd flown to Illinois from Italy to spend a couple of days helping with the search-and-rescue efforts. After all, he'd studied the changes Corbin had wanted and predicted they'd lead to structural failure, so he was reasonably certain of where and how the damage had occurred. With the city engineer out of town, Tyler had even signed a waiver and gone into the building to advise on the safest way to extract trapped workers.

What he didn't understand was why a particular concrete wall hadn't held. The thing had crumbled unexpectedly, bringing debris down on him and one of the firemen. Though injured, Tyler had pocketed a chunk of the concrete for later analysis. He'd given it to the lawyers he'd hired in Illinois.

Lawyers.

Tyler was struck by the irony. He'd never been

interested in his father's work, and now he was relying on a bulldog Chicago law firm to protect him.

But no matter what happened, nothing would take away the pain those construction workers had suffered or the fear their families had experienced as they'd waited for them to be found.

CHAPTER THREE

WHEN TYLER GOT BACK to the suite, he was relieved to see his brother had changed his clothes and was out in the garden.

Needing to accomplish something, he went inside and rang the rehab center to request recommendations for Nathan's treatment.

"I can give information to your brother, but not to you. Privacy laws are very strict," Dr. Chin explained.

Tyler gritted his teeth. "But you *have* talked to me, a dozen or more times since he went into rehab."

"Yes, but the release he signed has expired. Is Nathan there? He could give me permission. At the very least, I'd like to know how he's doing."

"Just a moment." Tyler went into the garden and held the phone out to his brother. "Dr. Chin would like to speak with you."

"Maybe tomorrow."

"He's concerned about your health," Tyler said tightly. "And he left a staff meeting to take my call. Please do him the courtesy of listening to what he has to say."

Nathan simply hunched his shoulders.

Tyler put the phone to his ear again. "I'm sorry, Doctor, my brother is being a jackass." Even as he said it, he remembered Sarah calling him the same thing.

Damnation, how had she gotten into his head?

"I'm sorry to hear that," Dr. Chin said. "I've been thinking, if you can't convince him to return, perhaps I…um, can send you some general recommendations. Ones that could apply to most of the recovering soldiers I've treated."

A faint sense of relief went through Tyler. He still thought Nathan should be getting twenty-four-hour care and the doctor appeared to agree, but any guidance would help. "I'd appreciate whatever you can give me." He provided his email address and disconnected, promising to call again if Nathan's condition worsened.

Tyler dropped the phone in his pocket. If he thought confronting his brother would do any good, he'd confront him. But he suspected it wouldn't, so he asked Nathan to take a walk with him instead. The idea was met with indifference and finally refusal. After that, Tyler suggested a game of chess. Nathan still wasn't interested.

Finally Tyler sat in a nearby chair and put a stern, I-mean-business expression on his face.

"Have you seen a doctor since coming to Glimmer Creek?"

Nathan gave him a dirty look. "*No*. I'm tired of doctors."

"I don't blame you, but I need to know what therapy program you're supposed to be following and any other information you and Mom have left out. How about that medication they were giving you for the nightmares? Don't you need refills?"

His brother shrugged. "It wasn't helping, so I stopped taking it. Anyway, I can't talk now. Kurt is showing me the Poppy Gold greenhouses today. I have to find out when he's coming."

Nathan got out his own phone but was obviously waiting for Tyler to leave before making the call.

Tyler finally went inside, hoping it was a good sign that his brother was carrying his cell. In the hospital and rehab center, Nathan had resisted being in contact with friends *or* hearing about the affairs of the world. Their mother had been the same, which was why Tyler had figured neither of them would have heard about the incident in Illinois. It helped that this sort of story, without any fatalities, usually wasn't in the news for long. And as it turned out, they also must have been busy getting settled into Poppy Gold.

Tyler massaged the muscles at the back of his

neck. The past two weeks had been rough. After being treated for his injuries, he'd returned to Italy and finished his work there, only to fly home and discover his family was gone.

But at least he'd broached the subject of medical care with Nathan, however unproductive the conversation had been. Perhaps they could talk about it as a family and figure out what they were planning from here…because he suspected they weren't going back to the East Coast any time soon.

KURT FULLERTON PARKED behind his daughter's catering business for his usual midmorning check to see if she needed anything.

"Hey, Dad," Sarah called as he came through the back door. He'd been there earlier, and she still looked so pale and tense that he frowned.

"What's up?" he asked.

"Just busy."

Kurt wasn't sure. Something told him something was going on, but she probably wasn't going to tell him; she'd inherited his ex-wife's slender grace and *his* pigheaded nature.

Wanting to taking care of his daughter was a tough habit to kick, especially since he hadn't been around much in her early years. After his wife had run off with another man, he'd brought Sarah home to his parents, convinced that caring for a toddler on an army base was impossible for a single father.

Now he knew that he'd given up too easily. Lizzie's actions had embittered him, and for a while he'd become the hardest-living son of a gun in the army. Instead he should have done his best to be a good dad.

"You hardly ever let me do anything to help around here," he complained.

"That isn't true," Sarah shot back. "You shop for me every week, and you're always finding something else to do. And that isn't even counting all the work you did remodeling the two kitchens. *Twice.*"

"That's nothing. I like being involved and knowing what's going on."

Kurt just wished he'd known more about Sarah's troubles with her louse of a husband.

A timer buzzed and Sarah hurried to remove loaves of bread from the ovens.

Kurt went to the front counter and got a cup of joe, then ambled down the short hallway to the office to visit with Rosemary.

"Good morning, Kurt. Don't you want something to go with your coffee?" she asked. "Sarah made poppy-seed muffins earlier. I've never seen anyone get as much done as she does."

"That's my girl. But I'd better not indulge, I already had her egg and ham pie when I brought over a batch of green onions from the green-house." He patted his stomach.

ROSEMARY TRIED NOT to laugh. Sarah had confided that her father, along with the rest of the male half of Glimmer Creek, wouldn't eat anything called quiche, so she'd put a puff pastry crust on top and called it egg pie.

"Working here is terrible for the waistline," Rosemary admitted. "I haven't tasted a single thing that isn't delicious."

"You've got a long way to go before you need to worry about your waistline," Kurt assured her. "Me, I've got a linebacker build, unlike my brothers. I'm glad Sarah didn't get my shape."

Kurt's large family intrigued Rosemary. Nine siblings, and most of them had several children, as well. It was sad that he'd never found someone else after his divorce, but she understood how difficult it was to risk loving again. After all, while her husband's death had been devastating, the grief had also renewed an old, wrenching sorrow…the loss of her first child.

One-year-old Kittie had been the light of their lives. Bright and full of fun, she'd brought joy to everyone. It was only after her death from spinal meningitis that they'd moved to Washington, DC, and Richard's dedication to his career had turned into an obsession. Rosemary hadn't handled the loss any better; she'd dived into fund-raising for nonprofit organizations. They'd even decided not to have more children, only to discover Tyler was on the way.

"Sarah has your eyes," Rosemary said, hoping her voice wouldn't break. It wasn't that she loved Tyler and Nathan any less, but it was wrenching to remember her daughter.

"Except they're pretty on Sarah." He grinned and drank a gulp of coffee.

Rosemary thought Kurt's eyes were nice on him, too. He was an attractive man, not classically handsome like her husband had been, but good-looking, with a reassuring manner.

"Do you ever think about grandchildren?" she asked wistfully. A year earlier, she'd had high hopes of becoming a grandmother. Nathan had been engaged and looking forward to fatherhood, then his fiancée had decided she couldn't handle being a soldier's wife.

"I'd love them," Kurt said, "but Sarah's marriage was pretty bad. I don't know when she'll be ready." He finished his coffee and got up. "Better get going. I wouldn't want my daughter to think I'm interfering with your work."

After a moment, Rosemary heard him in the kitchen saying goodbye to Sarah. She envied their close relationship. She'd seen it from her first day at the bakery when Kurt had delivered a load of supplies.

A thoroughly nice man, Rosemary had concluded after watching father and daughter together. She was glad for them, but it was a reminder that she didn't have a similar relationship with her own children.

Maybe that was why she'd gone along when Nathan insisted on leaving the rehab hospital… because she'd hoped it might bring them closer.

GREAT-UNCLE MILT came into the shop to see Sarah shortly before the lunch-hour rush.

"Hey, Uncle Milt, how about a sandwich?" Sarah nodded to Aurelia, who began packing his favorite meal into a bag.

"I should say no, but I won't. Just put it on my account. I mostly came to tell you about that fellow from yesterday."

"Oh?" Sarah said cautiously, hoping he didn't know Tyler had shown up again. "Let's go for a walk."

Aurelia handed Great-Uncle Milt his lunch, and they headed down the street.

"I spoke to Zach and he did a standard background check at the police station," Great-Uncle Milt explained as they strolled toward the city park. "It turns out Tyler Prentiss is connected to an investigation in the Chicago area."

Sarah nearly tripped. She didn't have a high opinion of Rosemary's eldest son, but she didn't think he was a criminal.

"What *sort* of investigation?"

"Earlier in July a building under construction collapsed and injured several workers. Prentiss was the original architect, though another architect took over the project in February and made changes. Nonetheless, the owner is blaming Mr. Prentiss. The investigation could take months to resolve."

Sarah wasn't surprised that Rosemary had been silent about the incident; it wasn't something you'd casually discuss. "It doesn't sound as if he *could* be responsible if changes were made to his original design."

"I realize that, and Prentiss's work is highly regarded, which I'm sure the authorities are keeping in mind. Other than this, his record is spotless. Not even a speeding ticket."

"I appreciate the update."

Sarah wasn't sure what to make of Great-Uncle Milt's revelation, though it actually made her feel more sympathetic toward Tyler. She knew what it was like to be to be exhausted and not thinking straight.

Within just a few months, his father had died and his brother had been seriously injured, and now his career was under siege. What did they say about trouble coming in threes?

Rosemary had talked often about her sons since starting to work at the bakery, and a picture of Tyler had emerged as an extremely cool and measured man.

Sarah had begun to think of him almost as a hermit crab, toting around an oversize shell into which he could withdraw. The mental image still fit what she'd seen of his personality—except for the bad temper he'd shown—but she hadn't expected his "shell" to be so…mouthwatering.

With a sigh, Sarah glanced at the clock tower on City Hall. "Sorry, Uncle Milt, but I have to scoot," she said. "See you on Sunday."

Sarah hurried back toward the sweet shop, and as bad luck would have it, ran into Tyler Prentiss going into the newly relocated Valentino's Pizza Pizzazz. In such a small town, encounters were to be expected. She just wished it could have happened on a different day.

He gave her an inquiring look. "I thought you weren't taking lunch."

"I don't take long lunches, though in this case I was discussing something with a relative, not eating." Sarah resisted the temptation to say she had the right to do whatever she wanted, regardless of what she'd told him. "Uncle Milt is the former Glimmer Creek police chief."

Tyler's expression didn't change. "Mom mentioned you have family in the area."

"That's right."

Grandma Margaret called their family an embarrassment of riches. Sarah thought that was apt. She was fortunate to have so many people who cared about her.

Of course, she hadn't always felt lucky when she was a teenager and couldn't get away with a tiny bit of rebellion—too many relatives to see it.

Being a little wild might have been fun, and maybe she wouldn't have made such a huge mistake with her ex-husband if she'd been able to learn from smaller mistakes as a teen.

"Is something wrong?" Tyler prompted.

"Nope. I understand you don't have any extended family yourself."

"It's just the three of us now."

Sarah couldn't imagine what it would be like to have so few relatives. Sometimes it seemed as if everyone in Glimmer Creek was related to her in one way or another.

"I'm sorry about your dad," she said, unsure if she should say anything at all. Some people didn't want to be reminded of someone they'd lost.

A mask seemed to come over Tyler's face. "Thank you. He was a great lawyer. Tops in the DC area."

"Oh. That's nice."

Despite her comment, she was puzzled. If she'd lost her father, even sympathy from a stranger would have made her declare how special and wonderful he was. Calling him a brave soldier or gifted horticulturist would only have occurred to her later.

She squared her shoulders. "Well, I won't keep you."

Sarah headed down the passageway between the sweet shop and the pizza parlor to go in through the back entrance. The front of the bakery was so crowded that there was a line out the door, extending down the street.

Yet a part of her mind wasn't thinking about the shop and everything that needed doing… It was thinking about Tyler Prentiss and the closed-off look in his eyes when he'd talked about his father.

SHORTLY AFTER THE lunch rush, Sarah was putting the final touches on a batch of wild blackberry tarts when Rosemary came into the kitchen.

"Sarah, there's a Mr. Seibert on the line for you, from City Hall."

Sarah hurried into the office and picked up the receiver. "Hey, Stephen." She didn't know him professionally—he'd started working for the city after the various renovations had been completed on her business—but they'd met at a few community events.

"Hello, Sarah. I…um… I'm sorry, but I need to schedule an inspection," he said hesitantly.

"Sure, but we don't have any remodeling planned."

Stephen cleared his throat. "Actually, I received a complaint saying your facility might not meet building codes for the number of employees. Also that the air-conditioning might not be up to par."

"A complaint?" Sarah tried not to react as she recalled Tyler saying he didn't want his mother in a hot, crowded kitchen. "From who?"

"It was anonymous. These things usually are, and they're usually a bunch of nonsense, but I still need to check. It's standard city protocol."

"Okay. Do you want to come today?"

"Tomorrow is fine. How about 2:00 p.m.? I'll also have to see your work schedules to know how many employees are present at any given time."

"Whatever you need."

Sarah got off and tried keep the frustration from showing on her face.

"Is there a problem?" Rosemary asked worriedly.

"No, the city just does inspections now and then."

"I heard you mention a complaint. Who would complain? Everybody is so happy here."

Sarah shrugged. "Stephen doesn't know—it was anonymous. I'm sure it's a misunderstanding."

On reflection, an anonymous complaint didn't sound like Tyler Prentiss. Of course, she couldn't think of anyone else it could be, either, though the memory of the silent calls she'd been having popped into her mind.

Don't be paranoid, Sarah ordered. It was unlikely the two problems were connected.

"I heard Tyler dropped by this morning," Rosemary said, still looking upset.

"Yes, he apologized."

Rosemary brightened. "I'm glad to hear that. He means well, but he's protective. The truth is, I was a complete mess after Richard died. I'd let my husband handle all our personal affairs and wasn't the least prepared when..." She swallowed. "Richard died of a massive stroke. He was older than me and should have retired years ago, but nothing could make him slow down."

"It must have been a shock."

"He simply wouldn't take care of himself. But I shouldn't keep you—you have enough to do."

Sarah smiled. She didn't mind the moments that she and Rosemary got to talking. Thanks to the older woman's ability to manage the business end of the sweet shop, *she* was getting more time to do what she loved most.

"Actually, I'm going to finish my blackberry tarts, then go home and take a nap," she explained. "I'll come back later to make fudge." Her candy chef had asked for an extra day off this week, and she didn't want to run low.

In the kitchen, Sarah found someone else had finished the tarts, so she gratefully left. At the house, she set the alarm and unplugged her landline before lying down. Theo delightedly jumped up with her and settled down, purring.

"Hey, baby."

It was crazy to feel edgy, even though she knew it was unlikely that anything weird was going on, but it still took time to drop off. The question kept revolving in her head—who could have complained? She easily met the county's guidelines for commercial kitchens.

Finally she began counting black cats in her head. Happy, playful black cats, and with Theo leaning against her shoulder, she drifted to sleep.

ROSEMARY WAS DISAPPOINTED she didn't find Nathan in the garden when she got home. She'd brought him a sandwich and salad at lunchtime, but he'd said Tyler was getting pizza so the food had gone into the refrigerator.

Nathan wasn't in the living room or his bedroom.

"Is that you, Mom?" called Tyler.

"Yes." She hurried out from Nathan's room. "Where is your brother?"

"Didn't he tell you? Mr. Fullerton took him to see the Poppy Gold greenhouses. I think they're spending the afternoon together."

"Oh, that's right. I forgot." Flustered, Rosemary put the kettle on for tea. "I heard you apologized to Sarah," she said finally.

"I asked her to lunch, but she didn't have time."

"She's always busy. Tomorrow will be especially hectic since she, um, got a call this afternoon from the city."

A thought had been nagging her...that Tyler might have made the complaint. It was dreadful to think he could do something like that, but she also knew he was unhappy about her job.

"Apparently someone made an anonymous complaint," she continued. "It's terrible that Sarah has to take time to deal with something like this. I can't imagine her violating any rules."

"Then the inspection shouldn't be a problem." Tyler's expression didn't reveal much. You'd think as his mother she'd be able to read more in his face, but it was no easier now than when he'd been a child. So unless she asked outright, she wasn't going to discover whether he was responsible. Surely not, though.

"What else did Sarah say?" Tyler prompted, breaking into her thoughts.

"Nothing. I'm just concerned about her."

"She isn't your daughter."

"I realize that," Rosemary returned sharply, though she knew her son wasn't trying to be cruel. He didn't know about his sister. Richard had insisted they never talk about Kittie, and since they'd moved to the DC area after her death, their new social circle hadn't known about her, either.

Would it upset Tyler and Nathan to learn that an important part of their family history had never been discussed, or would it help them understand their father a little better?

TYLER SUSPECTED HIS MOTHER wondered if he'd made the call, but the idea was offensive. It would have been purely to harass Sarah, and he'd never do that.

"The complaint must be a misunderstanding," he said.

"Of course. But it will take time to resolve, and Sarah already works appalling hours. Even worse than you, I think."

He didn't think his work hours were appalling, certainly no longer than his father's. Richard had rarely been at home when his sons were awake. Tyler hadn't faulted his dad for being a dedicated lawyer, but why have kids if he didn't like them? Just to have someone carry on the family name and follow in his footsteps?

Tyler didn't feel the need for children, and since his work took him all over the world, it wouldn't be fair to a family for him to be gone weeks or months at a stretch.

Frankly, he didn't intend to change.

He *liked* going full tilt. He wanted to leave his mark on the world by designing memorable buildings, not by passing on his genes.

"I'm sure Sarah will manage," Tyler said. "Besides, how long could it take? She doesn't need to go around with the inspector, just talk with him afterward."

His mother simply shook her head and walked upstairs.

Outside, Tyler saw his brother return with Kurt Fullerton and sit on the garden chairs, talking. It still amazed Tyler that Sarah was Kurt's daughter. While she had his green eyes, she was delicate and slim, with none of his square solidity.

Tyler stepped onto the porch, only to decide against joining the other two men. Instead he went for a walk around Poppy Gold. While he wasn't a huge fan of Victorian architecture, the place projected an air of gracious elegance. An hour later, he returned to the suite and found his mother talking to a man on the porch.

"I'm so sorry," she was saying, visibly distressed. "Maybe they can put it on my account here at Poppy Gold."

"What's wrong?" Tyler asked.

"I ordered food, but can't find my purse."

"No problem." He took out his wallet and turned to the deliveryman. "How much do we owe you?"

"Forty-eight even."

Tyler extracted three twenties and held them out. "Keep the change. Sorry for the inconvenience."

"Thank you, sir."

His mother's cheeks were pink as he carried the bags of food into the kitchen and put them on the breakfast table.

"I must have left my purse at work," she said. "I'll get it after dinner."

"Isn't it safe to leave in the office?"

"Of course it's safe. Someone is always at the shop, but I keep my blood pressure medicine in there. I'll need that tonight. And I…well, I keep your father's wallet in there. I like having it nearby."

"I'll go now. You and Nathan start eating without me."

Tyler didn't wait for her to agree. After losing his father to a stroke, he wasn't taking any chances with his mother's medication. The door was locked at Sarah's Sweet Treats, but he knocked until an employee came out from the back.

"I'm sorry, we're closed," the woman called pleasantly.

"My mother works here. Rosemary Prentiss. She left her purse and needs it."

"Just a minute, I'll let Sarah know."

She disappeared. A few minutes passed and Tyler wondered if he'd been forgotten, then Sarah came out and unlocked the door. She looked more rested than she had earlier, though still on edge.

"We keep running into each other," she said, stepping aside to let him enter and then locking the door again.

"Sorry for the inconvenience. Mom forgot her purse in the office."

"That's what Katie said. I phoned Rosemary, and she said it was okay to let you take it."

"Sarah," called a frantic voice. "I keep stirring this, but I don't know what else to do."

Sarah raced to the back of the shop. Tyler followed her through a bright kitchen filled with stainless steel appliances to one that was smaller but no less tidy. She was already at one of the stoves, stirring the contents of a large pot.

Chocolate, he realized. Obviously he'd come

at an inconvenient time, though he wondered if there was *ever* a convenient time with Sarah.

She checked a large thermometer and gave the mixture an extra stir before pouring it into a rectangular pan.

"It's fudge," Sarah explained, casting him a glance.

"Do you make all the candy you sell?"

"It's all made here, yes. But I have an employee who does most of it. She's taking a personal day, so I'm filling in. Usually I focus on developing new recipes. Tonight I may experiment with lemon meringue fudge."

Tyler frowned. "Fudge is supposed to be chocolate."

Her eyes narrowed. "Not the way I make it. Do you like cappuccino?"

"I suppose."

"Then come with me."

Sarah returned to the front of the bakery and turned on the lights in a display case. She cut a piece from a cream-colored slab and gave it to him on a napkin. "This is my cappuccino fudge."

He took a bite and the rich essence of coffee and cinnamon rolled across his tongue. Though he wasn't big on candy, he was disappointed when the last of it was gone. "That's pretty good," he admitted. "I concede that fudge doesn't have to be chocolate."

She served him another couple of samples, including one named Hogwarts Special.

"Hogwarts Special?" Tyler echoed.

"For the Harry Potter fans. The books talk about pumpkin juice, but this is mostly pumpkin spice. I haven't managed to get more than a mild pumpkin flavor in the fudge. Blackberry is easier because the berries are so tangy."

Sarah was clearly enthused about her creations, enough to indulge even *him* with samples when he must have been a thorn in her side for their entire acquaintance. Yet a thought kept tapping in the back of Tyler's brain...was she being nice because she thought he'd made the anonymous complaint?

She couldn't be worried about passing an inspection. From what he'd seen, both of her kitchens were modern, spotless and pleasant places to work.

"I don't cook and I've never met anyone who invented recipes," he said, genuinely curious about the process. As a kid, his mom had hired a chef or a caterer, and he'd relied mostly on restaurants as an adult.

"Chefs and bakers invent recipes all the time. I'll get Rosemary's purse."

Sarah left and returned a minute later. She put the purse inside one of the Sweet Treat's shopping bags before handing it to him, probably assuming he wouldn't want to walk back through Poppy Gold carrying a woman's handbag. It was true. While he didn't think he was irredeemably chauvinistic, he also wasn't exactly enlightened, either.

CHAPTER FOUR

BACK AT THE SUITE, Tyler found his mother had kept the food warm so they could eat together. It was an awkward meal that might have gone better if family dinners had been a Prentiss tradition. But even on holidays, his parents had attended social events.

After they finished eating, he cleared his throat.

"Nathan, as you know, I talked to Dr. Chin at the rehab center today. He's sending recommendations for you to follow while you're here in California. Since Mom has a job, I'll be taking you to your appointments. Unless you decide to return to rehab, that is."

His brother glared. "That isn't happening. And I don't need his recommendations. I'm doing fine. As for appointments, if I never see another doctor, I'll be happy."

Rosemary straightened. "That isn't what we agreed to when you wanted to leave the rehab center. I've let it go longer than I intended, but don't think I've forgotten."

It was nice to see she hadn't completely lost

touch with reality. Tyler had envisioned her believing that love and sunshine would be enough to resolve Nathan's PTSD and restore him physically. While it might be possible, he'd do a whole lot better with treatment.

Tyler leaned forward. "I don't suppose a tiny town like Glimmer Creek has many medical services. We'll probably have to drive to the nearest city for doctors and therapy."

His brother looked ready to argue, so Tyler fixed him with a hard stare. "In the hospital, you told me you wanted to go back on active duty. That isn't likely to happen without therapy. Or have you decided to leave the service?"

Resentment flickered in Nathan's eyes. "I don't want a medical discharge. The army is going to do a medical review in a few months to determine my fitness."

Tyler ached, suspecting Nathan questioned whether he could pass the review. Maybe he couldn't. Maybe he no longer *wanted* to return to active duty—after his personal tour of hell, nobody would blame him for deciding he'd had enough.

"We don't have to talk about this now, do we?" their mother asked in a shaky voice, and Tyler looked at her sharply. Her eyes were wide and her cheeks were pale.

"No," he and his brother said in unison. Taking care of her was an old habit.

Nathan put his hand over hers. "It's okay, Mom, I'm just feeling sorry for myself."

"You're entitled."

"Naw, but don't worry, I'll see a doctor. Right now I'm tired, so I'm going to lie down."

She smiled shakily. "Is there anything I can get you?"

Nathan shook his head and limped out of the kitchen.

Tyler turned to his mother.

"Did you *have* to mention him going back on active duty?" she asked tearfully. "He's sacrificed enough."

"It's important. Nathan has to *want* to get better. Deciding what he wants and how to get it will motivate him."

"I realize that. And I'm sorry I didn't get him to a doctor earlier. He's just so much calmer here, and I wanted to give him time. Besides, Kurt is good for him. They've shared a lot of the same experiences, and Nathan respects his opinion."

"Some of Nathan's doctors and therapists at the Walter Reed Medical Center were combat vets, too. What makes Kurt Fullerton different?"

"He just is."

She began clearing the table, shaking her head when he offered to help. So Tyler got out his laptop to send an email to his office, asking them to ship basic drafting equipment to him at Poppy Gold. He didn't know how long he'd have to be in California, but he had commissions with deadlines and couldn't sit idly by.

Yet he kept shooting worried looks at his mom, who was now fussing with the refrigerator. His relationship with his father might have been complicated, but his death had shaken Tyler to the core. When it came to his mother, he didn't want to confront feelings like that again for a very long time.

THE FOLLOWING AFTERNOON, Rosemary worked at the bakery's front counter to stay out of the way of the building inspection, but as soon as Stephen Seibert left, she hurried to the office and saw Sarah looking tense.

"Is something wrong?" Rosemary asked. "You can't have failed the inspection."

"I passed, but Stephen told me the county is expecting to implement new building codes next year. I meet the state codes, but not all the new ones that have been proposed for Glimmer County. So I'll have to remodel. *Again*."

"How long do you have to comply?"

"Within twelve months of the effective date. The problem is there may not be enough space to enlarge the kitchens. Stephen will send a detailed analysis in a few days." Sarah squared her shoulders and smiled brightly. "But don't worry, I'll figure it out. In the meantime, I'd better get busy with tasks that need doing today."

Rosemary kept wondering how she could help, but all she could think of was to get Tyler involved. He was a gifted architect, and he might be able to come up a plan.

Except Tyler might resist. He seemed determined to stay in Glimmer Creek as long as she and Nathan were here, but he was also uncomfortable with the idea of his mother working.

When Kurt had learned about Tyler's reaction to her job, he'd chuckled and asked if her son was worried about becoming a latchkey kid. It had made her laugh, as well, but it had also made her think. As a family they'd gone through a tremendous upheaval over the past year. Maybe that explained why Tyler didn't want to see his mother in a new way.

Would that affect his willingness to help Sarah?

There was only one way to find out, so as soon as Rosemary got back to the Yosemite suite after work, she told Tyler about the building inspector's news.

"She'll need expert advice from an architect," she concluded. "I wondered if you could take a quick look and tell her what you think."

Tyler sighed. "I have commissions to work on while I'm here. My office is sending a drafting table and everything else I need by overnight courier."

"Just consider it," Rosemary implored. "What they're asking seems terribly unfair, and you might be able to think of options the building inspector didn't."

"ALL RIGHT, I'LL make time," Tyler agreed reluctantly.

On the rare occasions he'd encountered his mother's friends since starting his career, he'd discovered they loved to get free professional services, no matter how wealthy they might be. Sarah would probably appreciate a free consult, even from him.

"Thank you, dear," his mother said. "What would you like for dinner?"

"Order whatever you want. I'm not hungry. I thought I'd explore the town. Maybe I'll stop by the bakery and see if Sarah wants to talk about the remodeling," he added impulsively.

His mother's face brightened. "That would be wonderful. She should still be there."

Tyler's mood was wry as he walked to Sarah's Sweet Treats. Volunteering his advice was the diplomatic thing to do. His mother hadn't accused him of calling in the complaint, but the faint doubt he'd seen in her eyes bothered him. He didn't expect blind faith, but she could have asked.

Or maybe he was just being unreasonable and the thought had never occurred to her.

After all, he *felt* guilty for what had happened in Illinois, if only for failing to convince the owner that the design changes weren't safe. Knowing it was the new architect's responsibility wasn't enough to absolve him of all blame. So maybe he was more sensitive than he needed to be.

Though it was late in the afternoon, the scents emanating from the sweet shop were richly tantalizing. Tyler opened the door and saw customers still crowding the small waiting and sitting area.

Sarah was working with two other employees, filling orders and chatting with the customers. She flicked a glance in his direction and her mouth tightened. A few minutes later, she flipped the Open sign to Closed, but it was another fifteen minutes before everyone was gone.

When it was quiet, she walked over to him. "Do you need something?"

"Mom mentioned you might need some renovations because of upcoming building code changes. She asked me to see if I can make some suggestions."

An interesting expression crossed Sarah's face.

"That isn't necessary. I don't even have the full analysis from the building inspector yet."

While Tyler had been reluctant to offer his advice, he also wasn't used to having his services rejected. "Then maybe when you get it."

"I don't—" She broke off and looked at her two front-counter employees. "Hey, guys, you don't need to stay and clean up. Put a half hour of overtime on your timesheets, and I'll see you tomorrow."

The pair left and Sarah sat opposite Tyler at the small café table. "I'm not sure why you'd offer, but it isn't necessary. I'll figure it out."

"Is there any possibility of protesting the changes? Usually there's a public comment period when regulations are changing."

"I…" Sarah started to yawn and clapped a hand over her mouth. "Sorry, I'm short on sleep. I *could* protest, but the proposed rules aren't bad. They only affect me because the restaurant and catering side of my business has gotten so huge. If I'd known code changes were coming, I would have bought a larger building to start with. Now I may need to relocate, which is too bad, because I get a huge amount of foot traffic from the tour buses."

"That's an even better reason for me to take a look," Tyler said, unsure why he was pushing the issue. "Besides, a year isn't that long when it comes to this sort of thing. If nothing else, it can be difficult to book contractors. You must have experience with that after your previous remodels."

"Actually, my father and other family members insisted on doing most of the work," Sarah murmured.

As TYLER NODDED, Sarah thought about the preliminary report the building inspector had given her. She hated the idea of going into debt again, but the worst part was not knowing if another remodel was possible. She didn't see how an extra inch of space could be gained without reducing the already-small customer area, and even that might not be enough.

"Do you think your family would be willing to help do the work again?" Tyler asked.

Sarah fought an unreasonable panic at the thought of losing her independence, which always came when she relied too heavily on family. She hadn't been married to Douglas for that long, but she was still repairing the damage he'd done to her self-confidence.

She'd let her father take charge of the previous renovations because it had saved her a ton of money and it meant so much to him. Yet it had also made her uneasy…she was just too aware of how easy it was to start depending on someone else. Maybe some people were naturally stronger, but life had already shown how easily she could lose herself.

"I'm sure they'd want to help," she admitted, "but they're busy and I hate inconveniencing them." She didn't add that it might be impossible to *stop* them.

"But it's good for the town, right? My mom mentioned this is the only bakery."

"Yes. I always thought we needed one growing up. Even when I went to college I wanted to come back here and open this place. The plan was derailed because…er…that is, for a while, but not forgotten."

Tyler's eyebrows shot upward. "Why not start a chain? You could bake in a central factory and ship everything to the different sites. If you plan it right, there could be Sarah's Sweet Treat outlets all over the Gold Country."

"I'm not interested in factory baking, that's why." Sarah was annoyed, even though she hadn't expected him to understand. "Maybe my dream isn't as grand as being a famous architect, with clients who are desperate to have my name on their building, but I don't *want* a business empire. I simply enjoy feeding people."

Tyler's face chilled. "Being able to call it a Prentiss building isn't the only reason people want my designs. I'm good at what I do."

Apparently she'd touched a nerve again.

"I'm sure you're an excellent architect," Sarah said, debating whether she should explain that she knew about the investigation in Illinois. *No,* she decided, taking another look at his arctic expression.

A gremlin inside of her wanted to goad him, but she didn't think it was wise. It might be like catching a tiger by the tail—both hanging on and letting go would be equally dangerous.

"Then you'll accept my professional assessment of your building," Tyler said.

Sarah lifted her chin. The offer of free advice was tempting, but she didn't want to be put under an obligation and couldn't afford to hire him.

"I'm not helpless and I'm quite capable of taking care of it by myself," she told Tyler. "I'm sure you have more important things to do with your time."

"You don't need to get huff—" Tyler stopped, apparently rethinking what he'd intended to say. "That is, I know you're capable. But you aren't an architect. I expect to be in Glimmer Creek until my mom and brother leave. Why don't I take a look at the analysis from the building office when it comes, along with the blueprints for your building? I'd be happy to make recommendations."

She knew quite well he'd started to say she was getting huffy and rolled her eyes. In her opinion, *huffy* was gender-specific. If she'd called *him* that, he would have felt his masculinity was being threatened. That was another point in Theo's favor—he didn't get in a tizzy about his manhood, though being a neutered cat, he might not feel he had that much to defend.

Sarah gave herself a shake. Her thoughts tended to drift when she was tired, and she still had to clear out the register and take care of a dozen other things before she could go home.

"That was sarcastic, not *huffy*," she returned, and Tyler looked faintly embarrassed. "But I'm not making any decisions until I'm more rested and have done more evaluation of my own."

"I understand. Maybe you can assist me in return."

Sarah was instantly wary. "How?"

"I've contacted over a dozen general practitioners in Stockton to get an appointment for Nathan, but the earliest slot for a new patient isn't for two or three weeks. Do you have any contacts who could help? Maybe someone in your family?"

"Go to the Glimmer Creek clinic. No appointment needed."

"I noticed there was a clinic in town, but I'd prefer someone in private practice."

Sarah gave him an exasperated look. "Give me a break. The GC clinic is brand-new and state-of-the-art. All of our medical professionals work out of it, but I'd recommend Dr. Romano for your brother. He was a reservist who served in the air force during the first Gulf War. Just call and ask when he's there."

Tyler nodded. "Okay. Do you mind if I wander around and take measurements, just in case you decide to accept my opinion on your renovations?" He pulled a tape measure from his pocket along with a small notebook.

"You brought a tape measure?"

"It's a habit. If you don't let me do some innocent checking, my mother's feelings may be hurt. She really hopes I can come up with a solution for you."

Invoking Rosemary's feelings was dirty pool. "Fine. Do some measuring. Just stay out of everyone's way. Would you like a cup of coffee before I empty the coffee makers?"

"Sure. Decaf if you have it, regular otherwise."

Sarah poured him a large to-go cup of decaf and cleaned the coffee makers, then put the now day-old baked items into plastic bags.

"Don't you have someone who can do that?" Tyler asked.

"Somebody comes later to clean, but we take care of the coffee machines immediately and bag the day-old items."

"What about those?" He gestured to the loaves of bread she'd kept separate.

"They'll be made into croutons. Croutons are

popular in the shop, and we also use them for our restaurant and catering needs."

Leaving Tyler to roam the building by himself, Sarah took the contents of the till back to the office and got it ready for the bank's night drop box. The shift supervisor cosigned the slip, and Sarah sealed the deposit in a large envelope.

"Hey, guys, I'll be right back," she told the kitchen crew. They waved, used to her going to the bank each evening.

The swing shift was the smallest, except when they were catering a dinner. Luckily in Glimmer Creek, there were plenty of people willing to work on an as-needed basis.

Tyler was sitting at a table by the front window, pouring over figures in his notebook, presumably the measurements. She just couldn't see what he hoped to do with them without knowing the proposed regulations.

"Um, are you done yet?" Sarah asked, wanting to push him out the door.

"I have a bit more to do. Your candy chef said she takes a break at eight, so I'm waiting till then to finish my measurements in the smaller kitchen."

TYLER FOUGHT BACK a smile at the harried look on Sarah's face. She hadn't agreed to accept his advice, but the more she resisted, the more he wanted her to take it. The situation was unusual for him, to say the least. He was no longer accustomed to pursuing clients and certainly not to being turned down for a free consultation.

"Fine. I'm going to the bank with the night deposit."

Sarah unlocked the door and went outside. Tyler found himself watching as she walked up the street, her hips swaying gently. The late sun glinted like platinum fire on her hair, and he shifted uneasily, more physically aware of her than he wanted to be.

As she turned to cross, a motorcycle came roaring up the street and veered toward her. Tyler jumped to his feet as the rider reached for the thick envelope she carried. The biker missed, but pushed Sarah hard enough that she went down.

Tyler ran outside as he dialed 911 on his cell. The emergency operator answered on the first ring.

"A motorcyclist just tried to rob Sarah Fullerton, half a block southeast from her business," he said concisely. "Across from the bank. They hit her and drove off."

"Yes, sir. Please stay on the phone while I dispatch officers to the scene."

Sarah was sitting up when he got there, dazed, but still clutching the envelope.

"I've called the police," Tyler explained, trying to determine if she was badly hurt. "Do you need an ambulance?"

"No, and I don't need the police, either. It was just a motorcyclist who doesn't know how to steer."

"Somebody tried to rob you, Sarah," he announced bluntly, anger burning through him. "I was watching, and there's no question the biker was reaching for the envelope. He also struck you and left. That's hit-and-run."

A hum of agreement came from the onlookers who'd gathered.

Sarah tried to get up, and he insisted she stay put. "You need to be checked first." Tyler heard a voice from his phone and put it to his ear. "Sorry, what was that?"

"I've dispatched paramedics, sir," the dispatcher said. "May I have your name, phone number and address?"

Tyler was providing them as a police car and paramedic unit came screaming to a halt nearby.

Two uniformed officers and a paramedic team came over, and it was clear from the way they greeted Sarah that she was either family or a good friend. One officer started directing traffic while the second took a report, speaking to the different witnesses.

A third vehicle arrived, and a tall, solemn-looking man got out, striding over to Sarah. She was now sitting at the end of the paramedic vehicle while they treated an abrasion on her elbow. Though he wore plain clothes, he had a badge attached to his belt.

"Hey, coz, what happened?" he asked.

"A motorcyclist brushed against me and I got knocked over. I wouldn't have even fallen if I hadn't been off balance. Everyone is making too big of a deal about this, Zach." Yet her voice had risen, suggesting she was more agitated than she wanted to let on.

"Somebody tried to snatch the bank deposit she was carrying," Tyler interjected. "I saw it clearly."

Sarah remained pale as he described the rider, which wouldn't help with identification. Despite the warm day, the biker had been wearing a bulky jacket, gloves and helmet. Tyler couldn't even confirm the person's sex. On top of that, nobody had spotted any distinguishing insignia on the rider's clothes or motorcycle.

"We have a bulletin out to watch for bikes of that description, but it's probably long gone now," Zach said.

The paramedics advised Sarah to see a doctor but didn't think she needed to be transported to the local medical clinic.

"Hey, Millie," she called, waving to a woman hovering at the edge of the crowd. Tyler recognized her as one of the cooks he'd seen working in the kitchen. "I'm all right and I'll be back in a few minutes."

Though Millie nodded and walked back toward Sarah's Sweet Treats, it was clear that she'd rather stay. Frankly, Tyler thought they had too many onlookers. The officers seemed to agree because they were urging the crowd to disperse.

Sarah was keeping a death grip on the envelope and looked at Tyler blankly when he offered to put it in the bank's night drop box, just a few feet from the paramedic's vehicle.

"Oh. Yeah." She glanced down, then held it out to him.

"Just a moment," ordered Zach. "Sarah, how much cash is in there?"

"Twelve hundred seventy-two dollars and fifty-three cents. Also some local checks."

"Who knew you were bringing the deposit down here?"

"Practically everyone knows I take care of it around the same time each evening."

Zach looked exasperated. "Routines make you an easy target, Sarah. Until we get this sorted out, call the station and I'll send an officer to escort you or come myself."

"I really don't think the rider was trying to steal it," she protested.

"That's your Pollyanna nature speaking. Witnesses say otherwise, and it's better to be safe than sorry."

Tyler took the envelope and dropped it in the deposit slot. If he'd thought a small town like Glimmer Creek couldn't provide any excitement, he'd obviously been wrong. But this was one form of excitement he could do without.

CHAPTER FIVE

SARAH WAS MORE SHAKEN than she wanted to let on in front of her cousin and Tyler Prentiss. She didn't want to believe someone had been trying to rob her, but the scared part of her—the one that had been getting silent calls at night and a complaint called into the city—wasn't so sure.

One minute she'd been enjoying the evening sunshine, and the next she was on the ground. Her arm hurt, and she suspected the rest of her body would protest once the shock had worn off.

Her own impressions of the motorcyclist were vague at best. She really hadn't been paying attention.

Glimmer Creek was wary of motorcyclists. A few years ago, they'd had two biker gangs meet up in town and get into a fight, but Sarah had friends in Los Angeles who rode motorcycles and they were nice people. They just liked the freedom they felt on a bike. While some were more unconventional, that didn't make them criminals.

"Shall I contact Kurt for you?" Zach asked, distracting her.

She shook her head. "I'll talk to Dad myself. It would scare the heck out of him if you call, and I don't need more drama tonight."

"Okay. Who is this?" he queried, looking at Tyler.

"Tyler Prentiss. He's staying at Poppy Gold, and his mother works for me. Tyler, this is Zach Williams, the Glimmer Creek police chief."

Zach's expression shifted almost imperceptibly as he shook hands with Tyler. He must have remembered Great-Uncle Milt saying that Tyler had caused a scene at the bakery.

"Hello, Mr. Prentiss," Zach said coolly. "I don't think Sarah mentioned that we're related." It was a not-so-subtle warning.

Tyler's return smile was equally measured. "I figured it out when you called her *coz*."

"Of course. Sarah, let me take you home," Zach said after a final look at Tyler.

"Nonsense. My car is behind the shop, and I'm okay to drive."

He hesitated, then nodded. "Very well. Call if you need anything."

Sarah was grateful when the officials and most of the onlookers had dispersed. She glanced at Tyler. "You'd better get going, too. I'm sure Rosemary wonders what's kept you."

"Mom knew I was coming here to discuss your

building. She'll be more concerned if I return too soon. Besides, I haven't finished measuring."

"Maybe another time," Sarah said firmly. She wasn't in the mood for dealing with anything but the necessities, and Tyler was far from a necessity. While he might be a great architect, she couldn't afford him.

He shrugged. "I'll still walk you back."

It was just a short way and the same direction as Poppy Gold, so she didn't object. But at the entrance of the shop she stuck up her chin. "Good night. Thanks for coming to help."

She quickly slipped inside and locked the door behind her.

"Sarah?" Millie called from the kitchen.

"Yes, it's me." Sarah went in and tried not to appear as frazzled as she felt. "Can you handle everything? I want to go home for a hot bath."

"No problem," Millie assured her confidently. "You don't have to stay every night. We know what to do."

"I realize that. There's just a lot of work."

"And you have *us* to do it."

Sarah didn't need more convincing. She locked up the credit card receipts, grabbed her purse and went out the back door. Each business on the block had a rear parking area, a perfect spot for the electric food-delivery vehicles. All she'd needed to do was install a special station for overnight charging—with few exceptions, Poppy Gold didn't allow modern gas-powered vehicles on-site.

Automatically, she plugged the catering vehicles into the charger, then got in her car and drove home.

Once inside with Theo on her lap, she started to call her father's cell, only to remember he'd said he'd lost it. So she dialed his home number. It was unusual to get voice mail—he was the early-to-bed type—but easier, too.

"Hey, Dad," she said brightly. "In case someone else calls and tells you about it, I wanted to let you know there was a minor incident on Mariposa Avenue this evening. A motorcyclist drove too close and I fell, but I'm perfectly all right. I'm home now and going to bed. I'll see you tomorrow. Love you."

Sarah disconnected and dialed into her own voice mail. There were several silent messages. She deleted them one after another, her stomach churning.

Earlier in the day, she'd signed up for the national Do Not Call list. It would take a while for her number to be processed…but if the calls weren't from a telemarketer, being on the list wouldn't do any good.

Theo was still hungry for attention, so she cuddled him for another few minutes before opening a can of his favorite food and going upstairs for a bath. The water lapped around her, soothing her tired muscles, and she closed her eyes.

Abruptly the phone rang. She'd put the handset within arm's reach—half expecting her dad to call—but the caller ID showed it was her cousin Tessa.

Sarah let out a sigh. Tessa had gotten married two years ago, so she generally didn't phone this time of the evening unless it was related to Poppy Gold Inns and a catering need. Marriage changed people, but even having a baby hadn't dulled Tessa's determination to make the facility an even bigger success than her parents had already made it.

"Hey, Tessa," she answered.

"Hi. Um, I just checked my email. We have a last-minute request to have a catered dinner on Saturday. It's for that big family reunion—the one you're doing a reception for tomorrow. I know it's a lot to ask, but is there any chance you can accommodate them?"

If Tessa hadn't been her cousin, Sarah would have screamed that the Poppy Gold website stated all catering requests needed to be made three weeks in advance, not less than two days. Instead she gritted her teeth. "How many people?"

"Ninety-seven, guaranteed. If it helps, they're offering to pay a 25 percent surcharge for the short notice. They want the wild salmon and prime rib menu."

Sarah's stomach rolled. She was allergic to seafood—even the smell made her nauseous—but salmon was so popular, she had to offer it.

"I'll check the schedule and contact the supplier in the morning to see if they can get enough salmon," she said. "I'll let you know tomorrow. Now go pay attention to your husband and stop looking at emails."

Tessa laughed, and Sarah heard a male voice rumbling in the background. She was glad her cousin was happy, but it was hard to imagine living with a guy like Gabe McKinley, a grim former navy SEAL whose hands were probably registered as lethal weapons. Still, he might be good with those hands in other ways...

Sarah grinned as Tessa said good-night.

Leaning her head back, she tried to relax again but couldn't. Theo wandered into the bathroom and meowed. Sarah held out her hand and he rubbed against her fingers, his loud purr rumbling like a poorly tuned motor. She'd once read that cats could modify their purr to get what they wanted, but it hadn't been a revelation...this was Theo's "come to bed" purr.

Bed was an excellent idea, so she got out and dried off.

The phone rang again and she checked. It

wasn't her father—it showed the caller ID was unavailable.

No way was she answering it. She needed sleep, and her imagination was already working overtime. There wasn't any reason to connect the calls to the anonymous complaint and motorcycle incident, but knowing and believing it were two different things.

KURT HAD A small side business repairing and servicing diesel engines, and he stayed late, catching up on work, only to be ready to spit nails when he got home and found the message from his daughter. More than anything he wanted to go over to the house and check on her, but Sarah had said she was going to bed.

He accessed the voice mail for his missing cell phone, his concern escalating at a message from Uncle Milt, one of his father's younger siblings.

"It's Uncle Milt. I heard on my police scanner about an incident involving Sarah near the bank. She isn't hurt, but a motorcycle knocked her over and took off. There's also some question about whether it was an attempted robbery. Call if you want to talk. I'll be up late."

Kurt stared at the phone. Attempted robbery? Why hadn't Sarah told him that part? He paced the floor, arguing with himself about what he should do.

Finally he dialed Uncle Milt.

"Hello," boomed Milt Fullerton after two rings.

"It's Kurt. Thanks for letting me know about Sarah. She left a message but didn't give much detail. Do they really think someone was trying to rob her?"

"From what I heard on the scanner, witnesses thought it was a possibility. Don't stress too much. Zach was on the scene, and he'll take care of whatever needs doing. Besides, knowing Sarah, a whole lot more fuss was made over it than she likes."

"All too true." Sarah didn't appreciate being the center of attention. "Thanks for the info."

"No problem."

Kurt's mood was grim as he disconnected.

It was typical that Sarah didn't want him to worry, but when would she realize that he wanted to know if something was wrong, no matter what? He *needed* to know. She was his daughter; protecting her was his job, not the other way around. He couldn't make up for being a lousy dad when she was a child, but he could do his best to be there for her now.

THE NEXT MORNING started with a bang when Sarah found her father waiting at the bakery at her usual 4:00 a.m. arrival time.

"Is something wrong, Dad?"

"Wrong?" he repeated, his tone filled with disbelief. "Your message didn't mention that the motorcycle driver tried to rob you, before running you over and escaping the scene. Uncle Milt provided that little tidbit."

She winced. "Don't exaggerate. Nobody ran over me, and the rest is speculation. The rider could have lost control, then panicked when I fell."

"Maybe, but we should ask the police department to run extra patrols around your business and the house."

"Dad, I don't need extra police patrols. Even if it was an attempted theft—which is questionable— they were after my bank deposit, not my glass paperweight collection. Don't overreact."

"I don't overreact."

Sarah snickered. "Oh, yeah? When you came home on leave when I was a kid, you'd drag me to the doctor if I so much as sneezed or skinned my knee. Everything got blown out of proportion, and nothing has changed."

"I just want you to be okay."

"I was fine then and I'm fine now, but *you* need sleep," she ordered. "You can snooze in the office. Put your feet up and get some rest." She would have sent him upstairs to the apartment above the shop, but it wasn't furnished.

Her father disappeared down the hallway, and Sarah quickly set to work. Four and a half hours later, the last batch of food had left for Poppy Gold, her dad had eaten and gone, and the shop's shelves and displays cases were filled, ready for their first customers. But she couldn't relax. They had hors d'oeuvres to make for the reception that evening. And now the Lindors wanted a prime rib and salmon dinner for ninety-seven people?

Sarah wrinkled her nose.

She'd heard from her supplier. Prime rib was always available, and he'd just gotten a shipment of wild salmon. But she would have to pick up the order herself, which meant a special trip to Stockton the next morning. Reluctantly she dialed her cousin's office at Poppy Gold Inns.

"Hey, Sarah. Do you have good news for the Lindors?" Tessa asked when she answered.

"Unfortunately, yes."

Tessa chuckled. "I know it's a pain, but thank you. I'll transfer the payment immediately."

The sound of a child babbling "Mama, Mama, Mama" came over the line, and Sarah smiled.

"When did Merri learn to say *Mama*?" she asked. Merri was Tessa's daughter, a toddler who was the darling of the Poppy Gold staff.

"Oh, that's right, you missed the big event. A few weeks ago, she stood up during Grandpa George's sermon, pointed at me in the choir loft and shrieked *Mama*, but she hasn't come out with *Daddy*, much to Gabe's dismay. I keep explaining to her that even *Dada* would be enough to make him happy."

"I'm sure she'll get that next. Give her a kiss for me."

Sarah got off the phone and let her staff know that the Saturday evening meal was officially a go, then returned to her baking.

Soon, loads of food would start going over to the historic Glimmer Creek Concert Hall where the reception was being held. Poppy Gold handled decorating and did all the setup, so mostly the catering staff just needed to refill the food platters as needed.

"Are you okay?" the shift supervisor asked as Sarah swallowed an aspirin.

"I'm fine. A headache is all," she fibbed.

She was achy from the previous evening, but she was trying to downplay the incident with her staff, not wanting motorcyclists to get an even worse reputation than they already had in Glimmer Creek.

KURT WAS STILL WORRIED about his daughter when he returned to the bakery at midmorning.

The kitchen was frantically busy, and he didn't try to speak with her, instead slipping into the office to chat with Rosemary. "Did you hear what happened to Sarah last night?" he asked, sitting down.

"*Yes*. She hasn't said much about it, but Tyler saw everything and told me. He was here to talk about the remodeling."

"What remodeling?"

"The building inspector told Sarah yesterday that the county building codes are changing. She'll need more space in the kitchens and another exit in the back, that sort of thing. He's sending a full report in a few days."

Kurt didn't like hearing there was *another* problem he hadn't known about, though to be fair, it could have slipped Sarah's mind after nearly being robbed. At any rate, he'd get the family together to handle the renovations, and she could use the commercial kitchens at Poppy Gold while it was being done. His niece would be happy to help out, and Sarah already used their kitchens whenever she catered a meal.

"Is there anything *else* I should know?" he asked.

Rosemary looked uncertain for a moment. "Well, Sarah is going to Stockton in the morning to get supplies for a last-minute dinner at Poppy Gold. Her grocery supplier has fresh salmon available, but they can't get it to Glimmer Creek in time, so she has to pick it up her-self, along with prime rib and a load of produce."

In spite of Kurt's concerns, he was pleased to learn there was a way he could help. "I'll take care of it. Would you or Nathan like to drive with me?"

"I'd love to, but Nathan is the one who needs an outing. I'm afraid he won't be in the best of moods, though. Tyler is taking him to see a doctor today, and he isn't happy about it. If you could convince him to go with you, I'd be aw-fully grateful."

"I'll see what I can do," Kurt assured her. "Then when I get back tomorrow, why don't I show you Poppy Gold's Victorian greenhouse? You haven't seen it yet."

"I'D LOVE TO," Rosemary said. She smiled deter-minedly. She'd felt ill ever since Tyler had spoken to his brother about the possibility of returning to active duty. It would be nice to have a distrac-tion on her days off.

At least Kurt understood what Nathan was going through. It seemed to help her son to spend time with someone who'd seen war and the de-struction it caused…someone who'd come out whole on the other side.

"I still can't find my cell," Kurt explained,

"but I'll call from work and let you know if Nathan decides to join me."

"Check around your driver's seat for the phone," Rosemary suggested. "That's where I always find mine. They slide into the oddest places."

"Good idea." He got up. "I'll tell Sarah I'm getting that fish. I wish people wouldn't order it. She's allergic to seafood and gets sick at the smell alone."

Rosemary blinked. Sarah hadn't mentioned she had a problem with fish. "There's bound to be odor, even in a cooler."

"Yup. She has special cold boxes to use when needed, just for salmon, so there won't be any chance of cross-contamination. She even has one of her chefs prepare it in a separate kitchen."

Whenever Kurt talked about his daughter, pride welled from every word.

"I'd better get going," he said. "They want extra flowers for that reception tonight at Poppy Gold."

He left the door open, and Rosemary could hear him in the kitchen telling his daughter that he would take care of the trip to Stockton.

"No," Sarah refused promptly. "It's my responsibility."

"Of course it is, sweetheart. But I need a few

things for my repair shop, and I may as well kill two birds with one stone."

Rosemary grinned at the excuse. It was unlikely he had a desperate need for anything since he drove to Stockton weekly.

"You're just making that up."

Rosemary's grin widened; obviously Sarah didn't believe him, either.

"No, I'm not," Kurt protested. "Besides, I'm inviting Nathan Prentiss to go with me. We have the best conversations. Some things have changed in the army since I retired, while others are just the same."

"Oh. Well, I'll pay for your gas."

"We can discuss it later. Love you, sweetheart."

A minute later, Sarah came into the office. "Did you hear?" she asked. "Dad is insisting on picking up the supplies instead of me. He's like a tornado sometimes."

"It makes him happy to help," Rosemary said softly. "At least he can do more for you than I can do for Nathan."

"Nathan isn't improving?"

"He has good and bad days. I wanted to give him space here at Poppy Gold—he was adamant that all he needed was peace and quiet—but I don't think he's even doing the exercises to strengthen his leg. Having your father to talk to is boosting his spirits, but he needs more than a confidant."

"I told Tyler that Dr. Romano at the Glimmer Creek clinic has experience with combat veterans."

"So I heard. He's taking Nathan there this afternoon." Rosemary fought back guilt. Once again she was relying on her eldest son to handle things instead of taking care of them herself. She'd truly believed that Nathan wasn't improving at the rehab center, but she also should have been more assertive about him getting medical support here.

Not that feeling guilty was anything new, especially when it came to Tyler. They should have seen his birth as a precious gift after Kittie died. Instead they'd dreaded the possibility of losing another child. Was that why he'd been such a sober, self-contained little boy? It wasn't that he hadn't been wanted, but he'd come too soon, before they could deal with their grief.

"You can take time off if you want to take Nathan yourself or go with them," Sarah said, breaking into Rosemary's thoughts.

"Thanks, but that would probably disturb Nathan even more."

"All right. I'd better get back to the kitchen now. The Lindor family ordered a mountain of food for their reception." Sarah smiled and walked out of the office.

Rosemary was grateful that Sarah was so nice. She could have gotten angry that Kurt had learned about the trip to Stockton. Perhaps telling him had been wrong, but Rosemary knew how unhappy he'd be to discover, too late, that there was something he could have done for his daughter.

She pursed her lips.

Her job wasn't important to her because of the money—it was just important. She *could* contribute something to make things easier for Sarah, and it was a gift to feel useful, particularly since she didn't feel that way with her sons. She was desperately proud of Tyler and Nathan, but neither wanted to hear it.

CHAPTER SIX

TYLER WAS PLEASED when his drafting table and other basic supplies arrived late in the morning. He would focus on his commissions whenever his mom and brother didn't need him.

His mother had suggested using the extra upstairs bedroom as an office, so Tyler set up his equipment by a south-facing window that overlooked the garden and the California hillsides beyond. It didn't have all the amenities he was used to, but it would be a good place to work on his contract with a group of developers. They'd purchased a tract of land with a private lake and wanted to build a commercial fishing lodge.

Yet before he could start working, an email arrived from the law office in Chicago, letting him know an article about the building collapse had just been published in a leading trade magazine. Tyler went to the website and frowned as he read. The author refrained from blaming anyone, while stating "prominent architect Tyler Prentiss" was connected to the investigation.

Well, at least Tyler knew his legal team was keeping on top of everything.

At lunch, Rosemary returned and reported that Sarah was cooking frantically and didn't appear affected by her brush with the motorcyclist. Tyler admired her grit, if not her refusal to accept that someone had tried to snatch the sweet shop's cash.

"I hope she'll be more careful when taking her deposits to the bank from now on," he commented.

"Me, too. At least she won't be going there tonight. We'll be too busy because of the catering job, so she'll have to do it before opening tomorrow," Rosemary explained.

Tyler made a mental note to go by Sarah's Sweet Treats in the morning. If Sarah had such a predictable pattern, she'd be an easy target, morning or evening. Then he shook his head—he wasn't a protector like his brother, he was an architect. And Sarah probably wouldn't appreciate an attempt at chivalry.

Nonetheless, Tyler found himself across the street from the bakery the next morning, sitting on a bench and drinking a cup of coffee, arguing to himself that he was just making up for the way he'd behaved his first day in Glimmer Creek.

At any rate, he preferred it to waiting for the next call from a client wanting to cancel or "sus-

pend" their contract with him. The calls had
started late the previous afternoon, prompted
by the article; nobody wanted their projects to
be tainted by the faintest hint of scandal.

At 8:30 a.m., Sarah stepped out of her shop,
carrying another large envelope. Tyler stood and
crossed the street as she locked the door behind
her. "Are you doing better after your tumble on
Thursday?" he asked.

She whirled around. "Did you have to sneak
up on me?"

"I didn't sneak. And considering what happened, you ought to be more aware of your surroundings."

"Still convinced the motorcyclist targeted
me?"

"More than ever. Come on, I'll walk you to
the bank, and you can try to persuade me that I
didn't see what I know I saw."

Sarah made a noise of derision as he fell into
step next to her. "Yeah, you obviously have an
open mind about it."

"More open than you, and I'm not the one who
was nearly robbed."

"That's my problem, isn't it?"

Tyler shrugged. "Sure, but a robbery would
have upset my mother, and I'm concerned about
her getting stressed out."

SARAH DIDN'T DOUBT it would have upset Rosemary. It was irritating…now that Tyler had declared his mother was fragile, Sarah was seeing hints he was right to a certain degree. Regardless, she didn't think her new office manager was ready to have a breakdown, just because Rosemary tended to be anxious about things.

Who could blame her with everything going on?

Life had a way of dishing out good things and trials in large scoops. Sarah remembered when Aunt Meredith had died. Shortly after that, a friend from Los Angeles had been killed in a hit-and-run collision, and a great-aunt had gone through a stem cell transplant for a condition nobody in Glimmer Creek had ever heard of. It got to the point that Sarah had hated answering the phone.

Losing her husband must have been the hardest blow to Rosemary. Uncle Liam had lived in a fog for almost two years after Aunt Meredith's death, though he was much better now that his daughter was happily married with a little girl of her own.

Hmm… Since Rosemary had spoken longingly of grandkids several times, she might respond the same way if her sons cooperated.

"What are you grinning about?" Tyler asked,

sounding suspicious. "You look like a cat caught with cream on its whiskers."

"I was just thinking your mom would benefit if one of her sons got married and started a family."

"You're my brother's type. Are you volunteering?"

Sarah rolled her eyes. "I'm not a 'type.' Besides, while I'd love to have kids, I used to be married to a manipulative creep. It wasn't an experience I'd care to repeat. Maybe someday I'll meet someone who's open and honest, who I can tr..." Her voice trailed off. She'd already revealed more than she'd intended.

"Trust?" Tyler finished, correctly guessing what she'd started to say. "Don't tell me someone with a Pollyanna nature has trust issues."

"Pollyanna?" she repeated.

"That's what your cousin called it when he was investigating your so-called accident."

Sarah vaguely recalled Zach saying something of the kind, but she'd been in shock and hadn't paid much attention. "He's wrong—I'm *not* a Pollyanna. If it makes you happy, I'll even concede that someone may have tried to rob me."

"What changed your mind?"

"I didn't change my mind, I'm just admitting the possibility. So, how did Nathan's visit to the clinic go?"

"Now you're trying to change the subject."

Sarah gave him a hostile look. "Would you rather talk about *your* marriage plans? I know several single women I could introduce you to."

"No, thanks. According to reliable sources, I'm poor husband material. Not that it bothers me. I like being a bachelor. Besides, my career plans don't have room for a wife and kids."

She didn't doubt it. Tyler probably rehearsed ways to warn women that he didn't want a long-term relationship. But she suspected there was more to his "I'm poor husband material" statement.

She turned to cross near the bank, but Tyler caught her arm, carefully checking both directions on the street, which was still quiet. His old-fashioned protectiveness was nice, if unnecessary.

"Do you always cross here?" he asked after she'd dropped the deposit envelope in the bank slot.

"Pretty much. We all do, even visitors. When Zach became police chief, he asked the city council if they wanted his officers to start writing jaywalking tickets, but the city council felt it would be bad for tourism. Instead they added crosswalks to blocks with high foot traffic."

"Eliminate the crime, instead of dealing with the criminal?"

Sarah cocked her head. "That's harsh. Jaywalking is hardly a major offense."

"It's still breaking the law."

She resisted calling him an uptight prig *or* admitting that until the crosswalk had been added, she'd gone to the corner. It was a safety issue, but she didn't see the point of being dour about the whole thing.

That wasn't to say Tyler's life *hadn't* been grim lately, so maybe there was some justification for it. Still, from what Rosemary had said, he'd been born serious and never changed.

To each their own, she supposed, but she preferred viewing the world around her with more joy. Laughter made everything better.

"I guess we just see things differently," she said as they went back across the street, not wanting to get into an absurd argument. "Did your brother go to Stockton with my father this morning?"

"They left around 7:00 a.m. I understand they're fetching fish and other supplies."

"We have a last-minute catering job tonight. I planned to go down myself, but Dad insisted."

He always insists, she added silently. It was sweet, yet frustrating at the same time.

They stopped in front of the bakery, and Sarah shifted from one foot to the other. Her grandparents had instilled strict rules about hospitality, and while she hadn't needed an escort to the bank, Tyler Prentiss *had* believed he was being helpful.

"Uh, do you want a cup of coffee?" she asked, unlocking the door. "The first batch should be brewed by now."

"Sounds good."

Sarah went behind the counter and checked the coffee makers. "What's your preference?" she asked.

"Poppy Gold special blend, if you have it."

"I couldn't stay in business if I didn't serve the Poppy Gold blend." She took his cup and filled it. "Cream and sugar?"

"Not for me. Mind if I sit and make a phone call?"

"No problem."

Sarah swiftly began setting out insulated pitchers of half-and-half and coconut milk creamer.

"I'll finish," said Aurelia as she breezed in from the back. But she looked confused when she spotted Tyler sitting at a table, phone to his ear. "Did you open early?"

"No. Mr. Prentiss witnessed my accident yesterday. He was concerned about the safety of my morning deposit, so he walked to the bank with me this morning. Now he's making a call."

Aurelia's expression turned friendlier. She'd heard about the motorcycle incident—the story had spread rapidly. No matter how strongly Sarah tried to downplay the idea of an attempted robbery, the possibility worried her staff.

It *could* have been a botched robbery. Her impressions were mostly of a rider veering toward her, but she'd been so distracted by thoughts of having to remodel again that she hadn't jumped out of the way in time.

An alarm chimed softly, reminding them that there were five minutes until opening, so Sarah left Aurelia and David, who'd arrived, as well, to handle the remaining tasks. The usual Saturday line of customers had formed outside the front door, and she waved before heading into the kitchen.

Yet all at once she shivered, realizing one of those customers could have been behind the helmet worn by the motorcyclist or be the one responsible for the anonymous complaint.

One of them could even be making the silent calls.

TYLER'S GRIP TIGHTENED on his phone as the president of the Lexington Consortium explained they were putting their building plans on hold for a while. He was barely aware of the cheerful chatter around him as people purchased baked goods and candy.

"The consortium is rethinking the project,"

Jeff Drake explained. "I'll let you know if they decide to move forward as is or if they're going in a different direction."

Tyler had been listening to his voice mail messages from the office when Jeff's call had come through. He'd taken it, knowing the consortium would probably back out of their deal because of that damned article. Not that Jeff was admitting it was the reason.

"I understand," Tyler said, trying to keep his tone even. "I'll return the fees you've paid." It was an absurd offer, but he was beyond thinking straight at the moment.

"Absolutely not," Jeff exclaimed. "You've done most of the work and the design is brilliant. I voted for the project to proceed, but the other members are quibbling about construction costs and other issues."

Tyler debated whether he should be blunt, but since his lack of diplomacy skills may have created some of the current problem, he decided to hold his tongue. Their relationship had always been cordial. Jeff had a clear understanding of what the consortium wanted, which wasn't always the case.

Now this?

They wanted to step back and reassess, but what other reason could they have except being worried about the situation in Illinois? Tyler had been working on the consortium's design for months.

His jaw hardened. "Well, thanks for letting me know. Hope your weather isn't too hot down there."

"It's July in Dallas, which says it all. I grew up in Nova Scotia and don't care for hot weather."

"I understand." Tyler forced a laugh. "Take it easy."

He disconnected before he said something he'd regret. Letting calls go to voice mail or having his assistant deal with clients was a possibility, but it smacked of cowardice. At any rate, part of him wanted clients to tell him directly why they wanted to back out. He wasn't in the mood to make it easy for them.

Technically they couldn't cancel their contracts—he wasn't in breach—but that didn't require them to go forward with building plans, just to pay for the work he'd already done.

Grimly he dropped the phone in his pocket and watched the stream of customers making purchases.

When his head began aching, Tyler instinctively put a finger to the scar at his hairline. The doctor had assured him it would fade and be barely noticeable, while a nurse had even made a joke that it was too bad it wouldn't be visible, since scars were almost fashionable. Neither of them had understood that he didn't care what it looked like. It was just a scar.

The first rush of customers had been served and Tyler got up, deciding he shouldn't keep monopolizing a table in the limited space.

He stepped to the counter when it was his turn. "A half dozen of the Italian meat sandwiches and a quart of the vegetable pasta salad," he said, holding out his credit card.

Aurelia smiled and bagged his order. "I gave you the employee discount because Rosemary works here," she explained as he signed the credit slip. "Enjoy your lunch."

"Oh. Thanks."

The idea of getting his mother's employee discount boggled Tyler's mind. He was still concerned the demands of a daily job would overwhelm her sooner or later, but there was nothing he could do about it except try to head off any trouble he might see coming.

"This is it," Kurt said, driving into a dreary industrial park on the far side of Stockton.

"Not much to look at," Nathan commented. After chatting for most of the drive, he'd fallen silent once they'd reached the city limits.

"It isn't impressive," Kurt agreed, "but Sarah gets good service from them, and they're normally able to deliver to Glimmer Creek on short notice."

The young man just shrugged.

Meeting Nathan had reminded Kurt of how *he'd* felt coming home from war to a world that no longer seemed to fit him. War wasn't glorious, the way some people believed. It was just death. For the most part, Kurt hadn't worried about dying. He'd worried about doing his duty and not letting down his buddies who were fighting alongside him.

He parked near the loading dock and got out.

A man appeared from the interior. "Hello. Are you from Sarah's Sweet Treats?"

"Yes. Sarah is my daughter. I don't remember meeting you the other times I've come here."

"I'm the owner, Grey Renault. I don't usually handle pickups, but we're shorthanded right now because three of my employees are National Guard reservists fighting the wildfire in Southern California."

Kurt grimaced. "Sorry to say it probably won't be the last one this year. It was a dry winter."

"I know. Apologize again to Sarah that we couldn't get to Glimmer Creek."

"No problem, I'm always happy to do something for my daughter." He glanced toward his truck and saw Nathan getting out. "I'd better get everything loaded," he said. "The coolers are in the back."

There wasn't an easy way to keep Nathan from

helping. Kurt just made sure he didn't lift anything heavy.

"As a rule, it's warmer in the valley than it is in Glimmer Creek," he commented on the drive back into the foothills.

"Both seem cool to me after the Middle East."

Kurt flexed his hands on the steering wheel. "Yeah, I remember what it was like there."

Nathan didn't say anything for a minute, then released a long sigh. "I went to the clinic yesterday for a checkup. Dr. Romano suggested image rehearsal therapy for nightmares. They mentioned it at the rehab center, but I didn't pay much attention. Do you know anything about IRT?"

"Some. It's supposed to be good for nightmares. Dr. Romano is a licensed therapist, so he could work with you on it, along with other post-traumatic stress treatment."

"I *don't* have PTSD."

Kurt snorted. "Son, you aren't an iron man. There's no shame in it. I had PTSD after my last tour and probably before then, except I wouldn't acknowledge it."

"You?"

"Sure. Simply couldn't get what I'd seen out of my head. Didn't have the nightmares, but during the day it was like a horror movie playing in my head, only this one was real. Restoring

Poppy Gold's greenhouse and learning how to grow things instead of fighting were what saved me. Also having my family's support. I say try whatever might work."

"I'll think about it," Nathan muttered.

Kurt didn't push, knowing it wouldn't help. Still, it had been good to hear Nathan mention a therapy program. Maybe it meant he was opening his mind to possibilities that could help.

"Should I drop you off at the lot near your suite first?" Kurt asked as they neared Glimmer Creek.

From the corner of his eye, he saw Nathan shake his head. "I can't be the only member of the Prentiss family who hasn't met your daughter. She sounds wonderful."

Pleased, Kurt called Sarah's cell phone.

"Hey, Dad," she answered.

"I'm almost there."

"All right, see you in a few minutes."

Sarah met them at the rear of the building and smiled at Nathan when he got out. "Hi, you must be Rosemary's son. Dad told me you'd offered to keep him company. I really appreciate it."

They shook hands, and it was plain that her smile and flattering remark had made an impact. Nathan's shoulders straightened and his chin went up. "I benefited more than Kurt."

"That's nice of you to say."

He made a diffident gesture. "Not at all. Never underestimate the value of good conversation."

"I still appreciate it." With another quick smile, Sarah checked the insulated containers. Then all the goods were unloaded into the respective kitchens and refrigerators.

Kurt realized he was prejudiced, but Sarah really *was* a fabulous cook and baker. And he was glad she'd achieved her dream of opening a bakery in Glimmer Creek. He just wished she didn't have to work so hard.

He also wished he could take a little of the credit for his only child turning out so well.

ROSEMARY WAS WAITING in the garden when Nathan and Kurt returned from the supply run.

"Ready?" Kurt asked her as Nathan sank onto one of the chaises, looking tired.

"Of course."

The greenhouses were located behind the maintenance area, and Rosemary's eyes widened as they approached the one in front. It was huge, with an ornate dome in the center and rounded sides that made her think of a Victorian birdhouse.

Going inside was like entering a different world. It was crowded with tropical plants and flowers, turning it into a tranquil jungle. The frosted glass ceiling was over twelve feet high

on each side and at least two stories through
the center.

"I could live in here," she declared. "It's so
peaceful."

"We're proud of it."

"Mmm. Were you disappointed when Sarah
didn't become a horticulturist like you?" Rosemary asked.

"Naw. And I'm not a horticulturist. I just grew
into the gardening job after I retired from the
army."

"I'm glad you don't mind that Sarah chose
something different. My husband had visions
of starting a legal dynasty and couldn't understand why Tyler and Nathan weren't interested.
Richard was a good man, he just couldn't get
past his wretched male pride. No offense," she
added quickly.

"None taken." Kurt bobbed his head. "Pride
is universal, but I'll admit my sex has a generous share. I was furious when my wife walked
out. Wounded pride was part of it, and I made
an ass of myself more than once."

Rosemary touched his hand. "Your heart was
hurting, too. Maybe pride becomes a disguise
when the pain is too great…like one of the car-
nival masks I saw in Venice on my honeymoon.
They were beautiful, but I remember thinking

that somebody could be weeping behind them and no one would know."

"Is that what your husband did—concealed his true self behind a mask?" Kurt asked.

Rosemary bit her lip. "It's complicated. Richard was always proud, yet after…" She stopped, but there was no longer a reason to stay silent. Her husband was gone and it hurt not to talk about her daughter. "My sons don't know, but they had a sister who died before they were born. Kittie was a toddler when she contracted spinal meningitis."

"Why don't Nathan and Tyler know?"

"My husband didn't want to speak about Kittie. *Ever.* I even took out a safe deposit box for her pictures and christening dress, for fear of what he'd do with them. Each year on her birthday, I've gone and looked through them alone. I even paid for the box in cash so he wouldn't find out."

"I'm sorry for what you went through," Kurt said awkwardly.

Rosemary was silent for a long moment. "I miss her every day and wonder what she'd be doing now—maybe she'd have a career, maybe she'd be married with children of her own. But I doubt Richard ever let himself think about Kittie. It simply hurt too much."

"Is that why he didn't want your sons to know about her?"

"Yes, and I worry how they'll react if they learn the truth someday and it didn't come from me."

"Are you going to tell them?"

"I'm not sure." She sniffed a fragile orchid hanging down from the ceiling. "I miss Richard desperately, but that doesn't mean I have to keep doing what he wanted."

"Perhaps he felt it would be too difficult for your sons to deal with death as children. Then it got harder to tell them the truth when they were old enough to understand."

Rosemary smiled wryly. "That's a generous thought, but I doubt it. As much as I loved Richard, he was self-centered. Maybe he needed to be that way to survive. You see, he grew up in the projects in Atlanta, and overcoming his background was desperately important to him. Even more after Kittie died. He was determined to be respected and make a huge amount of money. But he couldn't understand that more money wouldn't have saved our daughter. She had the best care…it just happened."

Over by the pond, a large green parrot blinked at Rosemary from a twisted tree branch, then moved back and forth along its knobby perch, turning its head from side to side.

She gazed at it, realizing her life with Richard had been like that bird's world…enclosed in a home that seemed safe and protected, but oblivious to everything outside its beautiful glass house.

It was okay for a tropical bird, but her own sheltered world had been smashed and there wasn't any way to put it back together.

CHAPTER SEVEN

By Sunday afternoon, Sarah felt as if everyone in the shop had run a marathon, cooking and serving food.

Her dad had shown up earlier that morning and insisted on taking the Saturday receipts to the bank, much to her annoyance. But they'd been so busy preparing a "down home" picnic for the Lindors that she hadn't objected too loudly. It could be tricky dealing with him. She didn't want to hurt his feelings, but she also wanted to be strong and not *need* his help. Sometimes she wondered if she would have ever learned to walk if he hadn't brought her to live with her grandparents.

After the last catering vehicle had returned from Poppy Gold, Sarah went into the office and collapsed for a few minutes. She needed to train catering managers to handle jobs from beginning to end, but there just never seemed to be enough time to do that *and* keep the business running. Perhaps it would be possible now with Rosemary running the office so well.

One option…

Sarah yawned. Though the silent calls had stopped coming, she was still having trouble sleeping. *Now* she kept wondering what else might take their place. It didn't make sense. She didn't know anyone with a grudge against her.

She shook herself and got up; she had to keep moving or she'd never get through the afternoon. But when she went to the front counter to see how things were going, she saw Tyler through the front window and made a face. He was measuring again.

"I'll be back," she told Aurelia and headed outside.

"*Still* measuring?" she asked.

"Just getting ideas." Tyler's face was more serious than ever. "I'm restless. Usually I'm far busier and until I see your floor plans, my own calculations are all I have to work with. This gives me something to do."

Sarah shifted her tired feet. "Not to beat a dead subject, but I don't have the final report from the building inspector yet. Besides, I'm not…that is, if you don't have other work, you should just enjoy being here with your family. Poppy Gold is a wonderful place to stay and relax. The activities staff make plans every day if you want something more structured."

"Planned activities aren't my thing."

He sounded so dismissive that she was annoyed. "You could study the local architecture. Poppy Gold has a wide variety of Victorian structures, and there are classic Arts and Crafts homes around town, as well."

"I'm getting the impression you don't want my help."

How did you guess? She had too much going on to add another complication. And Tyler was a huge complication, particularly with her hormones waking up. Just looking at him reminded her of how long it had been since she'd done more than date casually.

"I just think you have better things to do," Sarah said carefully. It was a wishy-washy response, but having grown up as the pastor's granddaughter, with strong expectations about her behavior, it wasn't always easy to be blunt. Well…unless her dander was up, the way it had been the day they'd met.

TYLER'S MOUTH TIGHTENED.

He suspected Sarah had heard about the incident in Illinois and didn't trust his abilities. Things were pretty bad when a business owner from a place like Glimmer Creek wasn't willing to accept a free architectural assessment.

"I suppose you've told my mother about the mess in Illinois," he growled.

Sarah lifted an eyebrow. "I'm not sure why

you're bringing that up, but are you saying Rosemary doesn't know?"

"She and Nathan have enough to deal with. But you know exactly why I brought it up— you think I'm to blame, which is why you don't want my advice. How did you find out? Online, I suppose."

"Actually, my great-uncle was concerned about the way you behaved during your first visit to the bakery and asked the police to run a background check on you. I don't have time to research people on the internet."

"Why is your great-uncle involved?"

"Aurelia was worried and phoned while you were huffing and puffing and making demands. Calling him is a habit. Uncle Milt was our police chief until he retired a few months ago. Zach is his grandson."

"Grandson? Only in a small town."

Sarah narrowed her eyes. "Glimmer Creek might be small, but that doesn't mean we aren't careful about our police force. Zach has fourteen years of law enforcement experience in different parts of the country. He may have gotten a boost because of the relationship, but he's well qualified for the job. Honestly, do you think everyone who succeeds here only did it because of nepotism?"

Tyler suspected he'd accidentally ventured into a sensitive area; Sarah seemed to have a fair dose of pride herself. After all, a branch of her family owned Poppy Gold Inns, so she'd gotten a "boost," as well, with the sweet shop.

"I apologize," he said. "That was uncalled for."

She looked slightly mollified. "All right. Let me be clear, I've dragged my feet about your offer because I can't afford to hire you and I don't like being under an obligation. It has nothing to do with the other matter, which I certainly haven't discussed with Rosemary. Besides, from the little I've heard, you're an innocent bystander. I mean, there was another architect who came after you, right?"

"The owner wanted changes I believed were unsafe, so I quit and he got someone else who made the modifications. But now he's claiming the error was in my original plan."

Sarah made a derisive sound. "Of course he's saying that. He's trying to duck legal responsibility, in case it comes out that the collapse was due to his changes. But even if they weren't, shouldn't the new architect have identified any existing problems before they continued? It seems logical that the other guy messed up."

Some of Tyler's tension eased and he smiled. "You have a straightforward way of looking at things."

"It's…uh…easy when you're on the outside looking in."

"I could say the same thing about your renovations," he pointed out. "Please let me make some recommendations as a more concrete apology for the way I've acted. You'd actually be doing me a favor since I don't like being inactive. I need something to do."

"Surely you have commissions."

His gut twisted. "Because I'm officially under investigation in connection to the building collapse, most of my clients have backed out of their contracts, or else they've put their projects on hold."

While it hadn't been necessary to explain, the information had burst out from a dark place. It was as if he'd wanted someone to know beyond an impersonal lawyer.

Sarah reached out a hand as if to touch him, then she drew it back. "That must be difficult for you."

"I certainly never expected any of my work to be connected to a structural failure. I even got a second degree in engineering because I wanted my designs to last forever."

"Is that your dream?" she asked softly.

Tyler thought about it for a moment. "I suppose you could put it that way. Look at the Egyptian pyramids. They've been there over four thousand years and will be there long after we're gone. The Great Wall of China is visible from space. And how about the Pantheon in Rome? It's stood for almost two millennia."

SARAH WAS BEGINNING to suspect an idealist might lie behind Tyler's dark eyes—numb and deeply buried beneath a lifetime of restraint. It gave her an odd sensation, almost as startling as the brilliant smile he'd flashed a few minutes earlier… a smile that had nearly taken her breath away.

"The problems in Illinois aside, how is your dream going?" she asked lightly.

Tyler shrugged. "Okay, except nobody wants to build pyramids any longer."

She bit her lip to keep from laughing, unsure if he was trying to be funny.

"I suppose not. Did you admire architectural treasures when you were a kid?"

"For as long as I can remember," Tyler said simply. "My favorite spot was the Lincoln Memorial on the National Mall. I'd sit and watch the visitors' faces as they walked up the steps. That's where I decided to be an architect—so I could design buildings so extraordinary they made eyes widen and hearts beat faster."

Sarah gulped.

It was a huge, sweeping dream, even bigger than she'd first thought. No wonder he wasn't looking for marriage; his career ambitions were taking all his focus. And the incident in the Chicago area was another threat to everything he wanted. Assuming he wasn't responsible for a flawed design, the damage to his reputation could still be substantial.

"I can see why you didn't think having a bakery in my hometown is much of an ambition," she murmured.

Tyler shook his head. "I shouldn't have suggested that. My only excuse is that I grew up with a father whose life revolved around monetary success and status. Dad was horrified when Nathan went into the army, and he dismissed architecture, saying real prestige was in law. If he was alive today, I can well imagine what he'd say about my name being connected to the building collapse."

"You don't think he'd be supportive?"

"Doubtful."

It was a single, flat word that revealed little. She sighed. What was that line…"just the facts, ma'am"? Most of the time that seemed to fit Tyler Prentiss—just the facts, with no hint of the emotions behind them. Even when he'd talked about designing great structures like the pyramids, she'd mostly guessed at his feelings.

She wasn't accustomed to people who kept things locked so tightly inside themselves; it was exhausting.

"Maybe he would have surprised you."

"I don't think so. The only place where Richard Prentiss surprised people was in court. He was a brilliant jurist."

If anything, the comment made Sarah feel worse for Tyler. She'd never experienced a mother's unconditional love and support, but she got it from her father on a daily basis. That love presented challenges, of course, and she worried that Kurt's life was too wrapped up with hers. She also felt guilty for wishing he'd *ask* if she needed something, rather than jumping in like a demolition team taking care of business.

On the other hand...it had been really nice during her divorce not to hear him say, *I don't understand why you married that creep in the first place.*

Just then a large group of chattering tourists turned the corner and came down the street, and Sarah suddenly realized how long they'd been talking.

"Sorry, I'd better get back to work," she said.

TYLER WAS DISCONCERTED to realize he wanted to prolong the discussion, though he didn't have a good reason to delay Sarah.

"Of course, but first let me thank you for telling me about the clinic," he said quickly. "Dr. Romano is quite knowledgeable about post-traumatic stress. He also recommended a physical therapist in Stockton, someone who's worked with combat veterans."

Tyler expected to hear, "I told you so," but Sarah just nodded. "One of my aunts is a doctor at the clinic, too. Emma Fullerton. She's great, but she doesn't have a military background like Dr. Romano. Anyway, tell Rosemary I'll see her tomorrow."

"Will do."

Tyler was troubled as he returned to Poppy Gold. He'd been interviewed dozens of times during his career, but he couldn't recall telling anyone about what he'd felt sitting on the Lincoln Memorial steps. And if he *had* told anyone his aspirations as an architect, he didn't think they'd ever asked how those aspirations were going.

He'd instinctively told Sarah things were okay, but *were* they?

And was *okay* enough?

Being a successful architect wasn't necessarily the same as doing the kind of work he'd hoped to do.

Tyler frowned.

Goals were practical, dreams usually weren't. People *didn't* build pyramids any longer, and all too often they didn't care if a building outlasted its profit-making potential. There were exceptions, of course, but aside from the private museum he'd designed in Italy, his work was becoming increasingly commercial in nature.

Not that there was anything with wrong that, but it was a long way from what he'd envisioned as a boy, sitting on the steps of the Lincoln Memorial.

OVER THE NEXT few days Tyler made a concerted effort to avoid thinking about Sarah and the innocent way she'd made him question what he was doing with his career.

It didn't matter anyway. Until the legal mess in Illinois was sorted out, he didn't *have* a career.

On Monday he stayed busy with phone calls and dealing with medical releases. Then on Tuesday he drove Nathan to his first physical therapy appointment—it turned out the therapist was a former Marine drill instructor who didn't mince words.

Sheepishly Nathan agreed to resume his daily exercises. Some of the exercises were to be performed in a swimming pool, so when they returned to Glimmer Creek, Tyler talked to the manager about letting them use Poppy Gold's pool at 8:00 a.m., before the regular opening time.

"I don't like getting special favors," Nathan grumbled as he finished his first workout on Wednesday morning.

Tyler tossed him a towel. "It's summer. The water will be packed with kids during the regular hours. You wouldn't be able to move, much less exercise."

"You're the one who's antsy around children, not me. If Pamela and I had gotten married, I might be a dad by now."

"Do you miss her?" Tyler asked, trying to make the question casual. It was tough to know what would upset Nathan.

"Some. I was pissed at the time, but at least she was honest about it. Some women don't want a military life."

Nathan ran the towel over his shoulders. He was thin, pale, and his skin was marked by scars. His physical appearance was one of the reasons Tyler had arranged for private time at the pool, not wanting his brother to deal with stares and curious questions until he was ready.

"Hello," called a voice from the maintenance gate to the swimming area.

It was Kurt Fullerton, and Tyler was interested to see Nathan square his shoulders. Maybe there *was* something to his mother's claim about Nathan respecting the other man and being able to talk with him about common experiences. But why hadn't he responded to the veterans he'd met in Washington?

"Hi, Kurt," Nathan called back. "What's up?"

"Not much. How did your workout go?"

Nathan pulled a T-shirt over his head. "My leg feels like rubber."

"Yeah, muscles take revenge when they aren't used enough."

Tyler expected his brother to get angry, but he just looked tired. "Yeah, but no more lectures. Okay?"

"Okay. I'll drop by after work." Kurt nodded and left the way he'd come.

"We'd better get going before the hordes arrive," Tyler urged.

They returned to the John Muir Cottage, Nathan silent and limping more heavily than he had on the way to the pool. He immediately sank onto a chaise in the garden and closed his eyes. Tyler brought his computer out to the suite's porch to deal with his email, recognizing one of Nathan's swift mood changes.

It might be a symptom of PTSD, but it wasn't easy to watch.

LATE THAT NIGHT Tyler was working at his drafting table, but his mind kept circling around the discussion he'd had that afternoon with Leonard Dalby, his lawyer in Illinois.

A special commission was being named to take over the investigation, and Dalby had petitioned to have the members drawn from outside the immediate area. He was citing conflict of interest since the county had approved the building plans and the contractor and owner were prominent local businessmen.

Tyler rolled his head from side to side to relax the muscles in his neck.

Dalby wasn't overly concerned, but obviously he couldn't make promises. Luckily Tyler had notarized documentation to show he'd advised against the modifications for safety concerns.

Just then, a sound from the ground floor caught Tyler's attention, and he headed down the stairs to investigate.

Nathan had fallen asleep on the couch, but he was stirring restlessly and their mother was bending over him.

"Mom, stop! Get away!" He sprinted down the remaining stairs and lunged between them as Nathan threw out a fist. It connected solidly with his jaw, a second blow followed almost immediately to his eye. For an instant the world dipped, then Tyler regained his balance and dragged his mother backward.

"What?" Nathan mumbled. He looked dazed and barely aware of what had occurred.

"Everything is fine. Go back to sleep," Tyler urged. He waited until his brother closed his eyes, then glared at Rosemary. "What were you doing?" he demanded.

"I just…" Her eyes widened. "You're bleeding."

"I'm aware of that."

There was a warm trickle over Tyler's left eye, and he went into the half bath off the hallway to take a look. The cut wasn't deep, so he pressed a clean washcloth over the spot.

"You need a doctor," his mother said at the door, her voice shaking. "I'll contact the front desk. They'll know who to call this time of night."

"I don't need a doctor."

"That's a lot of blood."

"I'm fine." He drew a calming breath. "Mom, you can't go near Nathan when he's having a nightmare."

"I know that, but it wasn't a nightmare. He was just restless. It cools off in the evenings, and I was pulling a blanket over him."

Tyler would have beat his head on the wall if hadn't already hurt so much. "I know you haven't seen one of his nightmares, but that's how they start. It doesn't matter anyway. Nathan is an expert in hand-to-hand combat and reacts instinctively when he's disturbed. The nightmares just make it worse because mentally he's already in danger."

Tyler went back into the living room and saw Nathan was thrashing around again with agitated mutters.

Nathan had never talked about the day he'd been injured, but he seemed to relive it in his sleep. Tyler shuddered. He'd had a few dark dreams himself in the past few weeks, but his memories of trying to rescue workers in a collapsed building couldn't compare.

He turned around. "Don't worry about it, Mom, go to bed. I'll keep an eye on Nathan for the rest of the night."

"You're hurt."

"I'm fine—it's barely a scratch. Besides, you have work tomorrow."

Even as the words left his mouth, Tyler felt a renewed sense of astonishment. He'd grown up with a mother who flitted from one charity event and fund-raiser to another, not one who reported to a job each day. He still suspected she'd get tired of it, but for the moment it was convenient. And maybe it *was* doing her some good. He was willing to admit his first reaction may have been a mistake.

Rosemary finally nodded. "All right. Come get me if you need anything."

"I'll do that," Tyler promised. "Sleep well."

After she'd ascended the staircase, he reevaluated the cut above his eye. The bleeding had stopped, but his jaw was dark where Nathan's first blow had connected. He was probably lucky to still have all his teeth.

Tyler started a pot of coffee in the kitchen and stood watching the restive figure on the couch. If he'd stayed home instead of going to Italy, would his brother have left rehab?

He clenched his hands, a familiar question rising—if he'd gone into law practice with his father, would Richard Prentiss be alive today? The thought had haunted him since the funeral.

Tyler didn't know the answer, but for some reason he wondered what Sarah would say about it.

It doesn't matter, he told himself bleakly. "Might have beens" were pointless. His father was gone, but his brother was still here, and Tyler would do whatever it took to ensure that Nathan recovered.

CHAPTER EIGHT

ROSEMARY SLEPT LITTLE the rest of the night, unable to let go of what had happened.

She'd gone downstairs to make a cup of peppermint tea, only to find Nathan on the couch again. Glimmer Creek was located fairly high in the foothills, and it was cool at night. He *had* seemed restless, but he'd always been a wiggly sleeper. Even as a baby it was impossible to keep him covered; he'd kicked and squirmed and ended up in the craziest positions in his crib.

Maybe she should have realized it was a nightmare. And maybe she should have tried harder to convince him to stay at the rehab center. Yet he'd been getting jumpier, refusing to eat, every little noise making him jerk. Shortly after Tyler had left for Italy, he'd announced he was checking out. Period. End of discussion.

An aide in General Pierson's office had already suggested a visit to Poppy Gold Inns when Nathan was released, so she'd called and they'd helped set it up.

Finally Rosemary got out of bed and dressed

for work. The reflection in the bathroom mirror was discouraging, and she made a face. Once she'd looked pale and delicate after a sleepless night. Now she simply looked older. When had that happened? She still *felt* like a girl. On the inside, she was the young woman in her wedding pictures.

In the kitchen she found Nathan dressed and sitting at the table. Tyler was setting out plates and food containers. A dark bruise had formed on his jaw and around his eye. They weren't talking, and the tension was so thick it made her skin crawl.

"Did you boys argue?" she asked nervously.

Nathan squeezed her hand. "It was simply a discussion. Tyler brought up going back east again, that's all. I'm still not interested, but he's right that you have to stay away from me when I'm asleep, Mom. It isn't safe."

"I know—I wasn't thinking. It won't happen again. What are you doing this morning?" she asked, anxious to change the subject.

Nathan gulped down a mouthful of coffee. "I'm going over to the Poppy Gold greenhouses. Kurt mentioned propagating plant cuttings. I don't know why he enjoys that stuff, but he suggested I give him a hand."

"He's proud of his work. The same as Sarah. I

think one of the reasons they're close is because gardeners and bakers have so much in common."

"Gardeners and bakers?" Tyler echoed, and both her sons looked at her as if she was insane. She didn't elaborate, knowing they'd probably always see her as flighty. But there *was* a similarity. Yeast and other leavening made baked goods rise. Water and sunlight made flowers grow. What's more, both required creativity, and both could smell heavenly.

Well…it might be a stretch, but it felt right.

Or maybe she just kept trying to find a reason she wasn't close to her own sons—a reason other than her mistakes as a mother. Having nothing in common would be comforting, because that was simply human nature.

"It was just an idea," Rosemary murmured.

"Mom?" It was Tyler, holding out a cup of tea.

"Thank you, dear." She tried not to look too closely at his bruised face.

The silence at the table echoed in her ears, and her few attempts at conversation were unsuccessful. She finished as quickly as possible and left for work.

The short walk was pleasant, and she called, "Good morning," as she went in through the back door. A chorus of greetings followed, but she didn't linger since the crew was getting the last breakfast orders ready for delivery to Poppy Gold.

Rosemary decided a thorough inventory of supplies was needed, so she checked, then focused on filling out purchase orders. Ordinarily Sarah left notes if she noticed any supply issues, but she was on edge, waiting for the report from the building inspector. It was a relief to sort the mail when it arrived and find an official-looking envelope from the city of Glimmer Creek.

Rosemary hurried into the kitchen. "Sarah, I think it's here."

SARAH WENT OUTSIDE to read the information Stephen Seibert had sent, not wanting the staff to worry more than necessary. They'd heard something big might be coming and it was a concern, no matter how much she tried to be reassuring.

The morning air was refreshing, so she sat on the trunk of her car and drew a deep breath to clear her mind. It didn't work. She still wasn't sleeping well, even though she hadn't gotten a silent call for a while.

Somehow that had made it worse.

She kept anticipating a call. Even though she'd turned off the phone, she couldn't help checking to see if there were any silent messages. She also had to make sure her cell was charged and nearby instead of relying on the landline, which was another reminder.

Still, the calls *had* stopped.

She could relax and forget about them, stay uptight, or get a new unlisted number to give her friends and family. Of course, then her dad would overreact because he'd want to know why...

Sarah shook her head and opened the envelope.

There were a number of technical terms, but it mostly boiled down to needing more floor space, a new cooling-heating unit, and other requirements that would be less problematic but still expensive. The new HEPA vac system alone would cost a fortune.

Stephen had written a separate note, apologizing again that he'd been the bearer of bad tidings and to let him know if there was anything he could do.

How about magically expanding my building? That would help. Sarah remembered the Harry Potter books where a tiny tent could be huge inside and a handbag could contain copious supplies. A solution like that would be wonderful. She could wave her magic wand and solve the problem.

"May if I take a look?"

The unexpected question made Sarah jerk so hard, she went sliding off her perch and might have fallen if Tyler hadn't caught her elbow. Thanks to him, she landed on her feet. "Don't sneak up on people," she scolded.

"I didn't sneak. Why are you so skittish?"

"You startled me, that's all. And I'm okay now. You can let go."

Tyler hastily released his grip on her arm. "Right. Mom called and said you'd gotten the report. She's convinced I can come up with a solution to the renovations you need."

"I'm afraid I need a miracle, not an architect." Sarah gave him a longer look and blinked. "Omigod, what happened?"

"It's a long story. I'd rather not go into it."

Hmm. He looked as if he'd been in a bar fight, but they rarely had that sort of thing in Glimmer Creek. Anyway, Tyler didn't seem the kind of man who *got* into bar fights.

"You may need stitches," she announced. "Rosemary can drive you to the clinic in my car."

"I don't need stitches *or* to be taken to the doctor by my mother," he returned coolly. "It just looks worse because it's on my face. Anyhow, I'm taking Nathan to an appointment in Stockton later and don't have time."

Why were men so stubborn?

Sarah rolled her eyes and got her first aid kit from the trunk of her car. "Sit," she ordered, pointing to the small loading dock.

"I don't need to be babied."

"That's good, because I don't intend to baby you. But you did a terrible job fixing that yourself, and you're going to scare people, going around like Frankenstein's monster."

"Is that how I look?" The corners of Tyler's mouth twitched. "Then it's a good thing I'm not sensitive about my appearance."

Sarah's stomach flip-flopped as she cleaned around the cut. It also gave her a close-up view of the healing scar at his hairline...and the strong, sensual line of his jaw.

Sensual?

She was insane to keep thinking that way about him. Yet she couldn't deny that even with a battered face, he was compellingly attractive.

And his smile when he really let it go?

She'd only see it the one time, but smiles like that could make a woman's heart go wacky. It was endearing, almost vulnerable, and had turned her inside out. But while he might have a real, no-holds-barred, completely charming smile that could knock a woman silly, he obviously didn't use it that often.

"Where did you get this?" she asked, lightly touching the older injury.

"In Illinois. The owner of the building that collapsed, Milo Corbin, asked me to come and see if there was anything I could do to advise the rescue efforts. My lawyer suspects the guy was already trying to shift blame."

Tyler's expression didn't reveal how he felt

about the matter, but Sarah suspected it was chewing him up inside.

"How would that help shift the blame?"

"Corbin now claims he just called to tell me about the structural failure and was surprised to see me at the construction site. He's given several interviews implying I came out of a guilty conscience."

A breath hissed between Sarah's teeth; Milo Corbin sounded like a bully. "Feel free to tell me this is none of my business, but maybe you should sue the guy for defamation. Show him you have teeth. That ought to put a sock in his mouth."

"My lawyer has mentioned the possibility of a slander suit," Tyler explained, "but worrying about my reputation seems petty compared to what those construction workers and their families suffered."

"Except if Corbin is responsible, he needs to be held accountable. Taking the high road is fine sometimes, but guys like that don't even *know* there's a high road."

"I'll think about it."

"Good, but you still haven't explained how you got injured."

Tyler shrugged, looking almost embarrassed. "The city engineer was on vacation, so I went in with rescue personnel to evaluate the best way to extricate trapped workers."

"And?" she prompted when he fell silent.

"And there was a concrete wall I thought would hold, but instead it came apart. A load of debris came down on me and one of the firemen," he continued in a tight tone. "But it *should* have held. The specifications on that wall were in my original plan, and it ought to have been fine even with twice as much weight on it."

"I suppose you've considered whether there was a flaw in the concrete."

The barest flicker of response crossed his face. "Yes. I've hired a Chicago law firm to protect my interests. I gave them a sample of the concrete that I managed to grab after I woke up. They're having it tested, but regardless of the results, they're reasonably confident about the outcome of the investigation."

"I'm glad."

"You are, aren't you?" Tyler asked in an odd tone. "Yet you've only known me for a few days."

"I care about justice."

"You can't be sure that I'm not at fault for those men being injured."

"Maybe I'm psychic," Sarah returned lightly.

She opened another square of sterile gauze, uncomfortable under Tyler's intent, questioning gaze. It was hard to explain, but she was convinced that he *wasn't* at fault, maybe because he hadn't spoken about the financial cost of the ruined building or bragged about his role in rescuing the workers.

Despite everything, she was starting to like him.

She finished cleaning around the wound and applied a butterfly bandage.

"I still think you should go to the clinic," she said unhappily. "This is close to your eye."

"I'll go if it gets worse. Honestly, you don't have to worry about me, Sarah. It's decent of you, but I'm okay. Now, about that report from the building inspector—do I get to see it?"

"I'll make you a copy. Wait here."

She grabbed the paperwork and went inside to the office. Rosemary looked at her anxiously. "What does it say?"

"I'm still digesting everything. Tyler is here and I'm making him a copy."

"Oh. I hope you don't mind that I called him. He might come up with something really innovative."

"We'll see." Sarah quickly ran the papers through the multifunction printer and tucked the original in her backpack. She hesitated, then asked, "How did his face get banged up?"

Rosemary instantly looked miserable. "Nathan did it. He didn't mean to, but he was having a nightmare. I thought he was just restless and went to cover him with a blanket, then Tyler yelled a warning and jumped between us. Everything seemed to go crazy, and Nathan hit him. Twice. I feel terrible."

Sarah patted her shoulder. "Don't feel *too* terrible—Tyler may have put Nathan into fight mode when he yelled. Dad says the fight-or-flight instinct is exceptionally strong for soldiers, whether they're asleep or awake."

"Really?" Rosemary brightened, only to have her face fall again. "Still, it wouldn't have happened except for me."

"Don't be so sure," Sarah observed wryly. "Dad had PTSD, and he says a loud noise can trigger a cascade of memories. It's probably worse for someone when they're asleep."

"I suppose. Honestly, I don't understand what makes either of my sons tick. Tyler has always been a mystery, and Nathan is like a different person since he was hurt. He was such a sweet boy, and so comforting after his father died. Don't get me wrong, Tyler was just as helpful," Rosemary added hastily. "He spent ages sorting out the finances and getting everything in order."

Sarah reflected that Tyler had offered practical support, and Nathan emotional encouragement. She wondered which one Rosemary had needed most.

"I'm glad they were both there for you." She held up the duplicates she'd made. "Tyler is waiting, I'd best get these out to him."

ROSEMARY FINISHED ENTÉRING purchase orders on the computer and sent them to the sweet shop's grocery supplier, but it was impossible to get her sons out of her thoughts.

And her husband.

Everything had changed in the months since Richard's death; the certainties had vanished, leaving the regrets behind. *If only I'd been stronger...* It was like a sad, unending mantra.

"You seem a million miles away," Kurt said out of the blue.

Rosemary yelped. "You nearly gave me a heart attack."

"Hey, I cleared my throat, but you must not have heard."

"I have a lot on my mind."

He sat down and put his cup of coffee on the corner of the desk. "Anything I can do?"

She smiled ruefully. "Actually, I may have *too* much help. As a matter of fact, I'm certain of it. My husband died almost nine months ago, and Tyler is still managing my finances. It was a relief to let him make the decisions in the beginning, but I have to start taking care myself. I just don't know how to tell him."

"Does he still think you shouldn't be working?"

Rosemary pursed her lips. "I'm not sure. He might be waiting to see if I fall apart and need him to rescue me."

Maybe she wasn't being fair, but Tyler didn't understand… The place where she felt *most* confident was her job at the bakery. Her responsibilities weren't that different from the fund-raisers she'd managed. Over the years she'd helped raise hundreds of thousands of dollars for important causes; so why had she freaked at the prospect of paying her own bills and balancing her monthly budget?

Kurt's brow creased in a frown. "You aren't going to fall apart—that's nonsense. I'll talk to him."

For Pete's sake, she had enough trouble with her sons. She didn't need anyone rocking the proverbial boat. "No, you won't. I'm grateful you've taken an interest in Nathan, but I'll do all the talking with Tyler. *Butt out.*"

Kurt's frown turned into a grin. "Butt out? I can't believe you just said that."

"Neither can I. You're corrupting me."

She shook her head as he left.

Kurt Fullerton was a big teddy bear who didn't know when to stop taking care of people. It might explain the underlying thread of exasperation she'd sensed in Sarah—she loved her dad and appreciated him wanting to help, but she was trying to be successful in her own right. Sometimes people just *needed* to do things for themselves.

Rosemary glanced at the desk where she'd put a photo of her husband. She'd let Richard make the decisions, and when he suddenly wasn't there, she'd been lost. Tyler's help had seemed like a lifeline at the time, but maybe she should have forced herself to take some responsibility.

THE NEXT EVENING, Sarah smiled at her dad across the restaurant table. "I realize you want to roll your sleeves up and start remodeling, but nothing can be decided right now."

"All right, but the family will help with whatever needs doing. Don't forget it benefits Poppy Gold, as much as it does you," he added quickly.

"I know everyone wants to pitch in, but nothing is final. Tyler is taking a look at the situation. He's offered to give me an opinion about what, if anything, can be done."

Her father nodded. "I can't get a handle on him."

Sarah looked down at her cheese enchiladas. She was having the same trouble. For the most part, she'd only guessed at the emotion flickering in Tyler's dark eyes. She kept telling herself it didn't matter. Either way, he was the last man she should find compelling. And yet she did.

It had to be a simple case of hormones. Perhaps if she dated more, she would be able to dismiss her response.

"Sarah?" prompted her father.

"Um, I think Tyler is just private."

"I prefer Nathan. Shame about his leg being so bad. While he hasn't said it outright, I can tell he's worried the army won't let him return to active duty."

"Rosemary has mentioned he's a career soldier, just like you were." Sarah clapped a hand over her mouth as she yawned. "Sorry."

Kurt leaned forward. "You seem more tired than usual, kiddo. Is the remodeling thing bothering you? I realize it's a pain, but we'll manage whatever needs doing."

"It isn't that." Sarah debated telling him about the calls and finally shrugged. "I was getting a bunch of silent phone calls that I thought were from a robocaller, then they started coming in the middle of the night. They stopped a few days ago, but my sleep patterns are still screwed up."

Her father's expression seemed worried. "Did you ever find out who complained about your kitchen? Maybe the two are connected."

"How could they be?" she countered.

"I don't know. But you mentioned that Tyler

Prentiss wasn't pleased about his mother working for you."

"I'm sure he isn't involved," Sarah said instantly. She was embarrassed that the idea had occurred to her and didn't want anyone else to think it now. However annoying and frustrating Tyler might be, he didn't seem the type of person who would resort to petty revenge. "Besides, the calls started before he arrived in Glimmer Creek."

"Then who could it be? Everybody adores you."

She repressed a snicker. That was her dad, totally unbiased. "I'm sure the complaint was just a misunderstanding or a practical joke that misfired."

"It wasn't funny."

Sarah reached over and squeezed his hand. "Dad, it's *fine*. Tonight I'm going to bed early and getting a good night's sleep. And thanks to you, I'm having a delicious dinner I didn't have to cook."

"Casa Maria sure makes a tasty chili colorado. Do you want flan for dessert or something else?"

Though dessert didn't appeal after baking all day, she nodded. Her father loved fried sopaipillas with honey, but he wouldn't order anything if she didn't.

"Flan sounds good."

They chatted about family the rest of the meal, and then he dropped her off at her house. Theo met her at the door from the garage, looking particularly pleased with himself, which made her suspicious.

"What have you been doing, Theo?"

He wound around her legs, oozing contentment. She understood when she found the toilet paper upstairs and down had been unrolled, the tissue dragged around and ripped to shreds.

"Got bored today, did you?" she asked as she gathered handfuls.

It was dark by the time she finished, and she promptly went to bed, already half-asleep.

She'd known the bakery would be hard work, but it hadn't been too bad until Tessa had asked her to provide breakfasts for Poppy Gold. The catering needs had grown from there. Definitely, she *had* to get employees trained and promoted. It would cost more, but it was the only way to be sure she didn't let Poppy Gold or her cousin down.

Sighing, Sarah turned on her side and listened to Theo's purr. She was almost asleep when her cell phone rang. Groggily she slid her finger across the touch screen to answer the call.

"Hello."

Silence.

Sarah bolted upright and looked at the display,

a sick sensation growing when she saw the number was unavailable.

"Hello?" she said again, not wanting to believe the whole thing was starting over with her cell phone.

Still nothing.

"You have the wrong number. Don't call again or I'll contact the police," Sarah announced, trying to sound more confident than she actually felt. She disconnected and drew a calming breath. The call *might* be a coincidence. Or a gag that had gotten out of hand. The kids in town usually didn't take things this far, but it was remotely possible.

She flipped on the light and saw Theo sitting on a corner of the bed with a disapproving expression. He didn't enjoy being woken up any more than she did.

"Come here, baby," she said, holding out her hand. He licked his paw and swiped it over his face before deigning to walk over and be petted.

With a sigh, Sarah leaned back. She couldn't turn off *both* the landline and cell phone—she had to be available if there was an emergency.

Okay. In the morning she would contact the phone company and ask if it was possible to stop calls like this one. In the meantime…she went to her jewelry box and found the police whistle that Great-Uncle Milt had given her when she'd left for college. She'd kept it on her key ring until returning to Glimmer Creek.

Sarah tossed the whistle up and down, then put it next to her smartphone. She crawled back in bed and was asleep, almost the minute her head hit the pillow.

SHORTLY AFTER 1:00 A.M., Sarah woke to the cell phone ringing again…though technically it wasn't a ring. One of her teenaged cousins had disapproved of her "boring" ringtone, so she'd downloaded the Star Wars theme song.

Sarah grabbed the phone and checked; as expected, no caller ID was displayed.

"Hello?" she answered.

When silence greeted her again, Sarah drew a deep breath and blew the whistle as hard as possible. A shriek sounded at the other end, but she couldn't tell if it had come from a man or a woman…her own ears were ringing from the whistle. She could imagine how her annoying caller felt.

"Take that, you imperial scumbag," Sarah said with satisfaction. "I *told* you not to call again."

CHAPTER NINE

SARAH'S INTERNAL ALARM BELLS went off when she found a message on her home voice mail on Saturday afternoon, but it turned out to be Tyler Prentiss asking if they could talk about renovation ideas, rather than the anonymous caller.

Sarah rarely left the shop early, but she'd decided to let the shift supervisor take over for the afternoon. It would have been pleasant to have the time for herself, but she had to admit Tyler might come up with ideas that another architect wouldn't consider.

He answered on the first ring. "Hello."

"It's Sarah. Your message said you wanted to get together. Where would you like to meet?"

"I'm sure the bakery is too busy, and there are people all over here at Poppy Gold. I'd rather not talk at the suite, so how about your place?"

She let out a breath, wishing she hadn't given him the choice. On the other hand, summer was one of the most hectic periods in Glimmer Creek; visitors were everywhere, which meant her house was best.

"Uh, okay," she agreed, petting Theo, who was ecstatic to have her home earlier than usual. She gave Tyler concise directions to the house.

"Sounds easy enough. I've got GPS on my phone if I get stuck. Is half an hour all right?"

"Sure."

Sarah got up, quickly dusting the surfaces in her living room. She spent so little time at home that there was rarely much housekeeping required except when Theo got bored and made a mess.

The doorbell rang exactly a half hour later. It wasn't a surprise; by all accounts, Tyler was a type A personality.

He has an amazing dream for his career, her conscience reminded her. When Tyler had talked about creating something that made eyes widen and hearts beat faster, she'd actually held her breath. People didn't talk like that much any longer. It was as if idealism belonged to preachers and poets.

With that thought she opened the door, only to suppress a gasp. While she'd seen Tyler's bruised face a few days earlier, it was still a shock.

"You…uh…"

"I know, I look like I've been brawling."

"I don't know about brawling, but you look like one of my cousins when he got whacked by a rake."

"Who was on the other end of the rake?"

Sarah chuckled. "His foot. He stepped on the tines to swing it upward, thinking he wouldn't have to lean over to pick it up. Russ could be lazy when he was a kid. Anyway, it popped up faster than he expected and nailed his face. Almost identical injuries, come to think of it."

"You must have a family story for every situation."

"Pretty much. My cousin Tessa is an only child like me, but most of my aunts and uncles have three or more kids. I saw it all growing up, good and bad. Do you want ice tea or coffee?" she asked.

"Coffee, if it isn't too much trouble."

"Not a problem."

Tyler followed her to the back of the house and sat at the table in the breakfast nook. "Where does Zach fit? You said he was your uncle Milt's grandson, but surely that wouldn't make him a cousin."

"Uncle Milt is actually *Great*-Uncle Milt. Zach is Grandpa George's great-nephew, which means Zach is technically a second cousin." She put water in a kettle and flipped on the heat.

"I would have expected you to have a bigger kitchen," Tyler commented, looking around. "But maybe you avoid cooking outside of the shop."

"Absolutely *not*," Sarah retorted. "This is

where I prefer developing new recipes and cooking for family gatherings."

TYLER NODDED. SARAH continually astonished him. Even her kitchen astonished him. It was fairly small and didn't seem to be overloaded. He would have expected her to have every culinary invention on the planet.

The kettle whistled, and she made the coffee in a French press, pouring it into a mug printed with "World's Best Kid." It was the sort of down-home gift his family didn't exchange. What would it have been like, growing up with parents who displayed their kids' A-plus school papers on the refrigerator? Or a father who used the clay pen holder his son had made in kindergarten instead of throwing it out?

Tyler pushed the thought away.

He didn't believe his father had intended to be hurtful; he just hadn't understood children. Nathan had been crushed to find the pen holder in the trash, so Tyler had said *he'd* like to have it. He still had the hideous thing; it was on his home office desk in Alexandria.

"Okay," Sarah said, sitting down with a glass of icc tca for herself. "What did you want to discuss?"

Tyler pushed less pleasant thoughts away and unrolled the blueprints he'd drawn, trying to ignore how desirable she looked. Her blond hair was like spun gold slipping from its thick braid, her eyes were a luminous green, and she was dressed in a snug T-shirt and faded shorts that showcased her figure.

It didn't make sense.

His preference was sophisticated brunettes, not slender blondes who ran around their house in bare feet. Of course, he had to admit that Sarah had very attractive feet. They were delicate, nicely proportioned, with slender toes and high arches. He'd never had a thing about a woman's feet or legs—feet were feet—but she had a particularly nice pair.

He cleared his throat. "There's a locked door here. Where does it go?" he asked, pointing to a spot on the diagram.

"That's a staircase to the second floor, which covers around half of the building. It's an apartment that hasn't been updated since the 1940s, though the plumbing is usable."

"I'd like to evaluate the floor plan. Moving the office upstairs would give you more space."

Sarah scrunched her nose. "You can check, but the steps are horribly steep. Definitely not to code. I lived up there for a few months, and it's hairy navigating the stairs."

"I still want to take a look sometime, if that's all right," he said. "Oh, I just remembered—this was on your front step." Tyler handed her the envelope he'd found tucked beneath the edge of her welcome mat.

"Is something wrong?" he asked, noticing a subtle shift in Sarah's expression as she checked the contents.

"It's just a coupon. One of my relatives probably thought I could use it. I'll have to remind everyone I come in through the garage." All at once Sarah frowned. "Is that the same bandage I put on you a few days ago?"

"Yeah, it's stayed on well. Even in the shower."

"You'll be lucky if it isn't infected" she said in an exasperated voice. "I'll get a fresh one."

With some women, Tyler might have wondered if she had ulterior motives, but not with Sarah. Anyhow, romance seemed to be the last thing on her mind. It wasn't that he'd object to a night together, but she didn't seem the type for recreational sex.

Sarah reappeared with a handful of supplies and removed the bandage she'd applied earlier in the week.

"This still looks nasty," she commented. "Getting it stitched might have meant a smaller scar."

"Scars don't worry me. Do you think it's infected?"

"I'm not a doctor, but I don't see anything suspicious and the swelling has gone down."

She carefully cleaned around the wound, giving Tyler a close-up view of her sweetly curved breasts and slim waist. His jeans grew tight and he restrained a groan.

For a woman who wasn't trying to entice him, she was doing an excellent job of it. As for her perfume? It was vanilla, cinnamon and chocolate, spiced with a dash of fresh-baked bread. He'd never imagined something so homey could be so alluring—maybe because he didn't associate fragrances like that with his childhood.

Almost as if Nathan was in the room with them, Tyler could his voice, *you're analyzing. Stop or your head will explode.*

"Did I hurt you?" Sarah asked out of the blue, startling him. "You're scowling."

"Just thinking. My brother claims I analyze too much. He could be right. An ex-girlfriend called me an ice man and said she felt sorry for any woman I got involved with."

"That's harsh."

"But accurate. I'm better with math and drafting tools than emotions. I didn't mean to shut Wendy out, it just happened. That's who I am."

Sarah gave him a long appraisal. "I don't know, you were pretty open with your emotions that day at the bakery."

Tyler doubted he'd *ever* live that afternoon down. "It wasn't my finest moment," he admitted.

Sarah shrugged and carefully applied a new

bandage. "You're forgiven. By the way, did you get a concussion along with this?" She gestured to the scar at his hairline.

"Yeah. They weren't happy when I checked out of the hospital and flew back to Italy. Well, after I met with a lawyer and hired him."

Sarah began laughing. "Omigod, it must be genetic."

"What?" Tyler demanded.

"Didn't you hear yourself? You checked out against medical advice…just like Nathan."

Damn. She was right.

A reluctant smile curved his lips. "You aren't going to tell my mother, are you?"

Sarah sat down and shook her head. "First I'd have to tell her about Illinois, so the answer is no, however tempting it might be."

"I appreciate that." Tyler tapped the blueprints he'd brought. "Back to your building… I'm guessing it isn't on the historic register."

"Actually, it's funny you mentioned that. Several weeks ago someone nominated Sarah's Sweet Treats for the state register. The application was inaccurate from beginning to end and recounted all sorts of lurid, bloodcurdling events that never happened anywhere in Glimmer Creek. The wildest story was that Joaquin Murrieta was killed by law officials there, rather than what really happened."

"Isn't Joaquin Murrieta just a legend?"

"*I* think he was real," Sarah asserted, "but some believe he's an amalgamation of several bandits, or that he didn't exist at all."

Tyler lifted an eyebrow. "You're intrigued by outlaws, huh? Is it the 'bad boy' appeal?"

"Wrong on both counts. While Murrieta is romanticized, in reality he was a vicious killer. Anyway, the application was incomplete. The state sent it back to me, because whoever filled it out put my address and name down as the applicant."

"Don't you think that's strange? Why would anyone both falsify the information *and* make sure you saw it?"

"At the time I…" Sarah's voice trailed off. "Yeah, it's strange. A lot of things are strange lately."

The back of Tyler's neck prickled. "Like what?"

"Nothing. That is, I shouldn't have said anything."

"It isn't nothing if it makes you look this scared."

SARAH DIDN'T WANT to look scared, she wanted to look strong and confident. But she'd forgotten about the historic register application. It hadn't seemed important at the time, and she'd dismissed it as a prank.

Now it was something else to question.

"What's going on?" Tyler prodded.

"You have your own problems, you don't need to hear mine."

"Wrong, it would be a relief to hear someone else's problems," he retorted. "This has been a lousy year for my family."

Sarah wavered. Tyler was a disinterested third party, unlike her father and half of Glimmer Creek. He might look at the situation with a fresh perspective.

"It'll sound ridiculous and a total overreaction, which is exactly what I'm always warning my father about."

Tyler made a sound of disgust. "Hey, I just confessed to checking out of the hospital early, which makes me an unparalleled hypocrite for jumping on my brother for the same thing. *Talk*."

Sheesh.

"Well, you know about the complaint called into the city."

"And the hit-and-run motorcyclist. What else has happened?"

Sarah didn't try to argue the motorcycle incident. "A week ago, I started getting flyers, catalogs and credit offers from stores all over the San Joaquin valley and San Francisco. Piles of them, with both my name and address spelled several different ways, so they couldn't have come from a single list. Basically it means somebody has been putting my name and address on sign-up lists. *And* they must have done it over a short period of time for everything to start coming at once."

"Is that why you tensed over the coupon I found on your step?"

She nodded. "I don't know anybody who'd leave me a coupon for a toy store in Sacramento. I haven't been north of Stockton in two years."

A hint of humor crept into Tyler's eyes. "Not even to shop at an adults-only toy store?"

Sarah nearly choked on her ice tea. A suggestive comment was the last thing she'd expected to hear from him. Maybe that starchy, uptight facade was hiding a wild side. Still…she grabbed his coffee cup and sniffed the contents.

His uninjured eyebrow shot up. "What's that about?"

"Just making sure you didn't add something stronger when I wasn't looking. It's hard to imagine the words *adults-only toy store* coming out of your mouth while sober. You have a persona that's very prim and proper."

The corners of his eyes crinkled. "I take exception to that description. Besides, you're deflecting. What else is going on?"

"I was getting strange calls on my home phone. Nothing obscene, just silence. They weren't a problem until they started coming in the middle of the night. The calls stopped for a few days, then on Thursday I got two, this time on my cell phone. One was around 10:00 p.m., and the other after midnight."

"It's hardly funny, so why are you grinning all of sudden?" Tyler asked.

"I...um, warned them not to try again when the first call woke me up. When the second one came, I blew a police whistle into the speaker. It may not stop them from harassing me, but it felt good to do something."

Tyler chuckled. "I'm sure."

Sarah nonchalantly waved her hand. "The calls should be over now, anyhow. I contacted the phone company yesterday, and they're going to stop calls when the number is unavailable, so I don't need to worry."

TYLER DOUBTED SARAH was as calm as she sounded, but he admired the effort.

He'd seen a fellow student being stalked when he was studying architecture. It turned out the perpetrator had conceived a bizarre grudge against the student, believing she'd cut him off in traffic one day. It had started with a few odd events and slowly escalated. He wondered if that was happening here, too.

"Have you talked to the police?" he asked. "They can help catch a stalker."

Sarah went white. "*No*. And I didn't say I was being stalked, just that some strange things have happened."

Denial, he decided, though admittedly it would be difficult for law enforcement to connect the events. And they *might* be a coincidence. As if rebutting the possibility, a motorcycle suddenly gunned down Sarah's street, so loud it made the doors rattle.

In silent accord they rushed outside, but the bike was gone.

"I haven't seen many motorcycles in Glimmer Creek," Tyler said, turning to Sarah. She was still pale.

"They...um, aren't popular here, though a cousin's boyfriend has one that he rebuilt when he lived in Sacramento. He doesn't use it very much."

"Any chance his bike is the one that hit you?"

Her strained expression eased. "None. Lance's bike is several different colors and quite battered. He pieced the thing together out of junkyards and it's unmistakable. I'm sure the motorcycle that veered at me was black and practically new. Do you want more coffee?" she asked with excessive cheeriness.

"I can't. Mom and Nathan are expecting me.

We're eating at the GC Steakhouse. It's the first time we've been able to convince Nathan to go to a restaurant instead of getting takeout. Maybe I could come over again later this evening."

Sarah gave him a quizzical look. "Do you have anything else to discuss about the remodeling?"

"Er, no." Tyler was thrown, realizing he just wanted to see Sarah and be sure she was all right. Perhaps he was more like his brother than he'd thought—when Nathan was himself, he had a penchant for taking down pirates and tilting at windmills. "That is, there's *always* something to discuss with this kind of thing."

"Mmm, I'm not convinced. You wouldn't be concerned about me, would you?"

Heat crept up his throat. "Is there something wrong with that? Anything that affects you could also affect my mother."

"I know, but I'm fine. I've got an evening of cooking and baking planned and don't need a babysitter."

Tyler gave her a slight nod. His white knight instincts might be rusty, but he was concerned… and not just about his mom.

SARAH WENT INSIDE and briefly sagged against the door after closing it, feeling tired to her bones. Scared, too, though she kept telling herself that a bunch of weird little events didn't necessarily mean anything. Of course, if the attempted theft by the hit-and-run motorcyclist was connected, that changed everything.

She looked around for Theo, hoping to cuddle him, but he'd gone into hiding the minute Tyler had arrived. He wasn't fond of strangers.

Distractedly, Sarah returned to the kitchen and began taking out various pans and bowls. She'd volunteered to bring desserts to a baked potato feed after church and also needed to cook for a meal with her grandparents. They'd been hosting Sunday dinner with the Fullerton clan for over sixty years, but last year Grandma Margaret had finally let the meal become potluck, instead of making it all herself.

Before long, Sarah had apricot cobbler, corn bread and pans of lasagna baking in her two ovens, along with chili in the Crock-Pot. The peace and quiet was wonderful, and she hummed as she prepared a large pasta salad. Cooking was the best stress relief for her, and after dealing with Tyler, she needed a *lot* of stress relief.

Ice man?

She considered the description again. While he cared about his mom and brother and was struggling with what had happened in Illinois, he did come across as cool and unemotional most of the time. But how about the adage, "still waters run deep"?

Maybe.

Mostly Sarah knew *facts* about Tyler, though she'd gotten a brief glimpse of his professional vision. She even sensed depths in him, but it felt as if she was peeking around corners and looking through a rain-streaked window, trying to catch a glimpse of something he wanted to keep hidden.

All the same, calling him an ice man had been cruel, even though she understood how frustrating it would be to fall for a guy who couldn't share himself. Heck, Tyler hadn't even told his family about the events in Illinois.

Her pulse jumped when the phone rang, then she saw her father's ID information on the screen and answered the call. "Hi, Dad."

"Hey, sweetheart. Your grandmother asked me to tell you not to go overboard cooking. You aren't, are you?"

Sarah glanced around the kitchen and squirmed. Maybe she could take the chili to the baked potato feed instead. "I'm fixing a few things. Not a big deal. You can take the leftovers home to eat this week. I don't get to Sunday dinner often enough and want to contribute."

Kurt chuckled. "That's means you're cooking for twenty. Okay, I'll run interference with your grandmother. See you tomorrow."

"Thanks. Love you, Dad."

Sarah disconnected, feeling unaccountably

sad. Her father could make her crazy, and she *had* to find a way to get him to back off some of the time, but it wasn't a big deal compared to what Tyler and his family were going through.

She should remember that her issues were comparatively minor.

CHAPTER TEN

"WE SHOULD GO to church today," Rosemary announced the next morning as Tyler drank his third cup of coffee, trying to wake up.

His eyes widened. "Church?" His mom had worked on fund-raisers for churches when he was a kid, but he didn't remember her attending.

"Yes. Sarah's grandfather is the pastor and her uncle is the youth pastor. It's good manners to go."

"Mom, you don't have to attend because your boss is the preacher's granddaughter." He didn't mention that he would rather not go with his bruised face—his brother felt bad enough already.

"Will Sarah be there?" Nathan interjected, a flicker of interest in his eyes.

"Probably," Rosemary said. "They're having a baked potato feed to raise money for the youth group, and Sarah is providing cake and cookies for dessert."

"Yeah, let's go," Nathan agreed immediately.

The enthusiastic tone startled Tyler, though it shouldn't have. His brother had a thing for blondes.

Yet a flicker of unease went through him. It didn't make sense, because while he was attracted to Sarah himself, he didn't plan to act on it. Both she and Nathan were free agents.

Stop analyzing, Tyler ordered himself as he ate a mouthful of French toast.

"The service starts at eleven," said his mother, visibly pleased. "Let's go early and visit with people beforehand."

Visiting wasn't his thing, but however illogical his concern might be, it was a way to check on Sarah.

The sanctuary at the church was crowded and Tyler watched his mother and brother converse with different people. Nathan wasn't as comfortable as he usually seemed in a group but was doing all right, while their mother appeared to be in her element.

Sarah arrived just before the service started. She sat at the front next to her father and an older woman. Her hair was loosened from its usual French braid and tumbled over her shoulders in thick cascades of pale gold that kept catching Tyler's eye.

The opening scripture was read, but his

thoughts drifted, and it didn't seem long before everyone was heading into the social hall.

"Hi, everyone," said Sarah from behind them.

Nathan smiled broadly. "Hello. It's good to see you again. I've never gone to a baked potato feed. What do we do?"

"Just get into one of the lines. There are tons of toppings, including different types of chili, veggies, cheese, cheese sauce, salsa, sour cream, bacon...you name it."

"What did you make?"

"A white-bean-and-chicken chili. And I contributed to the baked goods. Go enjoy yourselves. The youth group is participating in a coastal cleanup, so they're raising money for expenses. Donations can be put in one of the baskets."

"Is fifty dollars enough?"

Sarah laughed. "It would be an amazingly generous gesture, and you'd have their undying gratitude."

Nathan winked. "I'd much rather have yours."

He was acting so much like his old self—charm capped off by easy flirting—that Tyler stared. It was as if those dreary months in the hospital and rehab, the multiple surgeries and physical therapy sessions had never happened.

"Smooth talker," Sarah shot back. "You'd better get in line before the sour cream is gone."

"Yes, let's eat," Rosemary agreed.

They got in line, leaving Tyler alone with Sarah. "Don't you want some?" she asked.

"Sure, I'm just surprised to see you here. Can the shop manage without you?"

"It's fine. I come to church whenever possible, which isn't often this time of year, I'll admit."

"I'm glad you could make it. You know, I think my brother likes you," he said awkwardly.

Sarah shook her head. "I think your brother just likes flirting. He's making up to my cousin Vickie at the moment."

She pointed, and sure enough, Nathan was chatting with one of the women serving the potatoes. She appeared to be in her early twenties, had long blond hair in a high ponytail, a curvaceous figure and bubbly personality, judging from the way she was laughing and flirting right back.

"Are all the women in your family blonde and enthusiastic?" Tyler asked curiously. When asking about the swimming pool, he'd met Tessa McKinley, the owner-manager of Poppy Gold, who'd introduced him to another cousin, Jamie Fullerton. Sarah had also mentioned that the woman who worked the front counter at the sweet shop was family. They all seemed to have the same fair looks and vibrant personality.

Sarah shrugged. "A few have golden-brown hair or darker. As for 'enthusiastic,' I suppose we're energetic, but that's because we have so much to do."

"Don't the men help?"

"We all work hard, but we also enjoy ourselves. Right now, I'm going to enjoy a baked potato."

She got into one of the lines, which had shortened. Tyler followed and chose "five alarm firehouse" chili to top his potato, while Sarah's bowl resembled a salad when she was done. There weren't many chairs left in the social hall, so they went into the courtyard and sat on a bench under an arbor.

"Did anything else happen last night?" he asked quietly after a few minutes. "Any calls or other problems?"

"No," she replied in an equally soft tone. "I finished baking before 8:00 p.m. and went to bed. Everything was quiet."

"It isn't even dark by eight this time of the year."

"Yeah, but I go to the bakery at four in the morning."

Tyler winced. "I'm usually still up working until then."

"In that case, I wouldn't suggest becoming a professional baker," Sarah advised.

She dug a forkful of broccoli and cheese sauce from her bowl and munched it down. Tyler's body reacted as he watched her lick a trace of sauce from her lips, a response that didn't seem appropriate given their location. What's more, she wasn't trying to tease him—she was simply relishing her lunch.

"When did you leave the shop this morning?" he asked hoarsely.

Sarah covered her mouth as she yawned. "After nine. I wouldn't have gone in at all, but the shift supervisor needed time off to visit a sick relative in Oregon."

"Surely your staff knows what they're doing."

"Yes, but somebody needs to have final responsibility, keeping an eye on the clock and making sure we don't fall behind. Now that Rosemary has the office whipped into shape, I'll have time to get more supervisors trained, also some catering managers." Suddenly Sarah looked guilty and glanced around.

"Is something wrong?"

"Not exactly, but I wouldn't want anyone in the family to hear me say something like that," Sarah answered in a low tone. "Aunt Babs was helping in the office, but she doesn't have Rosemary's gift for juggling everything. Then she broke her leg. She had to stop working while it heals."

"How did it happen?"

"She was doing a 12K run when one of the other runners tripped her."

"Oh." Tyler's vision of a gray-haired lady with osteoporosis and balance problems instantly vanished. He should have known better, seeing as she was related to Sarah. "Then my mother's job is temporary until your aunt returns."

"Not exactly." Sara smiled impishly. "Aunt Babs has wanted me to find a replacement for her, so Rosemary has the office manager's job for as long she wants it. Sorry, I know that isn't what you hoped to hear."

"I'm learning to be philosophical about it."

Tyler still wondered if his mother would get to a point where the stress was overwhelming, but right now she was reveling in her success. Nathan was harder to evaluate, though he'd finally agreed to start doing image rehearsal therapy with Dr. Romano, and he was doing the recommended exercises. On the other hand, he continued refusing medication. Tyler understood not wanting to continue taking the one for nightmares if it didn't work, but there were others that might help the PTSD.

"Hey." Sarah tossed a wadded-up napkin at him. "Your face went blank."

"Just thinking."

"What's going on behind that mask?"

Mask?

Tyler had never thought of it that way. "I was thinking about my brother," he admitted. "He refuses to take medication to help the post-traumatic stress."

"I understand Nathan hopes to return to active duty. Maybe he's worried how taking meds will look on his record."

Tyler frowned. He should have thought of that.

Sarah poked at the contents of her bowl; she'd eaten the toppings, leaving most of her potato behind. She jumped to her feet. "I'm going back for a refill. Want some more?"

He went with her and saw there was plenty left, despite the large turnout. "How often do you have events like this?" he asked curiously.

"Once a month, though sometimes it's pie day or finger food. There's always something going on."

The servers had left their posts, presumably to eat, so Tyler took another baked potato and loaded it with chili and cheese, while Sarah added a fresh assortment of veggies to her bowl.

Nathan was in a corner, still flirting with the blonde he'd met at the serving table, and their mother was deep in discussion with a group of women on the opposite side of the room. They both seemed quite happy without him, so Tyler stayed with Sarah as she joined her father, standing nearby with several other men.

"Did you get enough, Dad?"

Kurt patted his stomach. "I'm doing okay. Good afternoon, Tyler," he said, nodding.

"Hello, Mr. Fullerton."

"Please, it's Kurt." He smiled, but Tyler didn't think the older man cared for him. Aside from what Sarah may have said, it couldn't have helped that his initial reaction to Kurt had been distrustful. Tyler still wondered if the relationship with his mother went beyond friendship, but he no longer had misgivings about the other man.

Kurt was, in his own way, helping Nathan more than any doctor.

BELATEDLY, SARAH REALIZED she should make introductions.

"Everyone, this is Tyler Prentiss. Tyler, you know my father, but this is Reverend George Fullerton, my grandfather. Reverend Daniel Fullerton, one of my uncles. He's the youth pastor here. And this is Milt Fullerton, one of my great-uncles."

A general chorus of greetings followed, and Grandpa George struck up a conversation with Tyler.

Sarah focused on her food. Tyler attending church and the baked potato feed had startled her. She suspected he didn't socialize that much, so he must have come for his mom and brother's sake.

"Dad, I ran by your house before church and put an apricot cobbler in the fridge," she told him between bites. "I was going to bring it to dinner tonight, but thought you might like to have it instead. Just don't eat the entire pan in one sitting."

"Thanks, darling." Kurt's eyes gleamed. She didn't sell old-style cobbler at the bakery, but he loved it.

"I like cobbler, too," Uncle Daniel complained.

"Maybe I could give Dad the lasagna instead."

Uncle Daniel shook his head. "On second thought, I'm sure my brother deserves a treat."

Sarah chuckled. He shared cooking duties with Aunt Emma, but they no longer made lasagna... not since he'd forgotten a batch was in the oven and had gone to play a spur-of-the-moment softball game with the youth group. The volunteer fire department called it the Great Lasagna Inferno and never failed to bring it up at annual fund-raising events.

Uncle Daniel checked the clock on the wall. "I need to make sure the youth group is helping with cleanup. I'll see you later, Sarah."

A few minutes later, Tyler said Nathan looked tired and that they should leave. Once he and his family were gone, Great-Uncle Milt frowned. "So that's Tyler Prentiss. He looks like a prize-fighter with those bruises. I wonder what the story is behind them."

"It's nothing to worry about," Sarah assured him hastily. "His brother is an army captain who was injured in a bomb blast and has PTSD nightmares. There was a mix-up about whether Rosemary got too close when Nathan was asleep. Tyler jumped between them and got hit."

"What about the incident at the shop?"

"Incident?" Kurt asked.

"I told you about it, Dad," Sarah said lightly. "Tyler was concerned when he learned Rosemary was working for me. He thought she might have taken on too much. That's all."

KURT RECALLED ROSEMARY saying that Tyler had wanted her to quit her job, but he hadn't imagined anything more dramatic than a young man having problems seeing his mother in a new light.

For himself, he'd grown up with working parents and his childhood couldn't have been better. Margaret Fullerton had been elected mayor of Glimmer Creek more times than anyone could remember. At seventy-five, she'd finally insisted on retiring. His dad was still senior pastor at the church, but contemplating retirement, as well.

Kurt knew some of his attitudes might be outdated, but not about women in the workplace. Well, initially it had been strange to serve in the military with the opposite sex, but he'd learned to respect them as fellow soldiers, with just as much courage and dedication as any man. And having them around had reminded him of what he was fighting for back home.

"Tyler was under a huge amount of stress when we met the first time," Sarah explained. "He's apologized."

"If you say so," Uncle Milt said. "And I suppose the business in the Chicago area doesn't mean anything here in Glimmer Creek. I just don't like having *anything* come up on a background check."

"Stop worrying. I'll see you all later, I'm going to help with cleanup." She blew kisses at them and hurried away.

Kurt looked at his uncle. "Chicago?"

Uncle Milt's frown deepened. "A building complex in Illinois collapsed a few weeks ago while under construction. Tyler Prentiss worked on the initial design, then another architect took over before the work started. The building owner is trying to implicate Prentiss, though nothing I've read suggests there's much basis for it. Still, I'm reluctant to see Sarah accepting his architectural advice until everything is resolved."

Kurt made a face. "I agree, though you know how stubborn she is. I wonder why Rosemary hasn't mentioned the incident. She's talked about Nathan's difficulties, but nothing about Tyler."

"Nathan is a soldier and was injured through no

error of his own. Mrs. Prentiss can't be a hundred percent certain about her other son. She might not want to discuss the situation for that reason."

Perhaps, but Kurt wanted to speak with his daughter. He wasn't comfortable about the late-night calls she'd been receiving, either, even if they *had* stopped.

"Is something else wrong?" asked Uncle Milt.

"No, no. Sarah says I worry too much."

Uncle Milt laughed. "We never stop worrying about our kids. You didn't believe me when I told you that all those years ago, but you've learned it now. The trick is learning to let go."

Kurt remembered when Uncle Milt had told him that…the day he'd enlisted and seen his mother with red eyes. She hadn't tried to prevent him and had been proud that he wanted to serve, but she'd worried for his safety.

"You were right," he admitted. "Thanks for the info, Uncle Milt. I need to check on something. See you soon."

He went straight to the kitchen to ask Sarah why she hadn't told him more about Tyler Prentiss.

"WE NEED TO TALK, sweetheart."

Sarah looked up and saw her father wearing his outraged protective expression.

"Okay, just a minute." She finished washing the insert to her slow cooker and dried her hands. "Yes?"

"Why didn't you tell me that Tyler Prentiss was in trouble in Illinois?" he asked in a low voice.

Sarah shot a quick look around the kitchen. A number of the women and kids from the youth group were still cleaning up, so she reassembled her cooker and held it out. "Carry this to the car for me and then we'll talk."

She grabbed another container filled with baking pans and platters and led the way to the parking lot. Once everything was stowed in her trunk, she turned and gave her father a stern look.

"Listen to me, Dad, Tyler isn't in trouble. There's just an investigation into who might be responsible for a building that collapsed."

"That sounds like trouble to me. If they decide he was negligent, he might go to jail."

The thought gave Sarah a queer sensation in her midriff, even though she believed Tyler *couldn't* be responsible.

While she rarely looked up people online, she'd read several articles about the building collapse. A special commission was being convened to investigate and a flurry of lawsuits had been filed, but none were specifically against Tyler except the one filed by the owner, Milo Corbin. Tyler was considered a hero by the press and rescue crews, and the injured workers had lauded him for helping to save their lives. The only sour note seemed to be Corbin and the second architect, who were trying to shift blame.

Rather fishy, in her opinion.

Sarah shook herself. "They're probably including Tyler's name in the investigation as a matter of form. The second architect made changes to the design that Tyler had advised weren't safe. I don't see how he could be responsible—if I change a recipe and it doesn't come out, that's my fault."

Kurt didn't look convinced. "Where there's smoke, there's fire."

"That isn't fair, Dad. Why are you so prejudiced against him? Tyler was uptight about Rosemary working for me when he first arrived, but shouldn't you approve of him staying to help Nathan?"

"I suppose. But I'm going to have another architect review any advice or blueprints Prentiss gives you."

Sarah counted to ten. While she loved her father and wanted him to be happy, she also wanted him to respect her choices. A lot of the time he just took action without discussing it with her or finding out if she actually needed something done.

What about *his* life?

He hadn't even taken a vacation since she'd

opened the bakery, because he wanted to "be here" in case she needed him.

"Dad, don't worry about it."

"An army buddy's son is an architect in San Jose. I'll have him take a look at your building."

"*Listen to me.* I'll handle whatever needs to be done. By the way, Rosemary and Nathan don't know about what happened in Illinois," Sarah said, partly as a distraction and partly to warn him.

"He should have told them."

"Maybe, but he asked me not to tell his mother. It's uncomfortable, but there are complications to telling Rosemary, too. He's concerned that it would be too stressful."

Her father scowled. "Rosemary mentioned that Tyler tries to make decisions for her."

"You do same thing with me," Sarah told him carefully. She didn't want to hurt his feelings, but she also needed him to understand.

"No, I don't." Yet his expression churned. "Uh, well, maybe. Once in a while. But I wasn't there when you were a little girl and I want to make up for it."

"We've talked about this a hundred times. There's nothing to make up for. I had a great childhood. And when I visited you in Japan and other places, I got to see parts of the world I might never have seen otherwise."

"What's wrong with me doing things for my daughter?"

"Nothing, but I think you still see me as that frightened little kid whose mother abandoned her. I'm not. I'm grown up and happy and don't need my hand held all the time."

"That isn't what I'm doing." He stuck his chin out and Sarah knew he hadn't changed his mind.

She kissed his cheek. "Just think about it. You're so busy trying to take of me, you aren't taking care of yourself."

And you're driving me nuts.

The silent admonition made her feel lousy, but they both needed their lives back.

SARAH ARRIVED AT the bakery later than usual on Tuesday morning and was dismayed to find the electric catering vehicles weren't plugged in. She thought she remembered taking care of it the night before as usual, but couldn't be positive.

Hurriedly, she connected the plugs to the charging stations and rushed inside.

"Did you hear anything odd outside last night?" she asked Regina, who'd returned the day before.

The night supervisor looked up from the dough she was making into cinnamon rolls. "Odd in what way?"

"I just found the catering vehicles unplugged. We probably won't have enough power to make all the deliveries—we used them a lot yesterday."

Regina shook her head. "Everything was quiet and the swing crew didn't say anything. I'll contact Poppy Gold and ask them to loan us carts to help. It'll be a pain, but better than being late with breakfast."

"I'll take over here while you make the call."

Sarah rapidly began filling pans with rolls, trying to put the problem with the catering vehicles out of her mind. The Poppy Gold breakfast included a large roll for each guest, which was a heck of a lot of cinnamon rolls every day. And that didn't count the ones they sold in the shop. Sometimes when she was trying to sleep, cinnamon rolls marched across her eyes in an unending succession.

It was a rough morning with breakfast barely getting delivered on time. They were only able to make a single trip with the regular catering vehicles and had to rely on Poppy Gold for the rest. Poppy Gold employees then also had to pick up food supplies for the two business conferences starting that morning, which couldn't have helped their own schedule.

Sarah felt terrible about it and sent a text to her cousin explaining that she'd pay for the time and trouble. Tessa swiftly sent a text back, refusing, but Sarah planned to ignore that.

Then her father came by before leaving on his weekly shopping trip to Stockton and learned about the problem. He had a fit, calling it vandalism and saying she had to make a report to the police department.

"*No*. I can't be positive I plugged the vehicles in last night," she told him. "I could have forgotten."

"Not likely."

"It's still a possibility."

Looking aggravated, he finally left, muttering about stubborn daughters taking too much after their fathers.

Sarah didn't think the day could get worse, but at 2:00 p.m., Aurelia walked into the kitchen with Tomoko Gates, who worked at City Hall.

Sarah waved at her. "Hey, Tomoko. What can I do for you?"

Tomoko looked miserable. "I have to do a surprise check as the health inspector," she explained. "There was a call…"

A call?

Sarah fastened a smile on her face as she gave

Tomoko access to every corner of the shop. Yet inside she was roiling. Strange coincidences were piling up faster than she could dismiss them.

CHAPTER ELEVEN

"Hello."

"Kurt, it's me," Rosemary said into the phone, trying to keep her voice down so Sarah and the inspector wouldn't overhear. "Something else has happened."

He cursed. "What?"

"Somebody called in a health department complaint about the bakery. It was anonymous, like the one about the building. The inspector is still here, checking everything."

"Hellfire. Sarah didn't want to call the police this morning, either. This can't go on, I'll have to call them myself."

A frisson of warning went through Rosemary and she straightened. "I don't think that's the best idea."

There was a long silence on the other end of the line. "Did Sarah say something to you?"

"No. What do you mean?"

"It's only that she...never mind. I just got back from Stockton. I'll come over and talk to her. Be there in a few minutes."

Rosemary put the phone down, her nerves jumping. Her mother's instincts had told her to let Kurt know about the problem; now she wondered if she should have. Sarah was a dear, but she was also a successful businesswoman and deserved respect.

A wave of the old helplessness swept through Rosemary and it scared her. She didn't want to be that woman again, the one who'd let someone else decide everything…the one with so many regrets.

She pushed back from the desk and went into the main kitchen. Through the window in the rear door, she saw Sarah on the loading dock, talking to the health inspector. The two women were shaking hands as Kurt drove in.

Wondering if she might get fired for being an interfering busybody, Rosemary went outside, as well.

"Thanks, Tomoko," Sarah was saying. "I'll put the new certificate in front with the others."

"Good. I'm sorry about the troubles you're having."

With a general smile that included Kurt and Rosemary, the inspector left.

"Sweetheart, what's going on?" Kurt asked urgently.

"A health inspection."

"You were certified last month."

"And I just got certified again."

Rosemary drew a shaky breath. She could tell Kurt was trying to protect her confidence, but she had to confess. "I'm sorry, Sarah, I called your father and told him about the health inspector. I realize now it was a mistake."

Kurt gave her an incredulous look. "No, it wasn't."

"Yes, it was. We're friends, but this is Sarah's business, and I work for her. I won't forget that again. I'm really, *really* sorry, Sarah."

SARAH COULD SEE the trepidation in Rosemary's eyes and gave her a reassuring smile. Glimmer Creek was a small town, and her dad would have heard about the inspection sooner rather than later. Yet Sarah understood how Rosemary felt— for the first time she was navigating life as an employee, and it couldn't be easy. It was something most people learned much younger.

"Thank you, Rosemary. Would you take this into the office while I talk to Dad?"

"Of course."

Rosemary took the certificate and hurried back through the door.

"Sarah, please call the police station and tell them what's happening," Kurt urged when they were alone. "I, er, thought about doing it myself, but Rosemary didn't think I should."

"She was right. I want time to evaluate before taking action."

"How about talking to Zach unofficially?" Kurt suggested. "He won't mind. We could go over to the police station together and have a private meeting."

Sarah tried not to get annoyed, but her father obviously wasn't paying attention. "I'm not talking to anyone until I'm good and ready."

"But—"

"No buts. You need to trust me."

Kurt's eyes widened. "This has nothing to do with trust."

Sarah wasn't sure, though it could be miscommunication. Her father still had a strong urge to protect her, and she wanted to know she could handle the bumps without his support. It wasn't a secret—she'd told him in a hundred ways—but she needed to make him understand.

"Dad, leave it to me," she said finally.

His expression told her he wasn't happy, but he finally nodded. "All right, sweetheart. I don't like it, though."

"I'm not enjoying this much, either. But I'm going to take care of it in my own way."

BY MIDAFTERNOON ON TUESDAY, Tyler was ready to climb the walls. He'd hoped Nathan's friendly behavior at the baked potato feed would mark a turning point, but he'd been rude and churlish ever since. He'd snapped at Tyler a dozen times, and worse, had snarled at their mother for simply offering to wash his clothes.

The physical therapist in Stockton hadn't bothered with diplomacy at Nathan's appointment that morning, telling him to get his ass together or have it handed to him. The rebuke had worked during the therapy session, but Nathan quickly reverted once they were back in Glimmer Creek.

"How about that girl you met on Sunday?" Tyler asked in desperation. "Did you get her number?"

Nathan glared. "Yeah, but she works in Davis during the week, and her classes will be starting in a few weeks."

"That doesn't mean you can't go out when she's free."

"You don't get it. Vickie is an athlete," Nathan growled. "Swimming, hiking, bicycling. For God's sake, she was going on a twenty-mile bike ride after the baked potato feed. Like she'd have any real interest in me. I can barely drag myself around the pool or get to Kurt's greenhouses."

Tyler felt as if a light had suddenly come on; his brother had seen himself through the eyes of a beautiful woman and gotten angry and discouraged.

"I doubt you could have done that a month

ago," he retorted. "And Dr. Romano is going to start working with you tomorrow on a therapy for your nightmares."

Nathan glowered. "It sounds like hocus-pocus. How can someone change a nightmare by 're-hearsing' a different ending to it when they're awake?"

"It's worth a shot," Tyler insisted.

Nathan just hunched his shoulders and stared out the side window.

Tyler was out of ideas to lift his brother's foul mood by the time their mother got home from work.

"Hello," Rosemary called as she came in through the kitchen.

Yet she seemed subdued and he frowned. "What's up?"

"Somebody is making trouble for Sarah again. They called the health department, and there was a surprise inspection this afternoon. We passed, of course, but someone also disconnected the electric catering vehicles last night. Sarah is trying to downplay everything, but I'm worried. Who could possibly have a grudge against her?"

"Has she called the police?"

"She wants to sleep on it. Kurt pushed, but that just made her more stubborn."

"Even *I* know pushing Sarah is a bad idea," Tyler said wryly. He checked his watch. "I've been planning to go over and do more evaluation on her building. Did she go home early?"

"She was still there when I left."

Tyler headed over to the shop and sat at one of the café tables while he waited for Sarah. She came out shortly before closing time, looking pale.

"I understand you had a bad day," he said.

"It could have gone better. Do you want to see the staircase now?"

"Unless you have something else to do."

She shrugged. "There's always something to do, but the swing shift can take over."

Tyler followed her to the staircase. She was right—it was far too steep to meet code—but Tyler still wanted to see the second floor. He had an idea knocking around in his head and wouldn't know if it would work unless he took a better look.

"Good lord," he said after they'd gone up. "It must have been a nightmare getting furniture up those steps."

"Luckily there's a built-in sideboard and bookshelves. Other than that, I mostly used an air mattress and folding chairs when I lived up here."

He looked around, assessing the space, including the flat expanse of roof over the front of the shop. Finally he turned to Sarah. "I'm starting to see options for the remodel, but they'll be expensive. You said your family might help. It would be a big savings."

"That's right, they're eager to rush in and rescue me, whether I need it or not," she replied in a dry tone.

"I can't imagine what it would be like having such a close family. It doesn't sound like a bad thing."

"I'm not complaining. I've always wanted to have the bakery here, but I'm still trying to find a balance with my relatives. Especially Dad. Didn't *you* want to succeed on your own? To feel you're responsible for your accomplishments?"

"Yes, though I didn't have much choice," Tyler admitted. "When my father learned I was studying engineering and architecture, he told me to switch to law or pay for the rest of my education on my own."

"That was unfair," Sarah said indignantly. "School is expensive, and I bet your dad's income kept you from getting grants and scholarships."

Tyler almost smiled. He was proud of having worked his way through school, but it was nice to hear Sarah's indignation on his behalf. He was becoming accustomed to the way she voiced her frank opinions…and he rather enjoyed it, to his surprise.

"Are you always this passionate about the injustices of the world?" he asked curiously.

"Injustices matter. Big ones and little ones. I guess it's because my dad was a soldier. My mother walked out when I was really young, so my grandparents raised me, but they made sure I knew he was out there to make the world safer."

"You two seem close."

"It took a while after he retired. I mean, he visited Glimmer Creek when he was on leave, and I would go see him, but it wasn't enough to know each other that well. Then I went away to college, not that long after he retired from the army. But we got there."

She fanned herself, and Tyler realized it was warm and stuffy in the small apartment.

Or it could be the effect Sarah was having on him.

There was no denying that was the real reason he kept coming around. His attraction to her was hard to resist, though he couldn't imagine two people who were less suited to each other. It was more than them wanting different things out of life. Despite a bad marriage and being abandoned by her mother, Sarah was still fresh and open, while he was a man who rarely shared anything with anyone.

Not a good mix.

Nevertheless, he was worried about her.

"Sarah, my mom told me what happened, about the catering vehicles and the second anonymous complaint."

"It was a peachy day, all right."

Tyler hesitated. Generally he didn't get mixed up with a client's life, but Sarah wasn't just a client. "You know, it isn't losing your independence to accept help if you're being harassed. I told you about that student who was stalked when I was in graduate school. After a while, she was failing classes and could barely function because she was so stressed out and sleep-deprived. It kept getting worse until she got the police involved, and the guy was arrested."

Oddly, the story seemed to make Sarah more uptight. Her cheeks went pale, and she crossed her arms over her stomach. "The police don't always believe you. Sometimes they just say it's your imagination. Especially when your husband tells them that you're just menstrual or prone to seeing shadows."

A cold anger went through Tyler. "That's what happened to you," he said flatly.

"I...yes. Turns out, the 'stalker' was my husband, trying to control me. Douglas wanted me to be afraid and isolated, to have no one but him. He even did his best to keep me away from my family or friends. There I was, in a city with millions of people, and I felt completely alone."

Tyler's outrage escalated, though he tried not to show it. "Could your ex be responsible for the trouble here in Glimmer Creek?"

She frowned. "I don't think so. He's remarried, and I haven't heard from him since our last court date anyway. A couple of friends showed up and explained in graphic detail what they'd do if he ever bothered me again. Douglas was so scared, I'm pretty sure he wet himself."

"Then he didn't succeed in ending *all* your friendships."

The color came back into Sarah's face, and she smiled. "I managed to hang on to a few. Look, Tyler, one part of my brain says somebody is trying to make trouble for me. Another part thinks the idea is ridiculous. I don't have any enemies or rivals that I know of. If anyone else wants to start a catering business, I'd be happy to let them have the contract with Poppy Gold. With Tessa's approval, of course."

"Isn't the contract with Poppy Gold lucrative?"

"Yes, but without it I'd have more time to develop recipes and just bake. I also wouldn't need to remodel the building and most of my employees could transfer to the new caterer."

Tyler tried to clear his head.

They were discussing a hypothetical situation, which was ridiculous. For one, the breakfasts that Sarah provided to Poppy Gold were excellent, and it was unlikely her cousin would want to rock the boat. It was equally unlikely someone else was interested in going through the expense and hassle of setting up another restaurant and catering business in such a small town.

"I doubt this is connected to your contract with Poppy Gold," he said quickly. "There doesn't have to be a logical reason for someone harassing you."

"Assuming it isn't just a series of bizarre coincidences."

"Do you honestly believe that?"

"No. I'll probably call Zach tomorrow, unofficially, but can we *not* talk about it now?"

"Sure. How about a walk?" Tyler suggested, hoping to distract himself from the way Sarah was creeping around his senses. She didn't wear makeup, not that she needed any. She was wrapped in a chef's apron, and her gorgeous hair was in a snug French braid…yet he was acutely aware of her.

SARAH WAVERED, BUT only for a second.

"A walk sounds great."

Downstairs she checked with Millie and was told nothing critical was going on, so she dropped her apron in the laundry bin.

In a curious way, Tyler was becoming a friend. But unlike her other friends and family, he didn't seem to have an agenda, at least not since she'd made it clear she wouldn't encourage Rosemary to take Nathan back to the East Coast.

Sarah's feelings about Tyler were mixed. He remained hard to read, yet the tiny glimpses of emotion in his eyes and the way he was sticking around Glimmer Creek to help his brother were deeply appealing.

Bad idea, warned her instincts. She already knew she had a weakness for enigmatic men. Maybe because they were so different than the outgoing family she'd grown up with. But Tyler was a visitor to Glimmer Creek, forced into a short detour on his quest for professional greatness. He would quickly get back on track.

Still, going for a walk with Tyler wasn't the same as jumping into bed with him or handing over her heart.

Outside, the late afternoon rays from the sun were less intense and bathed Glimmer Creek in golden light. They wandered into the residential area, debating their preferences on historical architecture.

"What kind of house have you designed for yourself?" she asked curiously.

"Me? I never thought about it."

She blinked. She wasn't an architect, but she'd know exactly what she'd want if she could build her own home.

"Think about it now," she challenged. "Start with where you'd put it. Don't be realistic, just pick a spot where you think it would be great to live."

TYLER WAS FLUMMOXED. Sarah asked the darnedest questions. "The city."

"You have to be more specific," she urged. "*Which* city?"

"Er, Paris. My French is better than my Italian."

"Okay. If you could have any location in Paris, what kind of house would you build? I'm not talking about practicality, what does the kid inside of you want?"

He gave her a dampening look. "I'm not a kid any longer."

"According to your mother, you never were." Sarah's cheeks promptly turned pink, and she scrunched her nose. "Sorry, Rosemary wasn't criticizing—she just mentioned you were a serious child. Didn't you ever have a silly, fun side?"

"I'm afraid not."

Yet Tyler wasn't being entirely honest. He hadn't thought about it in years, but now he remembered drawing castles as a boy, fantastical, labyrinthine castles populated with dragons and trolls and princesses in danger. He'd been a knight, but instead of slaying the dragon, they'd formed an alliance and worked together to save the princess.

He had a sneaking suspicion that if Sarah had been the princess, she would have knocked the troll over the head and rescued herself.

"Okay, forget being silly," Sarah said, looking disappointed. "Tell me about your perfect place in Paris."

"A loft," Tyler replied, saying the first thing that came into his head. "On the top floor of a tall building. The outside walls should be all windows. Not too large, open concept, with a three-hundred-and-sixty-degree vista of the city. I'd want spectacular views, especially at night with the lights. That way I could clear my mind and simply work."

"Oh." She blinked. "Then you'd live there alone."

"You know how I feel about marriage."

"Yeah. When you think about having this ideal Paris loft, does it feel like home?"

Tyler understood what she meant. Warmth. Welcome. Belonging. A sort of mystical place where you were loved and felt safe.

"What's home to you?" he countered, knowing "home" had to be a much more important concept to Sarah than to him.

"A big, comfortable place with fireplaces and cozy corners to read, with happy, active children and an easygoing guy who loves me," she said promptly. "It needs tons of outdoor space for the kids to romp and have picnics and explore with their cousins and friends. I also want a spot in the garden where water trickles over rocks and around ferns into a pool…a place where the wood faeries can come and wash their hair when everyone has gone to bed."

It seemed typical that Sarah knew exactly what she wanted without having to stop and think. And she hadn't needed to say her ideal house was located in Glimmer Creek. That part was obvious.

As for the wood faeries?

She'd probably said that to get a rise out of him. Or maybe not. Sarah could pass for a wood faerie herself in the right clothes, and he didn't question she had a playful side. Stress might even be bringing it out more prominently.

"You didn't mention a great kitchen," Tyler said.

"Okay, add a great kitchen," she agreed. "By the way, a few blocks over we have a house that Julia Morgan designed. It's unusual to see her work outside of the Bay Area, and it's the closest thing I've seen to my dream house."

"I'd love to take a look," he said. "I've always admired Morgan's work. She was a gifted architect. Lead the way."

Tyler was grateful for the change of subject. He'd almost expected Sarah to ask how he planned to design something great and memorable if he didn't have more imagination. Maybe he should have told her that he wanted to live in a crystal bird's nest over a cloud city.

They walked down several streets lined with large houses, predominantly built in the Craftsman style.

"Here it is," she announced.

Tyler gazed at the structure. It sat on a huge lot and took advantage of the rolling terrain. The other houses on the street were nice, but this one had a radical distinctiveness. More than anything, it looked natural, as if it had grown up out of the land.

"Nice," he said, impressed.

"It belongs to my uncle Daniel and his wife— you met Uncle Daniel at the baked potato feed. Anyway, they bought the property when Aunt Emma was doing her medical residency with Dr. Romano. That's when everybody knew they'd stay in Glimmer Creek, instead of going somewhere else."

"She would have made more money in a city."

Sarah gave him a stern look. "Money isn't everything."

Tyler felt as if the Ghost of Christmas Past was tapping his shoulder. *Money isn't everything,* he'd told his father when they'd argued about law school. Richard had agreed, claiming that influence and power were equally important, neither of which his son was likely to earn in architecture. He'd never changed his mind, despite Tyler's success.

"Are you okay?" Sarah asked. "You seem tense all of a sudden."

"I was just thinking about my father," Tyler explained, surprised that she'd detected anything. "To be honest, I simply didn't know him very well. I can't remember a single time we ever just sat and talked."

Sarah's gaze was sympathetic, and Tyler wished he'd kept his mouth shut.

"It must hurt, knowing you can't ever get to know him now."

Tyler sucked in a harsh breath.

She was too perceptive.

He didn't regret the way he'd worked for his education; it had taught him the value of earning his own way. Yet it hurt to think about his father. Richard Prentiss's death meant that nothing could ever be resolved with him.

"We probably couldn't have fixed our relationship, no matter how much time we had," Tyler admitted. "We were too much alike."

Sarah had an unfathomable look on her face.

"You called yourself an ice man. Is that how you saw him?"

"In a way. I never understood what drove Dad, or what he cared about beyond his career. Maybe my mom did, but I didn't."

"You're also letting him influence whether you want children," she said. "A few days ago, you mentioned being too much like him to be a good father."

Tyler prayed for patience. "The reason I don't want children is because I'm uncomfortable around them and they feel the same way about me. I also travel too much to make a family happy and like my life too much to change it. Of course, since marriage is out, having children is unlikely. Unless I get careless, that is, and I'm never careless."

If anything, Sarah's eyes became even more mysterious. "I'm sure you aren't."

"That said, I'm aware my father was a lousy parental role model," Tyler added firmly. "I'd probably make all of his mistakes and more of my own."

He frowned, deciding Sarah was dangerous to his peace of mind—somehow she'd gotten him to say things he'd never said to anyone. He didn't *want* to become a touchy-feely guy with his emotions on his sleeve. It would make him vulnerable, and there were too many risks in that. Sarah didn't seem to understand the risks, though she'd obviously been hurt in the past, including a hideous marriage and being abandoned by her own mother.

Tyler looked at Sarah, suddenly curious. "How do you feel about your mom leaving like she did?"

Her green eyes darkened. "I think she must have been a really unhappy person. I heard Dad and my grandparents talking about her when I was a kid. After the divorce my father saw my mom in a bar when he was on a layover in Hawaii, and he said she seemed so alone and pathetic that he stopped hating her. I was shocked. Dad was a knight in shining armor, saving the world. How could he hate someone? It took time to understand how much she'd hurt him. Now I mostly feel sorry for her."

Tyler focused on the Julia Morgan house again, not knowing what to say. It was a common problem when he was around Sarah. "She hurt you, too."

"I suppose, but I had a great childhood, surrounded by people who love me. Occasionally I'd spot an unknown woman who seemed to be watching, and I'd wish it was my mom, checking to see how I was doing. Mostly I wish Dad had found someone else to make him happy."

Sarah sounded more forgiving than Tyler would have felt. Whether or not she remembered the trauma of her mother leaving, something like that would have affected most people. Instead she'd chosen to see it in a different way. The urge to put an arm around her crept over him and he stuck his hands in his pockets. He was just a hard-nosed architect, and it was becoming clearer by the day that he shouldn't have anything to do with someone as sweet and joyous as Sarah Fullerton.

He was still mulling it over when a woman walked down the driveway, calling, "Sarah, what are you doing, just standing out here on the sidewalk instead of coming in?"

"Hey, Aunt Emma. This is Tyler Prentiss. His mom works at the bakery. He's an architect, so I wanted him to see your house."

"Welcome, Tyler." Emma Fullerton smiled cordially. "Come in and explore."

They went through a side door and into the kitchen where he saw Sarah's uncle stirring a pot on the stove.

"What a treat, kiddo. I'm lucky to see you once a week, much less three times," Daniel Fullerton told his niece. "Hi, Tyler, nice to see you again. I hope you'll both have dinner with us. I'm making my deluxe spaghetti."

Before Sarah could say anything, Tyler shook his head. "That's nice of you, sir, but I have a commitment."

He spotted the faintest roll of Sarah's eyes. She was so outgoing and friendly herself, she probably couldn't imagine what it was like to be in his shoes. Social occasions with large numbers of people were challenging enough, but he rarely made a good impression in more personal settings.

"I don't remember if told you that Tyler is an architect, Uncle Daniel," Sarah interjected. "He's offered to consult on possible renovations to my kitchens. He also admires Julia Morgan's work, which is why I brought him over here."

Daniel nodded. "Wasn't she incredible? What an extraordinary talent."

Emma laughed at her husband's enthusiasm. "What's this about renovations, Sarah?"

"The county is considering new building codes. If they're implemented, I'll need to remodel again."

"Let us know what we can do to help."

Her husband nodded. "Whatever is needed, we'll be there."

SARAH GAVE HER aunt and uncle a strained smile. "I know. I told Tessa about it, and she said not to bother, just to use the kitchens at Poppy Gold.

But I'd hate to divide my attention between two or three locations."

Aunt Emma nodded. "It's a tough choice. Do whatever you think is best."

"We can make something happen," Uncle Daniel declared. "I'll—"

"Why don't you finish dinner?" Aunt Emma interrupted, giving him a stern look. "This is something Sarah has to decide."

Sarah hugged her. "Thanks," she whispered. Aunt Emma understood how the Fullertons could overwhelm someone with help and advice. Emma often likened her husband's family to a well-intentioned tsunami.

"Sarah, why don't you show Tyler around?" Aunt Emma suggested.

"Great idea."

Sarah practically dragged Tyler out of the kitchen.

"I didn't see a historical marker outside," he commented after they'd explored the ground floor and were climbing the central staircase. "This is the kind of place that belongs on the historic register."

Sarah's stomach tightened with the unintentional reminder that someone had nominated her shop for the register. She'd truly thought it was a joke at the time, but now everything had a sinister undertone.

She drew a calming breath. "Uncle Daniel and Aunt Emma plan to nominate the house when they get a chance. They even have the original blueprints in a safe deposit box so they can prove it's a Julia Morgan design. Do you want to see the reproductions?"

Tyler nodded, and she took him into Uncle Daniel's home office, gesturing to the walls where framed copies of the blueprints were hung. He eagerly went to look at them.

Sarah crossed her arms over her stomach and made a face at his back. There was no doubt that Tyler was getting to her more than she wanted him to. Half the things he said were opposite to her views. Even his perfect place to live sounded cold and remote…living alone in a glass loft, watching the city lights?

If she lived in Paris, she'd want to explore every side street and sample the bakeries and shops. The museums and galleries would be second homes, and she'd go to outdoor markets like the Marché Bastille and make friends with the merchants and customers alike. But Tyler hadn't mentioned any of that.

You asked, Sarah's conscience reminded her. A question he'd obviously never considered. It wasn't fair to pass judgment on his answer.

"As an architect, I'm sure those blueprints

speak more to you than the rest of the family," she said in an effort to regain Tyler's attention.

He didn't answer, and she wondered what he'd do if she tried to invite a kiss…would he even notice?

"Julia Morgan was remarkable," he said finally. "I studied her work in college. Her use of native materials, especially redwood, was wonderful."

Jealousy tugged at Sarah. He was standing there, lost in admiration of a woman who, though amazing and talented, had been gone for sixty years. It was stupid. Tyler wasn't interested in her, yet she still had a wicked impulse to brush against him or do something else to get his attention.

If nothing else, she needed to remember they were in her aunt and uncle's house.

Sarah moved closer to the framed blueprint Tyler was examining with so much fascination. It was just a bunch of lines and writing to her.

"I'm sure Uncle Daniel would let you look at the originals sometime," she suggested.

Tyler dropped his hand from where he'd been tracing a section of the blueprint. "Thanks, but I wouldn't want to take a chance of damaging them. They may be fragile after so many years. It's enough being able to see copies."

Wow.

Scans of century-old blueprints had put that look of wonder on his face. Their gazes locked, and deep in his dark eyes Sarah saw a flicker of heat. She was on the verge of forgetting herself when she heard a downstairs door open and close and footsteps come running up the staircase.

Sarah jerked backward. "Um, you told Uncle Daniel you had a commitment this evening. I wouldn't want to keep you."

"Right, we should go. Mom and Nathan are expecting me for dinner," Tyler muttered.

His eyes still held a hint of warmth, and longing went through Sarah. But it wasn't just sexual. A part of her wanted to pull him into a world of love and laughter and simple pleasures.

Bad idea, she warned. Tyler didn't want his life to change. He'd told her so himself.

CHAPTER TWELVE

TYLER'S CHEST WAS TIGHT as he walked toward the sweet shop with Sarah. He'd wanted to kiss her, partly out of appreciation for showing him something amazing, but also for the simple reason that she was beautiful and intriguing. Her vivacious nature, her family's close ties, this small town… They were a bigger mystery to him than anything he'd encountered.

"We should get together some evening and discuss kitchen design," he said. The words had popped out of his mouth without forethought and a mental groan followed. Wanting to see Sarah had little to do with kitchen design.

"I suppose," she said slowly. "But to be frank, I'm not sure that someone who doesn't cook can plan a proper kitchen unless it's by accident. Still, I'm happy to listen to your ideas, provided you listen to mine. I've dealt with two other architects, and I swear, nothing got through to them."

It was a reminder that she'd remodeled once when opening the business and again after signing the contract for Poppy Gold. She had to be sick to death of the entire process.

"I'll listen," Tyler promised, more confident now that he was talking business. "But are you certain you don't want to use the Poppy Gold kitchens permanently? It would be much less costly than remodeling or buying a different building."

"When I used Poppy Gold's facilities during the second remodel, it felt as if I was running a factory. That isn't what I want to do."

"I remember your opinion on factory baking," he said. "I promise to listen to what you want. I don't know if you can get the space you'll need out of your building, but if you have to go through it again, I want to be sure the extra square footage is useful."

SARAH KEPT HER GAZE forward, unsettled by the sincerity in Tyler's voice. She'd been trying to keep the conversation light, but the undercurrents were too strong.

"I have all the paperwork on my building blueprints at the house," she said slowly. "It's fine if you want to come over tomorrow night to see them."

"Great. I'll get takeout."

"That isn't necessary, I'll bring something home from the shop," Sarah said.

Tyler was doing her a favor; she couldn't let him provide a meal on top of that. Not to mention the "favor" still bothered her. He claimed it was an apology and that he needed something to do, but it didn't make her any more comfortable.

"Sounds good. Is six thirty too late?" he asked. "Nathan has an appointment tomorrow afternoon, and I don't know long it'll take."

"It's fine."

He continued down the street toward Poppy Gold as Sarah went inside the shop. She quickly locked up the daily receipts and collected her purse and keys.

With deliberate care, she walked around the catering vehicles, plugging them in and testing the special connectors. They weren't likely to become *dis*connected by accident. She made a face, knowing that if she'd invested in a fast-charging station, they wouldn't have had a problem that morning. Instead the vehicles took an overnight charge.

A sound startled her, and she whirled around.

"Tyler, what are you doing out here?"

He looked embarrassed. "I wanted to make sure everything was okay, but you're obviously taking care of it."

Sarah didn't know whether to be amused or annoyed. In his own way, Tyler appeared to have the same protective streak as her father and other relatives.

But it wouldn't be wise to read too much into his behavior. His career was on hold while an investigative commission decided his professional future. Yet instead of staying in Illinois, he was in California, helping his mother and brother through *their* problems.

Boredom had to be influencing how he was acting, along with the need to protect his mother since she worked at the bakery.

"Plugging the vehicles into the charging stations is part of my routine when I leave in the evening," she explained.

"Except you aren't sure you did it last night."

"It's so automatic, I don't always consciously remember having done it. I've even called the shop a few times, asking them to double-check."

"Have you ever missed?"

"Once. So it's possible that with all the distractions lately, I just didn't get it done last night."

Tyler stood there, tall and sexy, and Sarah felt a traitorous tug in her abdomen. She shook herself. "Aren't Rosemary and Nathan waiting for you?"

"Yeah. How about eating with us? Nathan has been in a foul mood since Sunday. He might sweeten up if you're there."

Sarah tried not to laugh. Tyler wasn't asking

her for a date but for something just as personal…
dinner with the family. Some people might see it
as a meaningful step, but she knew better.

"I'll pass. Anyway, he'll be more comfortable
if it's just the three of you."

"I suppose. Well, good night."

"Good night."

Tyler turned and strode up the alley while
Sarah got into her car and debated with herself
all the way home. She could have asked him
to come over later…and tried to seduce him.
The temptation was enormous. Several of her
girlfriends who'd ended awful relationships ad-
vocated short-term liaisons as part of the recovery process. "Guys use us for sex—why not use
them?" they argued.

The idea bothered Sarah. If nothing else, how
could you be sure you wouldn't end up hurting
a nice man? She also questioned whether her
friends truly practiced what they'd preached. Not
that it mattered. She was no longer "recovering"
from her marriage. Douglas was behind her.

As for Tyler?

Getting involved with him would be like
sticking her hand in a fire and expecting not to
get burned. That didn't mean her body wasn't
in favor of the prospect, even though her mind
knew it was risky.

At the house, Sarah went through the ritual of

sitting on the couch while Theo ecstatically demanded attention.

"You're a pal," she whispered as he turned over on his back, exposing the small white spot on his belly. She stroked him, and a purr boomed out.

Sarah rested her head on the cushions as she rubbed behind his ears. In the morning, she'd call Zach and give him a heads-up about the harassment, but at this point a formal police report would still seem ridiculous.

Still seem ridiculous?

The words made her shiver, banishing everything else from her mind.

It implied that more problems were coming.

THE NEXT MORNING, Kurt showed up at the Yosemite suite shortly after six thirty. Rosemary had invited him to breakfast, saying she hoped he wasn't angry that she'd taken Sarah's side earlier in the day but she hadn't felt there was a choice.

Kurt wasn't bothered, at least now that he'd calmed down. He respected Rosemary taking a stance, even if it wasn't one that helped him.

Rosemary opened the door and gave him a tentative smile. "Good morning. Please come in."

Nathan hurriedly sat up on the couch. "Hey,

Kurt. I didn't realize…that is, I need to change. See you in a minute."

Kurt had only seen Nathan in passing since Sunday. Monday was a rushed day as Poppy Gold said goodbye to weekend travelers and greeted new ones coming in. And there were three large companies having conferences in Glimmer Creek, which took coordination from every member of the staff.

He glanced at Rosemary's anxious face. "Has Nathan experienced a setback?"

"More like a long temper tantrum," she said with exasperation. "Something must have happened on Sunday. The girl he was talking to seemed nice, and she even called last night to see if he wanted to do something this weekend, but he put her off."

Kurt instantly felt like a selfish bastard. In all honesty, he'd avoided talking to Rosemary on Monday, unable to decide how he should handle the information about Tyler's legal problems in Illinois. And yesterday he'd been oblivious to everything but Sarah's needs.

"As I recall, he was flirting with my niece Vickie," he said slowly. "Talented kid. Taking environmental studies at UC Davis and expects to have her degree next spring."

"I thought…" Rosemary's voice trailed as Tyler came into the kitchen. "Good morning, dear."

"Morning." He nodded at them both and stumbled to the coffee maker, only looking half-awake.

"Didn't you sleep?" Rosemary ventured.

"For an hour or two. Uh, I won't be here for dinner tonight. Nice seeing you, Kurt." He poured a cup of coffee and headed out again.

"I take it that neither of your sons are morning people," Kurt commented wryly.

"No, though before Nathan was hurt, he always got up at dawn when he visited. His military training, I think."

"It does that. Has anything else happened with Nathan?"

"He wants to cancel an appointment with Dr. Romano," she said softly. "They were supposed to start therapy sessions this afternoon."

"I'll ask Nathan to help me this morning and encourage him to keep the appointment," Kurt told her in an equally quiet tone.

"Thanks."

It was another few minutes before Nathan arrived, clean-shaven and showered.

Kurt didn't mind that Tyler didn't reappear for breakfast. He wasn't impressed by the young architect. Rosemary clearly loved both her sons, but her eldest was too reserved for Kurt's taste.

"How about helping me today?" he asked Nathan, who was stirring the food around his plate, barely eating.

Nathan scowled. "What could I do?"

"Plenty. I'm behind with starting the autumn plantings, and if I don't catch up, Poppy Gold will have to buy them. You can put seeds in potting soil, can't you?"

"I...sure."

"Good, because that's exactly what I need. My job includes producing plants for the garden beds and flowers for cutting. Now eat up. We have work to do."

Almost meekly, Nathan forked in a mouthful while Rosemary brightened and finished her cup of tea. "I'd love to stay longer," she said, "but I have to get going. Come over later and I'll buy you both lunch."

"Sounds like a plan." Kurt winked to reassure her.

As they were leaving, Tyler came downstairs carrying two of the pool towels Poppy Gold provided.

He gave Nathan a quizzical look. "Where are you going? You've got a workout at the pool."

"I'm going to skip it and spend the day with Kurt."

"Nonsense," Kurt interjected hastily. It had slipped his mind that Nathan exercised each morning. "I need to run over to the sweet shop, anyhow. Meet me at the second greenhouse when you're done, Nathan."

Kurt thought he saw a hint of appreciation in Tyler's eyes but couldn't tell for certain. Most of Kurt's commanding officers had been notoriously stoic, but even *they'd* shown more emotion than Tyler Prentiss.

"I'll put my swim trunks on," Nathan muttered.

After he'd limped into the back of the suite, Tyler nodded. "Thanks, Kurt."

"No problem. It gives me a chance to check on Sarah."

"How many times do you go over there every day?"

Kurt shrugged. "Once or twice usually, though I'll go more often until this harassment is resolved. My work schedule is flexible. I get things done, that's all my niece and brother-in-law care about. They're the owners."

"I've met them. Tell me something. Obviously this is a popular vacation spot—I've been wondering how my mom and brother got a suite on such short notice."

"Things happen. Cancellations and the like," Kurt said evasively, preferring not to discuss Poppy Gold's long-standing efforts to assist soldiers, veterans and military families in crisis. The John Muir Cottage was dedicated to that purpose.

"But it doesn't—"

Tyler fell silent as Nathan reappeared.

"See you later," Kurt said, hurrying out. He didn't know what was bothering Tyler Prentiss and would rather not find out; the information he'd already gathered was enough of a headache.

TYLER GOT IN the pool with Nathan to help with his workout. From their first session, it had been obvious why water therapy had been recommended. His brother instinctively relaxed, and there was little risk of further injury.

It was a warm morning already, and the cool water was pleasant. A pool might be nice to have at home, Tyler mused idly. Perhaps an infinity pool on a deck outside the loft he'd told Sarah about, built of Plexiglas, giving the sensation of floating through open space. It would be particularly remarkable at night.

Sarah would likely hate it.

The unbidden thought made Tyler frown. Actually, she wouldn't hate it, she just wouldn't see it as *home*.

Another mental picture grew of a secluded swimming pool with small islands and waterfalls and natural growth around the meandering edges…a place his ordered mind would dismiss as untidy and chaotic. *That* was the kind of swimming pool Sarah would undoubtedly appreciate.

He pushed the images away.

Sarah was getting into his head far too often.

To Tyler's surprise, Nathan exercised longer than usual before getting out and dressing. The mornings he'd spent in the sunshine already showed on his skin; instead of pallid white, his legs and chest had a hint of bronze.

"I'm going straight to the greenhouses," Nathan announced as he zipped his jeans.

"What about your appointment with Dr. Romano this afternoon?"

"We'll see."

Aggravated, Tyler grabbed the towels and took them back to the suite. Housekeeping was there, so he didn't shower, instead going upstairs to sit at his drafting table.

He stared out the window at the natural landscape beyond the confines of Poppy Gold. How had such a popular destination been able to accommodate his family for an indefinite period? In the long run, it didn't matter, but he still wondered how far ahead his mom and brother had planned this trip and if they'd intentionally left while he was in Italy.

Tyler tapped a pen on the table, determined to think about something else. Sarah had urged him to file a slander suit against Corbin, just as his lawyer had. What had she said…that taking the high road was great, but guys like Corbin didn't even *know* there was a high road?

Sarah was so passionate—how did she have the energy to care that much about everything? But she was also right. Staying silent might lead people to think he doubted his architectural skills. His feelings of responsibility stemmed from failing to stop the construction, not a concern that his design was faulty.

He took out his phone and called the law office in Chicago, leaving a message for his attorney.

His cell rang twenty minutes later.

"Thanks for calling me back, Leonard," he said. "I've been thinking about the countersuit against Corbin and discussing it with a friend. I want to move forward with the suit."

Friend?

Tyler was amazed to realize the description was true. Sarah *was* a friend—an exasperating, overly emotional, opinionated friend. And all of that might be fine if she weren't uncomfortably desirable, as well.

"Excellent." Dalby sounded pleased. "I'm tired of watching Milo Corbin's interviews on the local station without doing something about it. Nothing has gone national, so I don't think anyone is taking him seriously, but he's annoying."

"He's trying to cover his rear end."

"If he'd listened to you in the first place, he

wouldn't be in this mess. It's a good thing he didn't try hiring me. Lawyers don't always have the luxury of defending the innocent, but I'll be damned if I'll represent someone my gut says is dirty."

A choked laugh escaped Tyler. He'd hired Leonard Dalby because of his reputation as an honest pit bull, but in the beginning, the attorney's bluntness had made him uneasy. Now he liked it. Maybe because it reminded him of Sarah. She wasn't blunt, but she was honest and forthright.

"I wish my gut had told me not to trust Corbin when he asked me to design his building," Tyler admitted.

"Hindsight is twenty-twenty. I'll get the paperwork filed. The damages I'm going to ask will definitely get his attention."

Tyler winced. "I don't want to look as if I'm trying to profit from this."

"Profit has nothing to do with it. You have the right to be compensated for lost income and damage to your reputation," Dalby retorted. "Anyhow, he's going to have a stroke when he learns you documented your concerns about the changes he wanted. I love that you predicted exactly what happened. If we discover that he cut corners on the construction, he'll be in even deeper trouble."

Tyler rubbed his forehead. "What I don't understand is why the county didn't tell him they'd gotten a notarized copy of my concerns before breaking ground. It should have been resolved before they signed off on the permits."

"That's another interesting question. This case is full of them. If it weren't for those men getting hurt, it would almost be fun. Got to go now—I'm due in court. I'll be in touch."

Tyler said goodbye and dropped his phone on the table.

His lawyer might relish the upcoming legal tussle, but he'd be glad when everything was over.

In the greenhouse being used for the fall plantings, Kurt worked next to Nathan as they filled the flats with soil and planted the seeds in a grid pattern. It was tedious, but that made it better for talking.

"I understand you put Vickie off when she wanted to do something next weekend," Kurt said.

"Mom shouldn't have told you that."

"She's a concerned mother who wonders why her son is backing away from a beautiful girl. You seemed interested enough on Sunday."

Nathan looked angry. "She's an athlete and

does projects like Rails-to-Trails and Habitat for Humanity. I don't want to be one of her causes."

"Vickie doesn't encourage a man that way if she isn't interested. You'd better call her back before she makes other plans. She's popular. But keep in mind, if you break my niece's heart, I'll break every bone in your body," Kurt returned with a pleasant smile.

A choked laugh came from Nathan. "I suspect Vickie would take care of any punishment for you. She seems direct."

"That she is."

They continued working, and Kurt was pleased to see Nathan looked less angry than before.

"Don't you get bored?" Nathan asked after a while. "I don't just mean planting seeds, but with all of it."

Kurt wasn't offended. It had taken him a while to appreciate how much he enjoyed working with his hands and the soil. While it might not be right for everyone, it had been right for him.

"No one is making me do this," he said mildly. "I enjoy being around growing things. I spent too much of my career in places where no life was valued."

"I suppose it's different for regular retirement," Nathan said at length. "You must need a rest then."

"I was forty-three when I retired," Kurt pointed

out wryly. "Hardly in my dotage, either then *or* now. But you might be partly right. I had more than my fill of war."

Nathan looked appalled. "That isn't what I meant."

Kurt sighed. "Son, it's tough becoming a civilian again, no matter how long you've served. None of my fellow soldiers liked fighting, but it put us on the edge. There's a surge in your blood that you can miss when it's gone. Then you feel guilty and wonder what kind of person that makes you. Hell, my daughter says that if she had her way, we wouldn't have war, we'd talk everything out over loaves of fresh-baked bread and fresh-churned butter."

"Hear, hear. I like Sarah's way best."

"She's a good kid. Makes me proud."

Nathan turned more serious again. "You're really okay, aren't you, Kurt? You got through it all and you're happy."

"Sure, but I didn't do it alone. Accepting help doesn't mean you're weak."

Nathan scooped potting soil into another flat before looking up. "Yeah, well, I guess Mom *also* mentioned I might cancel with Dr. Romano today. Do you honestly think IRT can do anything? It sounded good, but when I was talking to Vickie, I realized how I must look through her eyes. A banged-up guy who may always limp and whose career could be over."

Kurt opened another container of seeds, taking his time before answering. "There are never guarantees, but doing something is better than doing nothing. And if we can't change our endings, maybe changing how we feel about them is the best bet. Why not try to do it for a bad dream?"

"I guess that makes sense."

Kurt chuckled. "You know, I just remembered that one of the Egyptian pharaohs rewrote history after a defeat in battle. He simply came home and told a different story about what had happened. Everybody was happy."

"Whatever works, I suppose."

Kurt decided he'd said enough as Nathan nodded and bent over the flat he was planting. Time would tell, but IRT and other treatment could only be successful if Nathan put his mind to it and really tried. His physical recovery was only part of the healing he needed.

CHAPTER THIRTEEN

THE NEXT DAY Sarah packed cookies and sandwiches from the shop to take home as a meal. She already had a green salad in her refrigerator but figured Tyler probably would prefer something more substantial.

She'd barely had a chance to say hello to Theo when she heard a car pull up outside. He went racing up the stairs to hide. "Nobody is going to hurt you," she called after him.

She opened the front door and found a gift bag hanging off the knob.

"What's that?" Tyler asked as he came up the walk.

"I don't know." She looked inside and found a box of baby shower invitations, along with a pacifier. A creepy sensation crept across her shoulders.

"That's an odd present," he said. "Are you throwing a baby shower?"

"Hardly. I don't know anyone who's pregnant."

"Do you think it's connected to the other harassment?"

"Got me." Sarah looked in the bag again and

on the tag. "There's no note and my name isn't on it. Maybe they got the wrong house."

"Is that what you really think?"

Sarah wasn't sure. With all the hours she worked, she didn't hear most of the news in town.

"Uh, sorry, come in," she said belatedly, stepping aside for Tyler. "I'll call my grandmother and see if she knows about any upcoming baby showers."

She dialed Grandma Margaret, who hemmed and hawed around before finally admitting that she knew of six women expecting a baby and that four of the pregnancies weren't public knowledge yet. "It'll be a few months before baby showers are planned. Why?" asked her grandmother.

"Just wondering," Sarah said vaguely. "I keep hoping to hear Carlie is expecting."

"Oh, I…well…that is…" her grandmother stuttered and Sarah grinned, despite her nervous tension.

"Carlie is one of the six, isn't she?"

"I can neither confirm nor deny that."

"You don't need to. I've got to go—someone is here. But thanks for the good news."

It *was* good news, but it also sent a pang through Sarah. While she didn't begrudge her cousin's happiness, a part of her longed for love and babies of her own.

"What did she say?" Tyler asked as she stood still holding the receiver.

Sarah jumped. "Um, at least six women in Glimmer Creek are pregnant, but it'll be months before we have any baby showers."

"That's interesting."

Though Sarah was stressed, she laughed. "I find it hard to believe that babies and baby showers hold the slightest interest for you."

A sheepish look crossed his face. "True. Changing the subject, I called my lawyer today and told him to file the slander suit against Milo Corbin."

Sarah watched his face. "How do you feel about that?"

"Feel?" Tyler looked at her blankly.

"Yes, *feel*. Angry, relieved…what?"

"It was just something that had to be done."

Jeez. Sarah wanted to shake him. She still thought the "ice man" moniker was cruel, but in some ways it fit. On the outside, at least.

"Fine. Since we appear to be exchanging confidences, I talked to Zach this morning about the harassment. But only as my cousin, not to make an official police report."

"What did he say?"

"About what you'd expect." Sarah carried the gift bag into the kitchen and set it next to the pile of odd mailings she'd been getting. "The motorcycle incident concerns him since it goes beyond harassment. He agrees that someone unplugging the catering vehicles might be considered vandalism. And he isn't happy about the rest of this. But there isn't enough evidence to get a handle on, so we'll need to wait and see if anything else happens."

Sarah was glad Zach had been relatively low-key. She didn't want to read something significant into every little incident and start jumping at shadows. Usually there was a perfectly good explanation, and she'd spent too much time afraid and paranoid during her marriage.

"I've got sandwiches and salad," she said brightly. "I hope you're hungry."

TYLER WISHED SARAH'S COUSIN could have told her something more definitive, but he was glad *someone* in law enforcement knew what was happening.

The meal was tasty and he ate too much, something he suspected was a common problem when Sarah fed people. *She* mostly ate green salad and the chicken out of her sandwich, leaving the crusty French bread behind.

"Do you have any idea if the remodeling is possible?" she asked as she put a plate of cookies on the table.

"I'm working on some thoughts, including

ways to make the second floor useful. For one, the front section of the roof could be turned into a rooftop garden and seating area for customers."

"That's a great idea if it can work. What about my kitchens?"

"I have some thoughts about them, too. But how about going for a drive while we talk? I think we could both use a change of scenery."

"Or we could do something else."

From the look in Sarah's eyes, Tyler suspected he wasn't going to like the "something else."

"Such as?"

"If you recall, one of my cousins is the activities director at Poppy Gold."

"And I explained that planned activities aren't my thing. I'm not a group person," he amended, recalling her exasperation the last time the subject had come up.

"This one will be fun—it's a ghost walk of Poppy Gold and the pioneer cemetery. Your mom is going. I told her about it this afternoon and she invited Dad."

He stared. "You want to go on a double date with our parents?"

Sarah rolled her eyes. "No one is dating. But I'd like to attend and support Carlie. It's the first time she's offering the tour."

Tyler missed most of what she'd said; he was still processing his impulsive "double date" comment. The idea of dating Sarah was alluring. If they were dating, he wouldn't need to *fantasize* about kissing her; they would just kiss.

"Tyler," Sarah prompted.

"I don't know. Ghost stories?"

"Come on—didn't you ever do a campout in the backyard with your brother and tell each other scary tales?"

"No."

Sarah patted his arm. "Then this will help you make up for lost time. Think of it as getting in touch with your inner child."

Tyler wasn't sure he had an inner child, but he nodded. The tour would probably be jammed with kids and he'd be uncomfortable, but he couldn't turn Sarah down. And there was always a trillion to one shot she'd get scared by a ghost and jump into his arms.

SARAH SLID HER FEET into a pair of sandals. "We've got a few minutes, so I'm going to check on my cat. He gets freaked when someone is here that he doesn't know."

"Sure. I'll put the dishes in the dishwasher. I worked at a restaurant during college. Part of the time I bused tables, but the rest of the time I loaded the dishwasher, scrubbed pots and pans and mopped the floors."

"Really? I started at a caterer doing cleanup. It

was one of the really big guys in Los Angeles—
very posh and snooty—but I learned a lot from
him."

"How long was it before you got promoted?"

Sarah laughed. "A week. But that was pure
luck. A major client came in when everyone was
out on a catering job. I'd brought the ingredients
for my chocolate hazelnut torte, hoping to make
it and impress the owner. Instead I made it for
her. I could have lost my job, but she was thrilled
and her guests raved. Frederick liked my initia-
tive and made me a trainee pastry chef."

A smile spread across Tyler's face. "That
wasn't luck—that was talent."

Yikes.

It was the same smile that made her weak in
the knees—made her want to do her darnedest
to seduce him.

Breathless, Sarah started for the steps, only
to find a grumpy-looking Theo sitting halfway
down. "Hey, buddy. I thought you were hiding."

He deigned to accept a few caresses, only
to leave in a huff when he heard footsteps ap-
proaching.

"He's okay," Sarah said, meeting Tyler in the
living room.

"Good. I'll drive. About the gift bag," he
said, seeming to pick his words carefully. "Isn't
it something your cousin should know about?"

"I'll tell him tomorrow, but you're sworn to secrecy for tonight. I don't want Dad to hear about it from anyone else."

TYLER COULDN'T BELIEVE he was going on a ghost walk.

"Is this for serious ghost hunters or just for fun?" he asked as they drove the short distance to Poppy Gold.

"Entertainment only," Sarah explained, getting out.

Sarah hadn't needed to worry about the success of her cousin's ghost walk. A huge crowd had gathered to hear stories from Glimmer Creek's haunted history. His mother and Kurt Fullerton waved from the other side of the gathering, yet a tight expression crossed Kurt's face when he saw Tyler with Sarah.

"I don't think your father likes me," Tyler said softly. "Not that I'm complaining. I'm sure he's the one who convinced Nathan to keep his therapy appointment today."

"Rosemary mentioned that Nathan has been surly lately."

"Yeah. I'm afraid temper runs in the family," Tyler confessed. "I, uh, about earlier—you asked how I felt about going forward with the slander suit…"

Sarah focused on him. "You said it was just something that had to be done."

"That's because I didn't want to admit how much I hate being forced into this position. It really makes me angry."

"I'd feel that way, too. Why not say it?"

Tyler's embarrassment grew, but he'd started the conversation and might as well finish it. "The only time you've seen me lose control is the day I got to Glimmer Creek. I didn't want you thinking I was nothing but a jerk with a short fuse."

Sarah started laughing. "You call that losing control?"

"It was for me."

"I suppose it was. Well, don't worry about it." She slid her arm into his, and every inch of his body went on alert. "There may be ways you could lose control that wouldn't bother me in the least."

Just then a woman called everyone to attention and started talking.

Tyler didn't hear a word. He was too busy wondering what Sarah had meant.

ROSEMARY WAS PLEASED to see her eldest son and Sarah doing something together that wasn't connected to the remodeling. It would be lovely if they got together, she mused. Sarah would be the best daughter-in-law in the world. At the same time, she knew their temperaments weren't a good match.

"What are you smirking about?" Kurt whispered in her ear.

"I'm not smirking, I'm thinking about Sarah. You mentioned she takes after her mother. Is it difficult being reminded of your ex-wife?"

"Naw. Lizzie and I were never right for each other," Kurt admitted. "We met when I was stationed in Texas. We were moved around often by the army, which she hated, and she finally packed her things and left. She didn't even ask for custody."

"What about visitation rights?"

"No visitation, either. She walked out the day I was due back from an assignment. I think that's what made me hate her the most—she left our daughter alone in the apartment, divorce papers on the kitchen table. I was late, and Sarah was hungry and terrified. She clung to me and cried for hours."

"How awful," Rosemary breathed, horrified.

"That kid is my life. Even if Lizzie *had* asked for visitation, I would have fought it tooth and nail. No way was she getting near my little girl again."

"I would have felt the same."

But Rosemary wondered about what he'd said…*that kid is my life*. It was something most parents might say, but Sarah seemed to worry her father was *too* involved with her life and business.

The activities director was breaking the crowd into smaller groups, apparently having planned for a big turnout.

"Didn't Nathan want to come?" Kurt asked as the groups went in different directions, each led by a Poppy Gold employee.

"I invited him, but he's taking care of some homework the doctor had asked him to do."

Nathan's mood had greatly improved after spending the day with Kurt; he'd even called Vickie. They hadn't made plans, but had talked for nearly an hour. Yet once again Rosemary felt as if other people were taking care of problems for her.

She frowned.

Her son's recovery was too important to worry about who did what to help him. And if she wanted more control over her life, she could start by having Tyler explain the finances and hand them over for her to handle.

"What's wrong?" Kurt muttered.

"Nothing. Be quiet. I'm sure these ghost stories are old stuff to you, but I've never heard them before."

He grinned and let her be drawn into Glimmer Creek's spectral past. The tales were entertaining, spooky enough to give shivers, but not so terrible they were likely to keep anyone awake.

Of course, it might have been nice to blame her insomnia on a ghost.

IT WAS DARK by the time Tyler parked in front of the house.

Sarah had seriously considered throwing caution to the wind and trying to seduce him, but her brain was too tired to cooperate, even though her body was still in favor.

"That was fun," she said. "Thanks for going with me."

"Are any of those ghost stories true?"

"I haven't experienced any spirits personally, but the historical figures were real. And Tessa's mother once claimed she would have fallen down a flight of stairs, but something pulled her upright."

"Must have been Casper."

"Must have been," she agreed with a smile. "I'd love to, um, talk more, but I'm dead on my feet. No ghostly jokes intended. Four o'clock comes awfully early."

Tyler promptly got out and was at the passenger door before she could move. It was a gentlemanly thing to do, but she was less thrilled when he insisted on going inside to be sure everything was okay.

"I locked up when we left. I'm sure everything is fine," Sarah protested.

"Indulge me."

She curled up on the couch while he searched the house. Jeez, he was even checking windows. Her eyelids drifted down as she considered the effort required to go upstairs to bed. Maybe she'd just sleep here.

"Sarah, everything is clear," Tyler murmured.

She opened her eyes. He'd crouched next to her and looked so delicious, a renewed flicker of desire tightened her abdomen. *Mmm.* The cut was still healing over his eye, but most of the bruising had faded. The injury made him look rakish and just rough enough around the edges that his perfect looks weren't as intimidating.

"I really did consider seducing you," she said sleepily. "I wasn't just teasing earlier. I thought we could pretend it never happened afterward, but now I'm too tired."

He was close enough that Sarah saw his pupils dilate. "That would have been an interesting proposition. Do you have enough energy left for a kiss we can pretend didn't happen?"

"I guess."

Tyler kissed her gently, then more deeply, and her blood surged. His arms went around her and he deepened the caress. Her skin seemed to burn and his response was unmistakable. Yet as abruptly as the embrace had begun, it ended.

"I'd better go," he said hoarsely. "And you need to lock the dead bolts behind me."

With that, he lifted her to her feet.

At the door he stepped outside. "Lock the screen door, too," he instructed.

"Uh, okay." She started to turn on the front light, only to have her attention caught by an eerie glow. "Tyler, look."

She pointed, and his breath hissed out in a curse.

Written on the facing board of the porch roof was the question, *Why did you do it?*

SARAH MARVELED AT how quickly a little glow-in-the-dark paint could wake a person up, especially someone who'd just enjoyed a pleasant ghost walk and a really hot kiss.

Tyler didn't have to persuade her to call Zach. Her cousin insisted on coming over after he heard the story, his expression turning even grimmer than usual when he saw the message.

Why did you do it?

Do what?

Why was someone targeting her, and what could she have done to make them angry enough to write it in phosphorescent paint?

Zach took pictures and then checked the paint.

"It's dry. How long were you in the house after returning from the ghost walk?"

Sarah glanced at Tyler. She didn't think her cousin needed to know about the kiss.

"When we got back Tyler checked both floors to be sure everything was okay. I was locking the door after him, which is when we spotted the message. But it wasn't necessarily painted this evening. I don't remember the last time I was on the porch after dark, and the paint would blend in during the day."

"Show him the gift bag," Tyler urged.

With a sigh, Sarah led the way back to her kitchen. "I found this bag hanging off the doorknob this afternoon. Inside is a box of blank invitations and a baby rattle."

Zach put on crime scene gloves and began examining the bag and its contents, asking if she had any idea who could be responsible for leaving it.

When Sarah shook her head, Tyler stepped forward, looking impatient. "You should look into Sarah's ex-husband. From what she's said, he's the kind of guy who might harass her."

Her face went hot. Her lousy marriage wasn't a secret, but she didn't advertise it.

"Sarah?" It was Zach, and he was frowning. "How ugly was the divorce?"

"Pretty ugly. His name is Douglas Sheehan.

The last I heard, he was a vice president at the Bly-Smythe-Weston Corporation. But he's remarried, and I don't know why he'd bother with an ex-wife he hasn't seen in years."

Zach wrote the information in his notebook. "I'll check regardless. Also to see if he's stayed at Poppy Gold Inns in the past few months. In the meantime, I'll take the odd mailings you've received, along with the bag, and see what I can figure out."

He left, and the silence was awkward.

"I could spend the night on the couch," Tyler volunteered.

Some of the tightness eased in Sarah's chest. "That's sweet, but I'll be fine."

"Nobody in my entire life has called me sweet."

"What about when you were a baby?"

"Unlikely. I can't recall a single smile in any of my baby photos."

That seemed unbearably sad and Sarah wanted to cry.

She told herself it was just the pressure and fear of what was going on, topped with exhaustion, but she was afraid it meant more. A part of her was growing fond of Tyler Prentiss, and that scared her as much as creepy messages on her porch.

CHAPTER FOURTEEN

ROSEMARY COULD SEE the wheels turning in Tyler's brain on Saturday when she told him that she was going out to dinner with Kurt that evening. No doubt he was still wondering if their relationship was romantic, especially after seeing them together at the ghost walk.

Well, fine. He could think whatever he wanted.

She and Kurt decided on Giancarlo's Little Italy, where she ordered cheese ravioli and a side salad with the house dressing.

"The same for me," Kurt said to the server. "The ravioli is great here, and Sarah keeps saying I should eat less meat and more vegetables."

Cheese ravioli wasn't a vegetable, but Rosemary restrained a smile. "It's nice that she worries about your health."

"She's a great kid. I just wish she wasn't so stubbornly independent."

"There's nothing wrong with independence. It's better to be able to stand up for yourself, instead of always relying on someone else. Believe me, I know. I keep thinking how different everything might be today if I'd stood up to Richard. Especially about Kittie. We shouldn't have kept her a secret. Now I need to make all the decisions, and I don't have any practice."

Kurt had an odd expression on his face, but he just nodded. "I know the past few months have been rough."

They talked for another few minutes, then the server brought their meals. "Delicious," Rosemary said after her first bite. "They must make the pasta from scratch."

"That's what Sarah says."

DESPITE THE LIGHTER CONVERSATION, Kurt was restless.

The talk about secrets had made him uncomfortable since he knew about Tyler's legal problems in Illinois and she probably didn't.

"Rosemary, it's funny that you mentioned secrets," he said slowly. "Maybe it isn't my place to tell you, but I learned something the other day. If you haven't heard already, there was a problem with a building that Tyler worked on in the Chicago area. He had a disagreement with his client about requested alterations, and he left the project. Then the building collapsed in the middle of construction and several workers were injured. A commission is being convened to investigate who is responsible and whether any criminal charges should be brought."

Rosemary's fork clattered to her plate. "This happened recently?"

"A few weeks ago when Tyler was Italy, though he flew into Illinois for a few days to advise on rescue efforts. Apparently the second architect and the owner are trying to blame his original design."

"That's outrageous." Her eyes flashed in anger. "He would never make that kind of mistake."

"I think almost everyone agrees."

"How did you find out?"

"From my uncle," Kurt admitted, belatedly grasping the complications to revealing this particular secret. Sarah had mentioned those complications, but he hadn't paid attention. "Uncle Milt was the Glimmer Creek police chief until a few months ago and was concerned about an uproar Tyler caused at the sweet shop the first day he was here. So he did a background check. Do you know anything about that?"

Rosemary's cheeks brightened. "I told you about it. Tyler thought I should quit my job because he felt it was too much for me to handle. I know he generally keeps his feelings to himself, but he's protective and was worried."

"You mentioned he was unhappy about you working, not that he'd caused a commotion."

"It wasn't serious, and I didn't want you to be annoyed with him. He apologized, and that's why he's giving Sarah advice about the remodel, to show he regrets his behavior."

Somehow, Kurt doubted repentance was at the core of Tyler Prentiss's efforts. The young man was hard to fathom, but there was a spark when he looked at Sarah that couldn't be mistaken.

Kurt didn't like it.

There couldn't be two people more unsuited, even supposing Tyler Prentiss was interested in anything permanent.

"Er, yeah," Kurt muttered. "Anyway, I thought you should be told. You hadn't mentioned it, so I was concerned."

And my daughter told me you didn't know. He hoped Rosemary didn't ask any more questions, because he didn't know how to answer them.

Rosemary picked up her fork and pushed the remaining food around her plate. "I wish Tyler had confided in me. It's strange when your children begin protecting you, instead of the other way around."

Kurt nodded glumly. They were only in their fifties. Sure, he got involved when Sarah had a problem, but that was his prerogative as a parent. He didn't need to be shielded when she was upset or worried.

"I'm going to feel bad if you don't finish your

dinner," he said, gesturing to her half-eaten meal. "Did I make a mistake telling you about Tyler?"

"It's best for me to know."

ROSEMARY ATE MORE of the pasta to reassure Kurt, though her appetite had vanished. She'd thought something was distracting Tyler, but she'd naively hoped it was from falling in love with Sarah.

"I'm sure you can find more information about the investigation online if you want to know more," Kurt told her. "You're welcome to use the laptop at my house, but they also have computers available at the Poppy Gold business center."

"I'll go to the business center," she said quietly.

While Kurt had become a good friend, she didn't want him to be there when she was reading about Tyler's troubles. She'd feel too exposed.

"It's located in the old City Hall building and open twenty-four hours a day."

"You seem to know everything about Poppy Gold."

"I meet the guests while I'm working on plants or floral arrangements, so it's good to know what services are offered."

"What is your most common question?" she asked to lighten the mood.

"'Where can I buy those cinnamon rolls?'" he said promptly, and Rosemary forced a smile.

"The sweet shop sells unbelievable amounts of them," she said. "I'm trying to convince Sarah to do mail order for products like the rolls and fudge. Customers would love it. Some have even offered to pay for overnight shipping."

"If you stay in California, you might become part of a huge baking empire," Kurt joked.

The comment made Rosemary think. Tyler had asked if she planned to move to Glimmer Creek, but she hadn't given it much consideration. Was she ready for small-town life, nearly three thousand miles from where she'd been born and raised? It would be a huge step. She also couldn't stay at Poppy Gold forever, which meant finding a home.

"We're going to be friends, no matter what. Right?" she asked lightly, knowing it was time to give serious thought to the future.

"Friends are friends for life," Kurt replied. "I still stay in touch with my buddies from the army. They visit Poppy Gold, and we keep up-to-date with email and Skype."

"What about social media?"

"Nah. Skype is different. You can really talk, and I don't have to post pictures of my ugly mug for the world to see."

Rosemary grinned. "You're fishing for compliments, but I don't mind. I think you're very handsome. Not George Clooney handsome, of course, but there's only one George Clooney."

"What do women see in that guy?"

"Maybe it's his smile or his eyes or that gorgeous body. Or just the entire delicious package."

Kurt snorted. "Window dressing."

"I also understand he's a decent person. Socially conscious and all that."

They continued chatting and teasing each other, by unspoken agreement leaving more painful topics alone. Kurt was the first friend she'd made since Richard's death, and she was still learning how to navigate that friendship.

But one thing was becoming evident—it was *also* the first time since her marriage that she wasn't worried about what she revealed and whether her husband would approve. How could you have true friends if you never felt free to be yourself?

It made her sad knowing how much Richard's pride had cost them both.

OVER THE NEXT WEEK Tyler spent a few hours each evening at Sarah's house. She longed to kiss him again, hoping for more, but how could she be sure it was pure desire and not just a wish for him to spend the night and make her feel safe?

He was interested. She could see it in his eyes

and the way his breath quickened at times, but he also didn't make any attempt to kiss her again.

Mostly he seemed fascinated by the blueprints of her building, pouring over them like a cat inspecting a can of sardines that it couldn't open.

"What is so intriguing about those things?" she finally demanded.

"I've checked my measurements against the original floor plan, but something didn't seem to add up. So I went to the city and checked the plat maps. There appears to be a hollow space in the wall between your building and the one next door that isn't included in any of the plans. You've never noticed?"

Sarah frowned. "If anything, I would have assumed they closed a gap between the two buildings for appearances."

"Perhaps, but I wonder if your shop could have been used as a speakeasy. It was built right after the start of Prohibition, and the hollow area may be a staircase or hiding place in case of a raid."

The possibility of a hidden space in her building was exciting, and Sarah tried to recall what she'd been told when buying the property.

"If I remember correctly, my building and the one next door were originally built by two brothers," she said slowly. "They had a huge fight before opening their respective businesses. Supposedly they never spoke again. Both defaulted on their mortgages after the banks failed during the Depression. The properties were repossessed, and they left the area around the same time."

"What were the two businesses?"

"Got me. But if one of them operated as a speakeasy, the other brother *must* have known."

Tyler grinned at her. "Want to go look for secret passageways?"

Sarah hesitated. No other packages had been left, but it still would be uncomfortable returning to her house late. On the other hand, she couldn't let fear paralyze her.

"All right. We can both drive, and that way you don't have to come back here."

"Let's just go in my rental."

Trying not to feel relieved, Sarah went out to the car with Tyler. He drove to the shop, and they went in through the back to the storeroom where he promptly began checking the wall adjacent to the neighboring business.

"Hear how hollow that sounds?" he asked, tapping various spots.

"Couldn't it just be a poorly insulated space?"

"Sure, but the outside dimensions of the building are definitely wider than the inside dimensions."

Sarah eyed the plaster he was tapping. "That's great, but you aren't going to start knocking holes, are you? I don't think the health inspector would approve."

"Of course not, but let's go upstairs to the apartment. I didn't take enough measurements to know whether the discrepancy exists up there."

Sarah shrugged and unlocked the door to the staircase. They went up, and Tyler seemed to forget her presence as he measured and calculated, checking the small notebook he always seemed to have with him.

"The discrepancy is here, too," he finally said in an absent tone. "You'd probably see it if you got onto the open section of the roof and started comparing."

"I'll take your word for it."

Tyler began examining the bookshelves attached to the wall in question and finally the floor.

"There are drag marks along here."

He pointed, and she saw a faint wear pattern in the hardwood floor that she hadn't noticed before. They looked interesting and she began tugging at the bookshelf. "What about a hidden latch?" she asked after a minute.

"Possible." He ran his fingers under the decorative molding at the top. "Here's something." There was a click, but the shelves still wouldn't budge, so he continued checking. This time he pressed two places simultaneously and pulled sideways.

The bookshelf slid along the wall, and they saw a framed opening. Sitting inside was a bottle of amber liquid, with a yellowed sheet of paper beneath it.

Sarah blinked. "Well, what do you know?"

THOUGH TYLER HAD FOUND discrepancies in blueprints before, it was the first time he'd uncovered a hidden compartment. He stuck his head inside the opening and saw a staircase to the left, but it was too dark to tell much else.

Sarah brushed against him as she retrieved the bottle and sheet of paper. He ground his teeth. Kissing her had been a mistake because now he knew what she tasted like and how her fragrance filled his senses.

"Listen to this," she said, grinning, "'Dear Officer Bennett, you figured it out at last. Too bad we've left for greener pastures. Noble and I have a nice nest egg saved, not that the bank has ever seen it. Good thing, too, the way it failed. Have a drink on us. This is the finest whiskey money can buy. Don't ever say we didn't serve the best. Fred and Noble Millard.'"

Tyler chuckled despite his discomfort. "At least they had a sense of humor."

"I wonder what they'd say if they knew this staircase remained a secret all these years."

"Maybe it hasn't," he suggested. "Officer Bennett may have found the hidden door and didn't want anyone to know they got away from him."

Sarah held up the note. "And left this for future generations to find?"

"Maybe not."

"What made you think there may have been a speakeasy here?" she asked curiously.

"It was just speculation, but it seemed possible considering the period. Why else hide a space in a building except as an escape route? It's just the right size for a set of stairs. I also looked up old issues of the local newspaper. There were several editorials from the period urging the police department to be on the lookout for illegal drinking establishments in the downtown area."

Sarah held up her keys. "I have a flashlight on my key ring. It's small, but bright. Do you want to go down first as the discoverer?"

Tyler accepted the key ring. "Sure, but only to safeguard your fragile sensibilities from seeing the skeleton that may be at the bottom."

"My fragile sensibilities, huh? Do you think I'd come unglued that easily?"

Actually, Tyler was more concerned about the staircase being unsafe after decades of disuse, but he wasn't going to admit that to Sarah—she'd insist on going first. As for getting hysterical at the sight of a skeleton? He doubted it. He had a growing respect for her resilience.

"I just wanted to be sure you were paying attention," he said. "I'll go down first and come back with the light. If there's no skeleton, you can check it out for yourself."

"Ha ha."

Standing on the threshold, Tyler stomped the landing at the top of the stairs. It didn't quiver. The Millard brothers must have been as good at carpentry as they'd been at bootlegging. Nevertheless, he tested each step going down. They were rock solid. At the bottom, he flashed the light around.

"No skeletons?" Sarah called from above.

"Mostly dust. It looks as if there used to be a door into the other building. They must have covered it when they left town. There's also a small area down here where they could have stored some of their stock. I'm betting there's a storage area under the staircase, as well."

"That makes sense. In case of a raid by the police, customers could hide in the other building. I bet there was an opening into the apartment on the other side of the landing, too."

"Possibly. But do you know what this means?" he asked.

"Uh…my place of business used to be a speakeasy?"

"Yes, but it also means you'll be able to get the space you need for the remodel."

"Well, your mother *did* say you were a brilliant architect."

SARAH GULPED AT the sound of Tyler's laughter echoing up the stairwell. It was a no-holds-barred laugh and sent electricity surging through her abdomen.

Really inappropriate.

But she'd always thought laughter and sex were a delicious combination. It was too bad the empty apartment was such a dismally uncomfortable place. Of course, beds were more niceties than necessities. And since they weren't at the house, she was reasonably certain what she felt was pure desire, not a hidden need for a protector.

Tyler appeared at the top of the stairs and handed her a shoe. She blinked.

"There was a lady's shoe down there?"

"Yup. Imagine the stories that could have led to it being there."

Sarah tossed the shoe to one side and eyed him.

She'd never been that good at the games between men and women, but it seemed unlikely that Tyler would make a move. He'd been the starchiest kind of gentleman ever since they'd kissed.

Letting go of her inhibitions, she put her arms around his neck. "I can think of some possibilities. Do you think any secret lovemaking went on down there?" she whispered against his mouth.

His body instantly responded against her.

"You're playing with fire," he warned.

"I hope so," Sarah said as she kissed him. His hands slid down her bottom, pulling her tighter, and she moaned. All the reasons they shouldn't get more deeply involved didn't seem to matter, just the rush of blood through her veins.

She wiggled against him.

"I don't think your intentions are honorable," he muttered.

"No, and I'm counting on that preparedness you talked about."

"Oh, I'm prepared. But aren't you worried about your staff being downstairs?"

Sarah thought about it. None of her employees had a reason to come upstairs, so it shouldn't be a problem.

"No worries, I'm not a screamer…so I hope you won't be disappointed. Of course, all bets are off if you're a groaner."

TYLER FELT AS if he'd stepped from the edge of a precipice. "I don't groan."

With a saucy smile, Sarah stepped backward

and slowly removed her shorts and panties. Her T-shirt and bra followed.

Tyler groaned and she laughed. "Not a groaner, eh?"

"I've never seen you do a striptease before."

He took his own shirt off and pulled her to him. The contact of her breasts with his hot skin sent lightning through her body, a sensation that intensified when he lifted her against a wall and opened his mouth over her left breast, teasing the hard nub with his tongue.

She gasped and wondered if she might be a screamer after all.

After an endless moment, they slid to the floor and Tyler was able to give both her breasts proper attention, teasing and tasting with a skill she'd only guessed at before.

Ice man?

His ex had to be insane if she'd thought he could make love like this and not have a maelstrom of emotion inside.

Sarah explored Tyler's back and then eased the zipper over his arousal.

"In a hurry?" he whispered.

"Aren't you?"

"Hell, *yes*."

He groped and pulled out his wallet, quickly sheathing himself with a condom. Then grasping her hips, he thrust into her.

It had been so long, that Sarah's body instinctively resisted. Tyler stopped and caressed her until her tension eased. Slowly he set up a rhythm that made the world spin.

She came apart, her body no longer seeming to belong to her. Tyler collapsed next to her a moment later, gasping for breath.

CHAPTER FIFTEEN

MINUTES...OR MAYBE HOURS later, a loud thud came from the first floor.

"I should check on that," Sarah said, although she doubted it was anything dramatic. But it might get her past the awkwardness of wondering what to say. Maybe she simply wasn't modern enough to have a casual lover. Casual? She would have laughed if she hadn't felt so rattled. *Nothing* she felt toward Tyler was casual.

She collected her clothes and dressed, aware of him watching.

"Planning to sleep here?" she asked, smoothing her hair as much as possible.

"No, but I, uh, need a few minutes."

Sarah's gaze traveled over him, and she saw he'd become aroused again. Her legs shook. "Sure."

She hurried downstairs, wondering what she'd do if Tyler asked to spend the night with her. The question flew out of her head when she saw her father getting up from the floor, a pipe wrench in his hand.

"Dad, what are you doing here?" she gasped, feeling like a teenager who'd nearly gotten caught making out with her boyfriend.

"Working on the plumbing. A few days ago someone mentioned one of the drains might be slow. I knew it would be quieter tonight, so I cleaned the U-bend on all the sinks."

He'd been downstairs while she and Tyler were upstairs having sex? Sarah hoped she wasn't blushing. She had nothing to be embarrassed about; she wasn't a kid any longer.

She grabbed her father's arm and dragged him out to the loading dock. "Dad, the staff needs to talk to me about *everything* at the bakery."

"But it's okay—I took care of it."

"You don't understand. What if the health inspector had found something I didn't know about? Or if the sink had clogged in the middle of the breakfast rush?"

"You're right. I should have taken care of it right away instead of waiting a couple of days."

Sarah nearly screamed with exasperation. "The biggest problem is that *I didn't know*. I appreciate that you want to help, but I can't have my staff reporting issues to you instead of me."

KURT FINGERED HIS WRENCH, remembering something Rosemary had said...that there was nothing wrong with independence. He'd wondered if she was hinting something about Sarah, only to get drawn into a discussion about secrets.

He hadn't seen anything wrong with quietly taking care of things for his daughter, but now he wasn't so sure.

Uneasily he remembered the other repairs he'd handled after she'd gone home. Sarah's staff adored her. They knew she was under pressure with the business expanding so quickly and wanted to help, so they told *him* when there was something he could handle. His commanding officers in the army would have gone ballistic. *Follow the chain of command*, they would have thundered.

"Listen to me, Dad, you have to back off," Sarah said. "I love you, but you haven't even taken a vacation since I moved back to Glimmer Creek and opened the shop."

"Neither have you."

"But it's *my* bakery. You used to love visiting your old army buddies and seeing new places. What about *your* life? Do you know how much I worry about you missing out on the things you enjoy?"

"You don't need to worry about me."

Sarah sighed. "Remember all the times I've said the same thing to you? Grandma told me about the heated debates you had with Grandpa about being your own man when you were a teenager. She understood. You were becoming an adult and establishing boundaries. It didn't mean you loved them any less—just that you didn't want to be treated like a child any longer. Well, the same goes here."

Kurt winced, recalling the epic battles he'd had with his father. Growing up as a preacher's kid in a small town hadn't been easy. Why would he think Sarah didn't want her space and independence, as well, just because she was his daughter?

"Uh, I'll do better," he muttered. A noise caught his attention, and he saw Tyler Prentiss stepping out the door. "What's *he* doing here?"

"Tyler found a discrepancy in the floor plans and discovered a hidden staircase. It turns out my building used to be a speakeasy. It also means remodeling is possible," Sarah added. "The office can go upstairs, and I might even get more space in front for customers."

Kurt nodded to the younger man, trying to feel grateful. He *was* grateful, he just didn't like that someone else had found the answer Sarah needed instead of him.

Get used to it, he thought dismally.

THE NEXT MORNING, Sarah woke up in a reflective mood, her emotions churning.

Tyler had taken her home without saying anything about them making love, though he'd carefully checked the house. When he'd left, she'd reflected that there were pluses and minuses to being with a guy who didn't like talking about his feelings.

Especially when she didn't want to talk herself.

She didn't know how she felt about Tyler. She'd grown up in an outgoing family who interfered too much in each other's lives, but they did it out of love and with the best of intentions. Her father didn't mean to be a problem. He kept crossing the line, yet it was because he loved her.

But Tyler didn't love her, and they had little in common. He'd also made it clear what he wanted out of life, and it wasn't what she held near and dear to her heart, like a home and children and living in Glimmer Creek. While he obviously cared about his mom and brother, concern for family might be their only common ground.

Sarah was still thinking about it at work that morning when she noticed every tire on her catering vehicles was flat.

She stared in shock.

Nothing had happened for well over a week. Now this?

Forcing herself into action, she yanked out her cell phone and vaulted into the kitchen.

"What's wrong?" Regina asked, alarmed.

"The tires are flat on the catering vehicles. *All*

of them. Can you call Poppy Gold for help with delivering breakfast while I contact the police?"

"Right away."

Sarah dialed 911, and a patrol car soon pulled into the alley.

"I'm sorry, Sarah, the sidewalls have been sliced," Max Cantwell told her after a quick examination. "We'll check for fingerprints, but somebody with a sharp knife wouldn't have needed to touch anything. They could have gotten in and out within a few minutes."

Another officer took a kit from the trunk of the cruiser and began dusting for prints.

"We've been running extra patrols down the alley and haven't seen anything suspicious," Max continued. "The last pass was less than an hour ago, but if somebody was watching, they could have done it immediately after we left. Still, I wonder why it wasn't done earlier in the morning. Commuter traffic steps up about now, so they ran a greater risk of being spotted."

"Probably to give me less chance to have the tires replaced before breakfast," Sarah said bleakly. Everything that had happened at the bakery seemed calculated to disrupt her operations.

"It's possible. I've heard someone has been harassing you. This escalates the situation to an even higher level."

She nodded.

Her dad was going to be beside himself. Great-Uncle Milt was away, but Zach would come over. Other people in town would likely show up, as well, both curious and concerned. She'd probably spend most of the day fending off advice and offers of help.

Max went to help gather evidence. Sarah rubbed her arms, knowing she should go inside and get busy, but she was too upset to focus on cinnamon rolls and hash browns at the moment.

"It's amazingly clean, as if everything was wiped down," Max said finally. "We've got one partial print, but I doubt it's enough for an identification. We'll keep it on file, though. Here's the case number for your insurance company."

"Thanks." She took the business card he'd written on and went inside to get an update from Regina.

Poppy Gold was sending vehicles over. To save time, they would collect food for the larger locations like the Gold Rail Hotel and provide drivers for the other deliveries.

Some of Sarah's tension eased.

"Thanks, Regina. Nice job."

Regina smiled sympathetically and went back to the cinnamon rolls she was putting in a baking pan to rise. Sarah began helping, but a few minutes later Tessa's husband arrived.

"Hey, I understand you had a problem this morning."

She should have known Gabe would show up. Since he ran the Poppy Gold Security Division, he was notified of any issues that might affect internal operations, including issues with their contractors.

"Bad news travels fast. Somebody knifed the tires on my catering vehicles. All of them. Do you know how expensive those things are to replace? My insurance company is going to have a fit."

"We'll need to increase security back there."

Gabe began prowling the small loading dock and up and down the alley. He was another tall, inscrutable man who showed little emotion.

Just like Tyler.

Sarah sighed.

Her brain kept going back to Tyler and the way he was getting mixed up in her life. The man was a country-hopping architect. Once his problems in Illinois cleared up, he'd be off, designing more great buildings and becoming as famous as Frank Lloyd Wright. And she *still* wouldn't understand a single thing about him.

Depressed, Sarah pushed the thought away.

"I'll install digital cameras with motion sensors," Gabe said. "They can be tied into the Poppy Gold security system. My crew will monitor any activity and get here quickly if they see anything suspicious."

"I can't impose," she told him hastily. "Just tell me what equipment to get. Someone is here twenty-four hours a day."

"It'll be easier for Poppy Gold to keep watch. Besides, my crew is trained for this. I'll come back after I get everything together."

He left so quickly she didn't have a chance to protest again…and he probably wouldn't have listened, regardless. Gabe wasn't gregarious like her family, but he shared one trait with the male Fullertons—doing what he thought best. It was *really* difficult to keep them all from riding to the rescue, though in this case, since Poppy Gold had a stake in breakfasts going out, he was slightly more justified.

Determinedly, Sarah called Gabe's office on her cell. When she got his voice mail, she left a message saying she expected to pay for the equipment and installation, and the same with the monitoring.

Next she called her father.

"What's up, kiddo?" he asked.

"I just wanted you to know there was trouble at the shop this morning. I'm fine and so is my staff, but someone slashed the tires on the catering vehicles. The police have been here, along with Gabe. He's going to install motion-activated cameras behind the shop and have his team monitor them. *Don't overreact.*"

"I want a security system at your house, too." Kurt was silent for a moment. "That is, a security system at your house sounds like a great idea. What do you think?"

Though Sarah was still reeling from the vandalism, her jaw dropped. He was asking, not insisting?

"It isn't an option, Dad. Glimmer Creek doesn't have a security company."

"Gabe might be able to put something together. Would…would you like me to talk to him about it?" he asked, almost meekly.

Sarah debated for a moment. She wanted to encourage her father's unusual behavior, but wasn't sure if agreeing was the right way to do it. Yet it might make him feel better. "I suppose you could ask if it's feasible."

"Love to, sweetheart. I'll let you know what he says."

"Okay. Bye."

Sarah disconnected, still astonished. Was it possible their talk the previous evening had gotten through to him?

TYLER COULDN'T REMEMBER ever enjoying himself as much he had while finding the hidden steps of the speakeasy with Sarah…and making love to her.

He wanted to understand Sarah, almost as much as he desired her. She was foreign to him, like one of the wood faeries she'd talked about— a take-charge wood faerie who enjoyed baking and cooking and didn't care that it wouldn't make her rich or famous.

Their few innocent kisses had put him in a near-permanent state of arousal, and now that he knew what it was like to make love to her, it would be even worse.

Yet regrets had crept in over a long, sleepless night.

He was fascinated by Sarah's spirit, but another part of him shrank from it. If nothing else, she asked damned uncomfortable questions. The questions weren't even that personal, but they reached into private spaces that he'd never shared. She also threatened the choices he'd decided *against*—a wife and children and being tied down.

They weren't idle decisions.

He'd reasoned things out, deciding what kind of life he wanted, and how to have it. Knowing he'd be a poor father and a worse husband just confirmed those choices. And nothing had changed. Nathan would get better, the crap in

Illinois would resolve itself and Tyler would get on with his career.

Simple as that.

But maybe he'd be a better person from knowing Sarah.

Yeah, right, jeered a voice in his head. Without her nudging, he'd probably fall back into the same old pattern of keeping the world at a distance. Problem was, the more time he spent with Sarah, the less attractive his old life seemed.

The morning was busy with Nathan's pool therapy and an appointment in Stockton with an orthopedist who felt his condition was improving. Naturally the news put smiles on both their faces.

It was when they were leaving the doctor's office that Tyler checked his phone and saw a text from his mother.

Tires slshd at shop but no one hrt lv mom.

"Something wrong?" Nathan asked.

"Yeah, vandalism at the bakery."

"We'd better get back."

Tyler pushed the speed limit on the drive into the foothills. When they reached Glimmer Creek, he left Nathan at the suite and hurried to the bakery. Going around the side, he saw a man up a ladder, installing an exterior camera. A tow truck was also there, changing tires on the electric catering vehicles.

"Are you supposed to be back here?" asked the man on the ladder.

"I'm Sarah's architect. Tyler Prentiss."

"I see. Gabe McKinley. Sarah is inside, talking to the police chief."

"Thanks. You're connected to Poppy Gold Inns, right? I'm staying at a suite in the John Muir Cottage with my family."

"I handle security. How is your brother?"

It was an interesting question. Or maybe not. No doubt it was Gabe McKinley's job to know everything that was going on.

"Better. He's doing a lot with Kurt Fullerton at the greenhouses and working gardens."

"So I've heard." Gabe finished attaching the bracket holding the video camera and adjusted it. "How is that?" he asked into a handheld radio.

"Looks good," said a voice over the speaker. "One hundred percent coverage."

Tyler stepped farther around the loading dock and saw two other cameras had been installed. Nobody would be able to get near the back of Sarah's Sweet Treats without being observed.

Just then Sarah came out the back door, followed by Zach Williams. "No," she was saying.

"It'll reassure everyone. An officer will be over this evening to take you home. And one will pick you up in the morning, even if I have to post someone outside your house all night."

"I don't need an escort, Zach. You can't justify using that many police department resources."

Zach Williams crossed his arms over his chest. "Somebody has a grudge against you. We don't know what that person is planning. I'm not talking about protective custody, just taking precautions."

"No, no, *no*," she repeated stubbornly, plainly not intimidated by her cousin's height or forbidding facade.

"Be reasonable, Sarah," Gabe urged. "I wouldn't allow Tessa to take chances."

"Allow? Promise to tell her that when I'm around. I'd love to hear what she says."

His hard face instantly looked chagrinned. "All right, that was stupid. But you need to be careful—this is a serious situation."

"Sarah knows that," Tyler announced, much to his own surprise. "She has to make up her own mind."

Sarah sent him a radiant smile that made him feel like a hypocrite. After all, he'd shown up to escort her to the bank and had come over to her house evening after evening. But he also knew she was determined to be strong and self-reliant. It was admirable.

"Stay out of this, Prentiss," Zach snapped.

"Tyler has a right to his opinion," Sarah said firmly. "I'm just sorry you don't agree with that opinion."

Tyler resisted grinning at the other men's expressions. They couldn't argue with Sarah without coming off badly. Didn't they understand her? He was far from an expert when it came to Sarah Fullerton, but issuing ultimatums was *not* the way to gain her cooperation.

"Fine," Zach ground out. "But at a minimum, let your father follow you home in his truck. Please," he added quickly.

"Maybe."

Gabe McKinley and the police chief both stomped away in obvious frustration.

"What happened?" Tyler asked when they were out of earshot.

"The tires were slashed last night on the catering trucks." Sarah's bottom lip trembled briefly before she raised her chin again. "My dad wants Gabe to install a security system at the house, tied into the Poppy Gold security monitors. The same as these." She gestured to the cameras on the wall. "I'm considering it. But now they want me to accept a police escort whenever I go. Glimmer Creek can't afford that."

"You're family."

"Yeah." She sat down on the edge of the loading dock with a heavy sigh. "I couldn't get the

Los Angeles police to pay attention when my husband was terrorizing me, though I didn't know it was him at the time. Here, everyone is freaking out."

"I understand, but, uh, is there any way you could meet them halfway?"

"I suppose letting Dad follow me home after work would make everybody feel better."

"Except you, right?"

Sarah released a long sigh. "I just worry that if I let fear take over again, I'll never *stop* being afraid. I don't want to be like that, jumping at my own shadow and wondering about perfectly innocent stuff."

Tyler nudged her. "Come on, the woman who called me a chauvinistic jackass? Not a chance."

"I usually don't resort to name-calling. When I was growing up, everybody knew I was the preacher's granddaughter, and they expected me to be well-behaved."

"Don't they say 'well-behaved women seldom make history'?"

She laughed and satisfaction swept through Tyler. It must have been a kick in the gut to arrive and find her catering vehicles vandalized.

"Surely there's a balance between using good sense and being independent, but I need to know for myself that I'm strong. It isn't easy after what happened with Doug. I can't believe I let him manipulate me the way he did."

Tyler surrendered to temptation and clasped her hand. "Maybe it isn't a question of strength. Maybe you mostly need to forgive yourself. We all make mistakes."

"I suppose that's possible."

He gently squeezed her fingers, unable to recall a time he'd ever just sat and held hands with a woman.

"Your ex-girlfriend was wrong, you know," she said after a minute. "You aren't an ice man."

"You haven't known me that long," Tyler warned.

She shoulder-bumped him. "We aren't always the best judges of ourselves. An ice man wouldn't have flown three thousand miles to California to rescue his mom and brother...whether they needed it or not. And you even got a black eye and jaw for your trouble."

Tyler grimaced. "Yeah. Apparently you told Mom that I may have set Nathan off when I yelled. She told Nathan, then *he* discussed it with Dr. Romano, who agreed. I'm in the doghouse all around."

"You can't be right all the time."

"Lately it doesn't seem as if I'm right *any* of the time."

Sarah arched her neck and rubbed it. "You're

the one getting Nathan to his appointments and making sure he exercises in the pool. And you found out about the speakeasy steps. On the whole, I don't think you're doing badly."

"Thanks. You know, we never took that drive I suggested," Tyler murmured. "We went to the ghost walk instead. How about it? Wouldn't you like to get away for an hour or two?"

Sarah pursed her lips, then finally nodded. "Let's go later this afternoon. I'll put a picnic together and show you the hillsides around here— I know *all* the back roads."

"Back roads? Is that a euphemism for axle-breaking ruts in dirt?" he asked. "I'm not sure my rental can handle that."

"There may be a couple of unpaved tracks involved, but they're usually in good shape this time of year. Even *my* little car can take them. Some of the roads are firebreaks, and others are maintained by mutual cooperation of the property owners."

"Are you sure the sweet shop can survive without you?"

Sarah tilted her chin at him in challenge. "Evidence to the contrary, I'm not a workaholic. I happen to believe in both working *and* playing hard. Besides, with everything that's been going on, I've asked several of my part-time employees to work more hours."

"Then we can go," Tyler said. He hesitated, wanting to kiss her, then glanced up at the video cameras. Perhaps not. Who knew how many of her relatives might be watching. "I'll come over at your house at four thirty."

Sarah had looked at the cameras when he did, and an impish look crossed her face. "Want to give the Poppy Gold security crew something more interesting to watch than an alley?"

"*No.* But I'm starting to understand your cousin's frustration. You must have been quite a handful when you were a little girl."

Sarah gave him a merry look. "I still am."

Tyler agreed, but he doubted they were thinking about the same handful.

CHAPTER SIXTEEN

SARAH WAS LOOKING FORWARD to the outing with Tyler so much that she went home immediately, eager to do something just for fun. Soon fried chicken fillets and macaroni salad were chilling in the fridge, and she had a batch of biscuits in the oven. She was taking them out when she heard the mail being dropped through the slot on the door.

There was nothing especially weird in the collection, though she wondered about a health magazine from a private hospital in Stockton. Still, hospitals advertised. It wasn't that unusual. The label was printed, and it simply looked like a bulk mailing addressed to "resident."

There also was a reminder that she had a package waiting at the post office. *Drat*, she thought, shoving it in her purse with the other she'd gotten that week. She kept forgetting to pick it up.

Looking out the window, she saw the postal truck still parked across the street, so she grabbed the slip again and ran over. "Surprise, Diego, I was home. Any chance you brought my package with you today?"

Diego laughed. "Hey, there's a whole bunch of them." He pulled out a plastic box, filled with parcels of assorted sizes. "Just leave the container on the porch, and I'll get it next time."

"Okay, thanks." Sarah carried the container into the house and looked through the items, her heart skipping unevenly. None of them had return addresses and the postmarks were from various valley towns.

Not now, she thought.

She didn't want to think about anonymous packages or slashed tires or anything else. She wanted to go on a picnic with a sexy guy and enjoy herself. She shoved the box firmly under the kitchen table and finished preparing the food. It might be denial, but right now she didn't care.

At precisely 4:30 p.m., the bell rang. Sarah hurried to the front with two bags slung over her shoulder and a folded blanket on her arm while Theo disappeared up the stairs so fast he was a blur of black fur.

She pulled the door open. "Hi, Tyler, I'm ready to go."

He frowned. "It's a good idea to check who's out here before answering."

"Please don't channel my father. Besides,

you're so punctual, why would I worry? You said four thirty, and it's four thirty on the dot."

"You enjoy giving me a hard time, don't you? Let me carry those."

He held out his hand and Sarah gave him the bags and blanket, resisting the urge to tease him further.

His laughter and pleasure while discovering the speakeasy stairs had turned her to mush. He'd astonished her even further when he'd supported her in the midst of family pressure.

"Do you want to drive?" Tyler asked, breaking into her thoughts. "You're familiar with the area and I'm not."

"Sure."

She took the keys and decided to head higher into the hills. Glimmer Creek sat on the margin of where the rolling foothills and evergreen forests began to blend. A few stands of pine had even survived the town being built and were tucked around Poppy Gold and the rest of the community.

"What is that scent I'm catching?" Tyler said, opening his window and inhaling deeply.

"Pine and deer brush, warmed by the sun. Maybe with elderberry and manzanita mixed in."

"Elderberry, as in the wine?"

Sarah shot him a look. "That's right. I've never made wine, but I've made elderberry jelly. Along with gooseberry jelly and blackberry jam. The youth group picks wild fruit to sell in town, and I'm on their regular sales route."

"Is that where you get your blackberries for the bakery?"

"Those have to come from a commercial source, I'm afraid. I buy from the youth group for personal use. Also to make items for the church bazaar."

Tyler shook his head. "I don't see how you do all that and run the shop, as well."

"It isn't always this bad. The holidays and summer are my busiest periods, and I put a lot in the freezer to handle when life gets quieter. Anyway, my new catering managers will take some of the pressure off. We've done three luncheons over the past week and they handled them from start to finish. I was thrilled. They got rave reviews."

TYLER GLANCED AT SARAH.

He didn't know what to make of her. Though she worked constantly, she was irrepressible. His mother had commented that Sarah seemed to magically get more done in the kitchen than anyone else; he suspected it was simply because she *liked* cooking for people.

"I'm glad your catering managers are working out."

"My cat is pleased, too. Theo doesn't appreciate me working such long hours."

"I didn't realize felines had such strong opinions. Aren't they self-sufficient?"

"In a way. They aren't always as obvious as dogs in their affections, but Theo gets grumpy when I'm not there enough. He's shy with strangers, which is why you haven't seen him."

Sarah turned down yet another hard dirt road, and Tyler reflected that it was a good thing she was driving. She'd already taken numerous turns, and he didn't have a clue where they were anymore. Then she went around a curve and he saw the town lying below them in the distance.

"Isn't this beautiful?" she asked, pulling to a stop. "My cousin and her husband bought the land earlier this year. Luke was living in Texas, but he decided to move here when he fell in love with Carlie. He has twin daughters from his first marriage, and they're making a fresh start."

"It's a nice property. Does the stream flow year-round?"

"Pretty much. I think this must be similar to what Glimmer Creek looked like before a gazillion miners descended in 1849 and began panning for gold. Well, it's flatter lower down, but you know what I mean. Peaceful and wild."

Tyler had always lived in cities, but could see the appeal of the open sky and natural setting.

The property was hilly, with outcroppings of rock and a mix of trees. The small stream meandered nearby, and a hawk circled lazily above. It almost seemed a shame to build on the property, though the right house might fit, perhaps something inspired by Julia Morgan. In his mind he automatically began sketching the outlines, a place with huge windows and broad decks supported by a foundation of native stone.

Lately ideas had been coming fast and furious. Though he didn't have any pending contracts, he'd spent hours getting those ideas down on drafting paper, with accompanying sketches to flesh out the vision.

"Let's eat here," he suggested.

"Okay."

Picnic for two, Tyler mused as they spread the blanket under a tree. Another romantic custom he'd never experienced before. Thanks to Sarah, he was starting to regret missing out on the things that many people took for granted.

He'd always considered flowers and picnics and dinner by candlelight to be impersonal tactics for creating a mood, but maybe they could be more than that. Just the other day he'd walked by the Argonaut Market and seen bunches of Dutch irises and roses for sale. He'd nearly bought Sarah some, just to make her smile.

This whole thing between them made him uneasy, even though he was trying to see it as a temporary interlude.

"What are you thinking about?" Sarah asked as she sat and stretched her legs out. "Your face has that look."

"What look?"

"The one you get when you're thinking about something and don't want anyone to know."

"I've just never had this kind of picnic. You know, two people, on a blanket under a tree."

Sarah grinned as she opened the insulated bags she'd brought. "If you say it's a cliché, I won't give you dessert."

"I wouldn't dare."

He accepted a plate, and his mouth watered as she explained that one container was filled with spicy fried chicken fillets and another was Southern-style. A third container held macaroni salad loaded with cheese and olives. Assorted fruit and fresh vegetables came out, as well. From the second bag, she pulled out biscuits that were still warm and filled with butter and honey. Dessert was chocolate caramel peanut candy with crunchy bits that turned out to be pretzels.

"A little magic with the microwave and they're done. No baking required," Sarah said, popping one into her mouth.

Tyler was in agony. He kept trying to ignore

the effect she had on him, but the sight of her pleasure was wreaking havoc on his self-control.

Sarah was still sitting upright, and he was tempted to pull her down next to him. It was a perfect setting to make love in the late afternoon sunshine.

"I swear you're corrupting me," he complained. "Usually I can't sit and do nothing."

"Glimmer Creek has a way of mellowing folks, which makes it a good place for a vacation."

Tyler wasn't sure if he'd been mellowed or seduced. "I'm not on vacation."

"Do you even *take* vacations?"

"Nope. I stay in the saddle, work, work, work."

"Stay in the saddle?" Sarah cocked her head. "Do you ever wonder where that expression comes from?"

"Probably from the image of the old cowpoke, dedicated to guarding his herd. I used to watch a lot of Westerns when I was a kid," he said when Sarah looked surprised.

"I never would have figured you the type."

"Where do you think I learned my poker face?"

SARAH SNICKERED.

She'd realized Tyler didn't have *that* great of a poker face. He kept everything locked inside, but someone watching closely enough could figure out what was going on.

She stretched, arching her back, and saw him tense. While she didn't know if she wanted to succumb again, it was nice to be reminded that she was a woman who could make a man's eyes glaze and his body react.

"Who's your favorite old-time actor?" she asked, pretending not to notice. Instead she put the leftover food back into the cold bag.

"Gary Cooper."

"You didn't have to think about it?"

"Hey, we're talking Gary Cooper. He's hard to beat. But maybe you've never watched classic Westerns. They're great. They have good guys and bad guys, and the good guys win. Most of the time, at least."

Sarah held back another smile. "When I was a teenager, Grandpa George and I watched old movies together every Tuesday night, including Westerns. I like Cooper, too. It may sound schmaltzy, but he usually played a character trying to do the right thing or redeem himself. That's my kind of hero."

"Where was your grandmother during these movie fests?"

"Usually at a city council meeting or doing something else as mayor. She'd come home and scold because I was up late, but she never seemed too upset."

Sarah realized belatedly that mentioning her grandparents probably hadn't been the best way to maintain a sexy mood, but the thought was interrupted by the arrival of a huge white SUV. It was Carlie and her husband, so it was just as well that nothing had developed beyond light conversation.

Annie and Beth, Luke's twin daughters, jumped out and ran over. Beth threw her arms around Sarah's neck while Annie sedately said, "Hi," and hugged her, as well.

"I didn't know you were coming up here this evening," Sarah told her cousin.

"We're just double-checking how long it will take to drive back and forth to Poppy Gold once the house is built," Carlie explained.

"It probably won't be too bad once the road is paved. Want some food?" Sarah asked. "We had a picnic, and there are lots of leftovers. I don't have extra plates, but you could take it home for dinner."

"Sarah makes the best chicken," Beth declared before her mom and dad had a chance to respond.

Carlie laughed. "We'd love to have it, thanks."

There was enough room on the blanket for everyone, though Tyler appeared desperately ill at ease with the way the twins plopped next to him, telling him their names and ages and asking the kind of artless, candid questions that adults learned to censor.

Sarah remembered him saying that he was uncomfortable with kids and they felt the same about him. Well, he hadn't met Beth and Annie. They were very determined children.

"Slow down, girls," Luke told them. He held his hand out to Tyler. "Luke Forrester."

"Tyler Prentiss."

"The architect?" Luke seemed suddenly focused, and Sarah kicked herself. *Of course.* Since Luke and Carlie were unhappy with the various designs submitted for their new house, they might have a healthy interest in meeting Tyler.

"Yes," Tyler replied in a clipped tone.

"Nice to meet you. This is my wife, Carlie."

Tyler nodded at Carlie. "I recognize you from the ghost walk, but there were so many people, we didn't have a chance to be introduced."

"It was quite a crowd that evening."

"It's lucky running into you this way," Luke said. "We both admire your work and would love to discuss the house we want to build."

If Tyler had looked uptight before, now he was rigid. Sarah leaned forward, but before she could say anything, Carlie smiled. "I hope you'll have time to speak with us, Mr. Prentiss. We're also looking for the right architect to design the hospital we're building in Glimmer Creek."

"My experience with designing medical facilities is limited. I interned with one of the top people in the field but haven't done much since then."

Luke shrugged. "We plan to have a team of consultants, no matter who gets the contract. But having the right lead architect is important." He took out a business card. "I'll give you my personal cell number, just in case you find a break in your schedule." He wrote on the back and held it out.

TYLER GLANCED AT SARAH, wondering if she'd set up the meeting with her cousin, trying to get him a local commission.

He put the business card in his wallet, taking note of the company name and realizing he'd heard of Luke Forrester. His first wife had been killed by sniper fire in the Middle East. The story had been carried by every news outlet on the planet—partly because she'd been a female soldier and partly because her husband was one of the wealthiest men in the United States.

Working with him would be a prime contract at any time, but right now, it would bring a particular satisfaction. Still, Tyler didn't want to have discussions with the Forresters only to have them back out because of the business in Illinois.

In the meantime…

He looked at Sarah, who was talking to the twins and felt a stab of longing. Her face glowed. She'd said she wanted children and would obviously be an amazing mother. It made the contrast between them even sharper.

After a moment Sarah met his gaze, and he lifted his eyebrows. "Maybe we should leave," he said, keeping his face neutral. "I should get back and see what's going on with Nathan and my mother." It was just an excuse—what he really wanted was a chance to speak to her privately.

"All right." She got to her feet. "Carlie, I'll get the containers and stuff from you guys on Sunday."

"I'll make sure to bring them or drop everything by the shop. Thanks for the food."

The two little girls promptly hugged Sarah goodbye.

Tyler didn't say anything until they'd reached a paved road again. "The children seem fond of you."

"I think the size of the Fullerton clan was overwhelming to them at the beginning, but Luke's sister moved here at the same time he did, which helped. I'm especially recognizable because I'm the cookie lady. That's what they called me at first."

"Why cookie lady?"

"They were here for the Christmas season last year, and my shop provides cookies and other treats for Poppy Gold activities. That's when Luke and Carlie met."

"They didn't seem overwhelmed to me—I couldn't have gotten a word in edgewise if I'd wanted to."

Sarah chuckled. "I know. They're competitive, though Beth is much more gung ho than her sister. I usually wait for the first rush of energy to ease off, then it's easier. Say, do you want to see the property that Luke and Carlie have purchased for the hospital? It's on the edge of Glimmer Creek and really nice."

The question was a reminder of what was bothering him...whether Sarah had told her cousin about him.

"Not right now."

SARAH WAS FOCUSED on the road ahead, but from the corner of her eye she could see Tyler's mouth had flattened into a straight line.

She parked in front of her house and handed him the keys to his rental car, but he got out when she did and headed up the walkway with her.

"Is something wrong?" she asked.

"I want to look around and be sure everything is okay."

"It's broad daylight."

"I'll still come in. We need to talk."

Sarah pursed her lips, fairly certain he wasn't playing the protective-man role. Instead she was going to hear what was upsetting him.

She unlocked the door, and they went inside. "What bee do you have in your bonnet now?"

Tyler scowled. "I don't have a bee in my bonnet. I want to know if you recommended me to Luke Forrester and his wife, and if it was some sort of repayment for consulting on the remodeling."

She put out her jaw, getting annoyed, as well. "No and no. I forgot they were looking for an architect until they were talking to you. But why would it be so awful if I had made a recommendation? Do you think I'd recommend someone I don't trust?"

"I guess not." Tyler sank down on the couch. "It's just awkward until everything is cleared up in Illinois."

"I realize that." Sarah sat next to him, wishing she knew what to say. "What's the latest news from your lawyer?"

"Corbin seems to have been stunned into silence by the slander lawsuit. He's cancelled all interviews and hasn't gone near a microphone.

That part is good. His attorney has suggested that he'll withdraw his lawsuit if I withdraw mine. My lawyer says to hold firm, that it's just part of the legal maneuvering."

Sarah made a face. "So it's still a waiting game."

"Afraid so."

"Why can't you sit on the commission's doorstep and insist they bring in experts to evaluate your original plan? Surely they can rule out your involvement without compromising the rest of the investigation. And it's only fair. If Corbin was smart, he'd want it, too. The longer this goes, the more he'll have to pay you."

"I'll talk to my lawyer, but I'm reluctant to leave Glimmer Creek right now."

"You aren't indispensable here," Sarah said bluntly. "Your mom or my dad can take Nathan to his appointments."

A curious expression filled Tyler's eyes. "I'll think about it. But off the subject, I've been wondering something about Poppy Gold."

She blinked. "What?"

"Well, it's obviously a hugely popular resort, fully booked, but somehow my mom and brother got a four-bedroom suite on short notice. How is that possible?"

"It isn't generally known, but the John Muir Cottage is special," she said slowly. "Poppy Gold keeps it for service members or their families who need a place to rest and recuperate, which means it isn't on the regular reservation schedule. You get in through referrals from specific commanding officers. In Nathan's case, it would have been General Pierson. Is that important?"

Tyler sighed. "Maybe not. I'd postponed my business trip to Italy a couple of times, then *had* to go or be in breach of contract. Things had settled down with Mom and Nathan, so it seemed all right. It was only for a few weeks, and I could call them every day and fly home if needed."

"But you still felt guilty for going," Sarah guessed.

He shot a glance at her. "Yeah. And now I'm wondering if they planned the trip to California even before I left. But maybe it plays out the same—they just couldn't tell me. I think that's partly why I was so upset when I got here, I couldn't believe they would do something like that and keep it a secret."

Sarah's heart ached for him. "Rosemary mentioned that your father used to decide everything for her. Maybe coming here has less to do with you and more with her need to make a decision."

"Dad *was* a control freak. There was only one area he didn't…" Tyler's voice trailed off.

"Um, yes?"

"I suppose it doesn't matter if you know. My

father enjoyed risky investments. Emerald and diamond mines, deep-sea mining, sci-fi technology. That kind of thing."

Sarah was relieved; she'd been afraid of hearing that Richard Prentiss had cheated on his wife. High-risk investments were nothing compared to infidelity.

"Maybe he needed it for the adrenaline rush." She paused, then straightened. "Tell me more about Illinois. You've told me some of the facts and I know you hate that those workers got hurt, but I'm getting the idea more is going on behind your stone face than you've said."

Tyler narrowed his eyes. "Stone face? You just said that to get me to talk."

"Did it work?" she asked hopefully.

"I suppose. The thing is, I should have done a better job of convincing Corbin that the modifications he wanted were unsafe, or worked on a modified plan that might have satisfied him. Instead I got angry and opted out of the contract. Now one of those construction workers may spend the rest of his life in a wheelchair."

Sarah swallowed. Beneath Tyler's stern exterior was a man with intense emotions. People could find all sorts of reasons to feel guilty. In the past year, he'd lost his father, and his brother had been injured… Maybe his grief and regrets over those traumas were adding to his guilt about the building collapse.

"The owner is responsible for what happened, not you. He's the one who chose to go forward with a design you told him wasn't safe."

"You must think I'm stupid to be bothered by it," Tyler muttered.

"It's human nature to question," Sarah said. "Decent people look at their behavior and wonder if they could have done something different. I respect that, but you have to stop tearing yourself up. You told the owner that the design changes were dangerous and then risked your own life to help when you were proven right. That's more than a lot of people would have done."

He pulled a sheet of paper from his pocket and showed it to Sarah. "There's more. I got a fax this morning from my lawyer. It's the report from the lab about the sample of concrete I snagged after that wall collapsed. The mix was way off. But I don't think it was a mistake; I think it was a cost-cutting measure. Who knows how many other shortcuts were taken? I should have been there, ensuring this kind of thing didn't happen."

Sarah crossed her arms and fixed him with a stern gaze. "Seriously? You can't be at every building site on the planet, looking over every builder's shoulder. Stop searching for reasons to feel responsible. I bet you even wonder if you'd gotten your law degree, you might have been able to convince your father to slow down. Now it's all gotten mixed up with your feelings about the building in Illinois."

Tyler sucked in a breath. How could Sarah do that? She seemed able to look into the darkest part of him and know things he'd only acknowledged to himself.

"It's true, isn't it?" he asked. "Dad might have retired earlier if I'd been there. He could have been alive and playing golf right now."

Sarah made an exasperated sound. "In the first place, the East Coast is in a different time zone—nobody is playing golf there, it's dark. In the second, you didn't owe him your entire life. And from what your mom has said, nothing could have made him slow down. Ultimately he might have seen you as competition, maybe even resented having you there."

That was true, too.

Tyler knew he was a rational, logical person trying to resolve impossible "what ifs." If he was more like Sarah, who acted from the heart, it might be easier to wade through the emotional quagmire.

"The more I learn about my father, the more he confuses me," Tyler admitted.

"I'm sorry," Sarah said simply, her eyes filled

with the warmth Tyler had grown accustomed to seeing there. He rarely had to question what she was feeling, and it was making him understand how difficult his own reserve must be for others to handle.

Blast.

Sarah was undermining all his resolve, all the decisions he'd made about what he wanted in his life. The problems in Illinois notwithstanding, he was *fine*. His career would recover. His life would be successful. He didn't need her to rescue him.

Or did he?

SARAH WASN'T SURPRISED when Tyler got up, making an excuse about checking on his mother and Nathan. She opened the door, only to freeze at the sight of another gift bag sitting on the steps of the porch.

"Gee, look at that. Another present from my secret admirer," she said, unable to keep the tension from her voice.

The bag was unexpectedly heavy, and glass tinkled inside when she lifted it. There were cartoon elephants dancing on the front and layers of pink tissue paper sticking artfully from the top, but Tyler caught her hand when she started to reach inside.

"Careful," he warned. "You don't know what's

in there. Maybe you should call Zach and let him take a look first."

"Not until I see what it is. I won't disturb any fingerprints." She found a large plastic container and carefully tipped the contents out...a shower of broken glass.

Tyler swore. He grabbed a pen from a holder by the phone and poked through the pieces.

"Those two look like they used to be champagne flutes," Sarah said, trying to keep her voice steady as she pointed at a couple of more intact pieces.

"But what are these?" There were a number of heavy chunks that seemed to have come from something else.

She looked closer and used the pen to nudge the largest pieces closer together. "The shapes look vaguely familiar. Maybe it was some type of art glass."

Tyler was standing nearby, and Sarah longed to lean into his warmth.

"I've noticed you have a number of paperweights," he murmured. "Are any of them missing?"

Sarah's pulse jumped as she recalled telling her dad that no one would be interested in her glass paperweight collection. "I don't think so, but I'll check."

She and Tyler did a quick circuit of the house.

It seemed unlikely that someone could have broken in, swiped one of her paperweights and left no other trace. But she'd learned anything was possible when Douglas had been trying to terrorize her.

"Nothing seems disturbed," she said finally.

They went back downstairs, and Sarah didn't need any urging to phone Zach.

"Hey, it's Sarah," she said when he answered. "I'm sorry to call when you're off duty."

"I told you to. What happened?"

She explained, and he said he'd be right over.

"He's on the way. You don't have to stay if your mother's waiting," she told Tyler when she hung up the phone.

He gave her an incredulous look. "You think I'd leave after you found something like that? I may have my faults, but I'm not going to run off when a friend is in trouble."

"Friend?"

"Yes, *friend*," Tyler said firmly. "And I'm short on those, so don't argue with me."

Sarah blinked, trying not to cry. "Okay."

Friendship was more than she'd expected, though her heart longed for more. When it came down to it, hearts weren't reasonable. They made their own choices, ignoring logic and good sense and the very real likelihood of getting broken.

Zach's knock jerked her out of the painful

thought, and she hurried to the door. Her cousin was in civvies but had attached his badge to his belt, so this was clearly an official visit.

"Let's see it," he said briskly.

"It's in the kitchen. By the way, I also got some packages in the mail you might want to check. There's no return address on them, and the postmarks are from valley towns."

Zach and Tyler both glared at her.

"You got anonymous mail and didn't tell me?" her cousin demanded. "Are you *trying* to make my job harder?"

"It isn't as bad as it sounds. They didn't fit through my mail slot, so the postman has been leaving package slips. I didn't think much about it, but I caught him this afternoon when he was in the neighborhood."

Zach growled something under his breath. "First I want to see the broken glass." He put on gloves and silently examined the contents of the plastic box. "I wish I'd seen the bag before it was disturbed. I'm concerned whether the glass was arranged with the intent of slicing your hand when you reached inside."

Sarah's skin went cold, and her fingers curled. In her mind, she saw the jagged tips of the broken champagne flutes rising up, hidden by layers of pink tissue paper.

"Hey, I think Sarah is scared enough," Tyler declared. He didn't look pleased.

Zach appeared equally annoyed at the challenge. Obviously, he and Tyler weren't crazy about each other.

"If you don't object, I'm going to take the packages with me," Zach said finally. "They should be opened under controlled circumstances."

"Absolutely *no* objections." She pulled the box from under the table, glad to see it go.

Zach took everything out to his vehicle and returned. "Sarah, I'm going to run extra patrols down your street. I don't know what's going on yet, but please be careful."

She nodded, not trusting her voice.

The door closed behind him, and she looked at Tyler again. "Well, this has been interesting."

"I'm spending the night on your couch."

It was nice that he hadn't assumed he'd share her bed, but she wasn't budging.

"No, you're going back to Poppy Gold to reassure Rosemary that everything is fine."

Over his continued objections, she pushed him out the door. There was too much chance that if he stayed, she'd weaken and invite him upstairs.

CHAPTER SEVENTEEN

ROSEMARY HAD BEEN EDGY all day about the vandalism and went for a walk to calm her nerves. Tyler was wrong, she *could* handle the stress of working, but the vandalism was a worry and she was concerned about her sons.

There wasn't a quick cure for PTSD, but at least Nathan seemed to be getting better. Still, she'd seen how a terrible experience could change someone. Her husband had become a different person after their daughter died. It was entirely possible that Nathan might never be the same.

As for Tyler?

The weeks at Poppy Gold Inns were the most time she'd spent with him since he'd left for college, but despite that, she didn't feel much closer to him. And now she'd learned he was keeping the problem in Illinois from her…? She needed to ask about it but knew she'd feel like a fraud since she'd been keeping an even bigger secret.

On the way back to Poppy Gold, she was stopped by a woman going into the Argonaut Market.

"You're Rosemary, right? We met at the baked potato feed."

"Yes, and you're Leah Benton."

"You've got a great memory. I know you've been staying at Poppy Gold, but since you mentioned working at Sarah's Sweet Treats, I keep wondering if you expect to move here."

"I'm considering it. I love Glimmer Creek."

Leah looked pleased. "That's wonderful. You know, I belong to a patchwork quilters' group if you're interested."

"I don't know anything about quilting."

"That's okay, I don't, either. I only joined a month ago, and it would be great to have another novice. We could learn together. I've done historical costuming, but nothing like this."

Rosemary laughed. "Thank you. I've also been asked to join some other organizations."

"We like getting people involved—that way you're more likely to stay. But feel free to attend the quilting group, even if you aren't moving here," Leah added. "My daughter sent a Poppy Gold guest to a meeting just last week."

"Your daughter?"

"You may have met her…Carlie Forrester?"

"Oh, yes, she's the activities director," Rosemary exclaimed. "I attended her first ghost walk. It was fun."

"I'll tell Carlie you enjoyed it." Leah took a

pen and an envelope from her purse and scribbled a note. "Here's my phone number. Call anytime. We have a garage apartment that's been empty since our daughter got married. My husband refuses to be a landlord, but if you need a place to stay while you're looking for something permanent, you'd be welcome."

"That's so nice of you." Rosemary put the envelope in her pocket, warmed by the other woman's open friendliness. "Would you like to join me for a cup of coffee? Poppy Gold keeps a pot in the reception area."

"I'd love to, but Mike will be home from work soon and I promised to make chicken potpie for dinner. Maybe we could have lunch this week. Just let me know when you're available."

With a nod, Rosemary said goodbye and continued back to Poppy Gold.

The encounter reminded her of how casual her relationships had been in Washington. Hundreds of people had come to her husband's funeral, but they hadn't called or visited after that. They weren't *friends*, they were just Richard's business associates and acquaintances. Others had known her through her fund-raising efforts, but genuine friendship had eluded her. Perhaps Glimmer Creek would be different.

Rosemary released a deep sigh.

She didn't think the little town was perfect.

The people were nosy and gossiped, but she liked them and they seemed to like her. Perhaps she *would* stay. She could always keep the house in DC in case she changed her mind at some point.

Rosemary returned to the suite and found Nathan asleep on a chaise on the porch, his face wonderfully peaceful. She slipped inside and went upstairs, hoping to find Tyler in the office, only to remember he and Sarah were having a picnic together.

"Mom?" Nathan called a short time later.

"In here, darling," Rosemary called back from the sitting room.

Nathan appeared at the door. "I'm hungry. Since Tyler is eating with Sarah, I wondered if you wanted to order something or reheat the stuff left from breakfast."

"I'm sure Sarah could do something gourmet with the leftovers," Rosemary said lightly, "but not me. Let's order."

"I'll call Casa Maria—they're fast. Then I'm going to the fitness center. The physical therapist thinks I need to work on my upper body strength."

Rosemary wasn't a fan of spicy food, but she was happy Nathan was showing an interest. "Get me a chicken quesadilla, no salsa or cilantro." It was the one dish she was comfortable ordering from Casa Maria, though Tyler had suggested trying the green sauce enchiladas, saying they were mild.

"Okay."

Obviously, this was one of Nathan's good days. She supposed PTSD was a little like grief. Sometimes she felt as if things were brighter, that the heavy, desperate weight of loss was slipping away, and the next morning the tears would start because she'd never wake up with Richard again.

One step at a time, she told herself.

The food came and Nathan ate with a reasonable appetite.

Casa Maria was familiar enough with them by now that they'd automatically included a generous amount of salsa for him. A new addition was a container of pico de gallo made of fresh tomato, onion, bell pepper and avocado, with a note saying it wasn't spicy and they hoped she would enjoy it with her quesadilla. Rosemary could have cried at the kind gesture. Busy as the restaurant must be, they'd made something special, knowing she didn't care for hot food.

"I don't understand why you don't like cilantro, Mom," Nathan said, breaking into her thoughts. He'd liberally sprinkled his meal with the fresh-chopped herb. "It's so mild."

"It doesn't taste mild to me. I've read that some scientists believe strong likes and dislikes to cilantro are genetic," she told him. "Like the way some cats respond to catnip and others don't."

A twinkle appeared in Nathan's eyes. "You mean we're like cats?"

"I'm sure they'd disagree. Sarah tells me they have a superior attitude."

"Like some people I've met." He ate his last bite and shoved the plate back. "I'll head to the fitness center now unless you need me for anything."

"Go ahead. I'm going to spend the evening with a book someone loaned me at work."

He winked. "Romantic?"

"Nonfiction, actually. It's called *Galileo's Daughter*. I doubt it has any romance since she became a pious nun."

"You're probably right."

Nathan kissed her forehead and left. While he was still limping, there seemed to be a spring in his step that she hadn't seen in a while. And that wink? Hope curled around Rosemary's heart, even though she knew a full recovery might mean he'd return to active duty. But if that was what he wanted, she would have to want it for him, too.

She'd cleaned up from the meal and was deep into her book when Tyler came in.

"Did you get something to eat?" he asked.

"Nathan was hungry and ordered food from Casa Maria."

"*Nathan* ordered?"

Rosemary smiled. "That's right. He suggested the restaurant and ordered for us both. Now he's at the fitness center. It'll give us a chance to talk."

Tyler's expression turned more guarded. "Oh?"

"It's important. Please sit down, I can't do this with you standing over me," she said, her heart fluttering.

TYLER SAT IN the chair opposite his mother, even though he wasn't ready for another intimate discussion. Sarah's insights had given him a measure of peace for the first time since his father's death, and he needed to work through what it meant.

Still, he wished she'd let him stay with her.

"Mom, what's up?" Tyler prompted.

"I…there's something you should have been told a long time ago."

His eyebrows shot upward. "What, I'm adopted?" It could explain his father's coolness toward him, though he looked enough like Richard Prentiss that it seemed unlikely.

"No." His mother twisted her fingers so hard he saw the skin whiten over her knuckles. As if he was hearing Sarah's voice in his ear, telling him what to do, Tyler reached out and put his hand on hers.

"It's okay, Mom, whatever it is."

"I'm not sure about that." A tear trickled down her cheek. "Before you were born, your father and I had a little girl. Her name was Kathryn Louise, but we called her Kittie."

Tyler stared. This was the last thing he'd expected to hear. "What happened to her?"

"She contracted spinal meningitis when she was a year old. The doctors did everything possible, but she died just a day after she got sick. Richard couldn't bear to think about her after that. He said we needed a new start where nobody knew about our daughter, so he sold his law practice in Boston and we moved to Washington, DC. He buried himself in work and insisted we never talk about her to anyone."

Tyler was struck by the pain in her eyes, along with the regret that he'd never known his sister. "I'm sorry," he said helplessly. There was nothing he could say to make it better. A part of him also recognized that this hidden sorrow explained a great deal about the past.

"I'm the one who's sorry. Oh, Tyler, we'd decided not to have more children when I discovered I was pregnant. It was too soon, and neither of us could open ourselves the way you deserved.

I loved you desperately, but we were terrified of losing you, too."

Tyler's mind was spinning, but his mother wasn't done. She went on to explain how his father had grown up poor, the first member of his family to ever finish high school, much less college. *Another* secret? Yet it made a curious sense. Richard Prentiss's drive for success had been obsessive.

"Wasn't he proud of how far he'd come?" Tyler asked.

His mother shook her head. "In the beginning, but not after Kittie died. Richard believed that if we'd lived in a nicer home or neighborhood, then she wouldn't have gotten sick. Or that the doctors could have saved her if we'd carried better health insurance. I think he always felt like a failure after she died, no matter how much money we had."

"How could he blame himself?"

"He just did. It wasn't his fault, but he kept trying to outrun the pain. He was still trying to outrun it when he died. I...I hope he has peace now."

"'Black care never sits behind a rider whose pace is fast enough,'" Tyler said quietly.

"What?"

"I found a bust of President Teddy Roosevelt in Dad's law office when I cleared it out. There was a brass plate on the bottom with that quote. I suppose that's what Dad was trying to do…move so quickly and work so hard, his grief couldn't catch up with him."

His mother wiped away a tear. "Except you can't escape what's inside you. Richard wasn't the only one who tried to run away—I stayed busy with my fund-raisers and foundations to keep from hurting."

"It's all right, Mom."

"No, it isn't. I'm not letting myself off over this, darling. I should have done something to help Richard face his grief, instead I went along with what he wanted. Our marriage was good, but I'll never know how much better it could have been if I'd stood up more for myself. And because of it, you and Nathan lost out. You deserved to understand how far your father had come and why it was so important to him to be successful."

"Dad was responsible for his own actions." Even as Tyler said it, he remembered Sarah saying something similar about Milo Corbin, and a small chunk of his guilt floated away.

"It still makes me sad. Just a minute, I want to show you something." His mother got up and soon returned with a man's wallet in her hands. "This was your father's. A few days ago, I found something in here that I didn't expect."

Rosemary opened the wallet and Tyler saw an

old Christmas photo of the family in the space normally used for a driver's license. She eased the photo free, turned it over and held it out. The faded picture of a little girl, maybe a year old, smiled up at Tyler.

"Kittie?"

"Yes." More tears flowed down his mother's cheeks. "Richard wanted all of her belongings removed from the house. He didn't know, but I saved what I could and put them in a safe deposit box after we moved to DC. Now I've discovered he carried a picture of her. So some part of him knew that he couldn't forget, that she would always be a part of us, the way you boys were."

Tyler knew he'd never see his father the same way again. Richard Prentiss had been flawed, but perhaps he'd genuinely loved his family.

"Why are you telling me about her now?"

"Because it's time. Because I found out about your legal troubles in Illinois and hate knowing you couldn't share it with us, the way your dad couldn't share."

Tyler's breath hissed out. "How did you find out?"

"Kurt's uncle told him, and he told me. I know you were trying to protect us, but I can't let you always be the strong one. That was part of Richard's problem, too. When I look at Kurt with Sarah, I see how things could have been with us as a family. Maybe it isn't too late to change that."

Tyler didn't know if *that* much change was possible, but it was a revelation to see his mother's steady gaze. She wasn't falling apart; she was moving forward.

"I didn't want you and Nathan to worry about Illinois," he explained. He looked down again at the picture of the sister he'd never known. "Have you told Nathan about Kittie?"

"Not yet. I thought it might be easier to speak with each of you separately."

He got up and handed the picture back. "Then I won't bring it up unless he does."

"Thanks. I also want you to go over my finances with me. It's time I take care of myself." Rosemary let out a small laugh. "I'm already doing some of it. I needed a place to deposit my paychecks, so I opened an account at the Glimmer Creek Bank. Since then I've gotten all the employees at the bakery to use direct deposit for their paychecks. It's a big savings for Sarah."

Tyler nodded, proud of how far his mother had come, even though it gave him a curiously hollow feeling to know she didn't need him any longer. "We'll do it soon."

"Great. And, um, I've also decided to stay in Glimmer Creek. It'll be a fresh start for me."

He wasn't surprised. Glimmer Creek had a growing appeal for him, as well.

"I'm glad you're happy here," Tyler murmured.

Upstairs he sat down and began work on another plan for Sarah's Sweet Treats, but his mind was only half on the project.

The other half was thinking about how close he'd been to becoming exactly like his father.

For the rest of the night, Tyler worked at his drafting table while he debated and analyzed his feelings. As daylight began creeping through the windows, he finally arched his back and stretched. The inescapable truth was that he couldn't weigh emotions on a scale like roofing nails from a hardware store.

Yet when he thought about Sarah's face when she was laughing or teasing or sexily tempting him, it seemed clear what he wanted. But loving her would require a leap of faith, and that wasn't something he was good at.

He closed his eyes, remembering how the two little girls had dropped onto the blanket next to him and starting talking a mile a minute.

Did he like chocolate or vanilla ice cream? They thought their new mommy was the best new mommy ever, but Sarah was awful nice, too. Was he going to marry her? How did his get face hurt? Who was his favorite, Dory or Nemo? Did he like their papa's truck? They called it Moby

Dick. Was he going to be there for Christmas, because Christmas was super great at Poppy Gold?

His ears had rung.

Still, while it had made him uncomfortable, the twins' exuberance and trust had been charming. They cut through all the nonsense, getting straight to what mattered to them. But the image that kept crowding everything else out was Sarah's face, alight while talking to the two little girls. She clearly loved children and could enter their world with ease. She'd be an amazing mother.

Was it *that* big of a leap to go from seeing Sarah as a friend to seeing her as his wife and the mother of his children? Little girls who would be just like her and little boys who'd adore her as much as he did?

Arrgghh.

Tyler rubbed his face and stood up. He needed a shower to clear his head. Being in love with Sarah didn't mean he would be a good father, though he'd certainly have a better chance with her help. It also didn't mean he'd be a good husband...just that he'd do his damnedest to make her happy.

But even supposing Sarah felt the same about him, it would take a whole lot to convince her.

A FEW DAYS after finding the bag of broken glass on her porch, Sarah went by the police station to talk with Zach…and bring him three more packages she'd picked up from the post office.

"Are you sure you want to know what we discovered?" he asked.

"Yes," she said, though she wasn't as confident as she tried to sound.

"All right. We X-rayed the packages before opening them and fingerprinted inside and out, but didn't find anything. This is a list of the contents."

Sarah took the sheet of paper. Assorted baby layettes. A sippy cup. Lotion. Petroleum jelly. A piggy bank. Diaper cream. A food grinder for preparing homemade baby food. And a smashed baby rattle.

"Do you think the rattle got crunched in the mail?" she asked, keeping her voice as steady as possible.

"No. We've also pieced together the glass from the gift bag. There were two champagne flutes, a sparkling cider juice bottle, and a paperweight in the shape of a baby booty. Obviously there's a baby theme here."

"That isn't hard to figure out, but the harassment with my shop isn't baby-related."

"I know. Maybe someone is angry at the bakery for whatever reason, and they're trying to misdirect us."

"Or the other way around."

"There's another possibility…in a way, the *bakery* is your baby."

Sarah lifted an eyebrow. "Isn't that a stretch?"

"At the moment, everything is speculation. We've checked out your ex-husband, by the way. He was at a conference in New York when the motorcyclist tried to swipe your deposit, and at another in Miami when the broken glass was left."

"I didn't think it could be him."

"We still had to check. I'd like you to sign a release to have all your mail come through the police station, including mail addressed to the sweet shop. We'll respect your privacy, but it'll go through fewer hands this way." He pulled out a sheet of paper and handed it to her along with a pen.

Sarah scanned the document and signed. As a rule she didn't get much mail. Bills came online and were paid that way, while her friends in Los Angeles preferred to call or email.

"Here you go." She handed the release back to him.

"Thanks." He sorted through the new packages she'd brought him. "I'll have these checked. Are you sure you don't have a glass baby booty paperweight in your collection? Or *had* one that's now missing?"

His face was bleak and Sarah winced, remembering his wife had been pregnant when she died. Babies must be a painful subject for him.

"I…uh, yes, I'm certain. Not that it's a collection exactly," she added, hoping to move the discussion away from babies. "Dad started bringing me paperweights when he was in the army because they didn't break easily in his duffel bag."

Zach nodded. "A heavy chunk of glass doesn't come apart without effort."

"Or rage."

"I didn't want to mention that, but yes. Please be careful, Sarah."

She got up. "Don't worry. I feel as if everyone in town is on guard duty. Speaking of which, I'd better get going, I'm meeting Gabe McKinley at my house for him to install a security system."

"Gabe told me about it. I'm glad."

Sarah left, unsure of how glad *she* felt. Thanks to her father and Tyler and everybody else, she was coming down with a raging case of cabin fever.

Her dad followed her home every night, and Tyler showed up within an hour of him leaving. Her neighbors were spending an inordinate amount of time doing yard work and had even called 911 the day Tyler swapped his rental sedan for an SUV. She rarely had a minute to herself except when she crawled into bed, and even then she was conscious of the patrols going up and down the street…along with the police cruiser that always seemed to be there when she left in the morning.

The worst part was knowing she did feel safer with so many people watching out for her. What did that say about her independence…and did it matter?

Maybe it *didn't* matter. Surely Tyler was right that accepting help with this harassment didn't mean she was weak.

"KEEP THIS WITH YOU in the house," Gabe instructed Sarah several hours later, handing her a gadget on a cord. "Just press the button and help will come immediately."

A panic button?

Instead of protesting, she smiled politely and let him show her how the system worked, also checking to be sure the exterior cameras wouldn't invade her neighbor's privacy.

"Thanks, Gabe," she said as he was leaving.

"I just wish you'd let me put it in sooner. This person might already be in jail."

Perhaps, but Sarah suspected the cameras would have just frightened the vandal away. Deterrence was part of the reason for a security system.

Her father showed up a short time later with a

load of fruits and vegetables he'd gotten for her and carried them into the kitchen.

"Want me to stay?" he asked hopefully.

"I'm fine, Dad. I've got the security system now, and nobody can get near the house without alarms screaming. Besides, you'd be bored to tears. I'll be cooking and canning, and Tyler is coming over with a floor plan for me to look at. Go home and stop worrying."

"Set the alarm," Kurt urged as he was leaving.

Sarah dutifully set the system, only to turn it off when Tyler arrived.

"Why are my eyes burning?" he asked as he walked into the kitchen.

"That's from the peppers." She gestured to the piles of bright red jalapeno and red Italian peppers she'd cleaned and seeded. She'd already blended some in the food processor and made a batch of her sweet-hot pepper sauce.

"Hmm. Fragrant."

She grinned. "It's worse when I make sriracha. The peppers and garlic have to ferment together for a few days. The garlic gets stronger and stronger and permeates the house. By the time it's ready to cook, you're ready to gag on the odor. I can only tolerate making it every other year."

"Something for me to look forward to."

Sarah nearly dropped her ladle. While Tyler had

been coming to the house for days on the flimsiest of excuses, she didn't expect it to continue. The idea that he'd be around by the time she was ready to make sriracha sauce was startling. And she hadn't even said *which* year she'd be making it.

Still, if he ended up designing her cousin's house, as well as the hospital, he'd probably be visiting Glimmer Creek often for a while. He might even check on the progress of her remodeling.

A flutter went through her stomach, and her mind began racing with questions.

She kept hoping Tyler would fall in love with her, but what if he did? What about his career plans? How could she fit in with them? She'd have to give up the shop and any thought of children. He'd want to live in a large, urban area close to clients and where he had access to a major airport. Obviously that wasn't Glimmer Creek. He would be gone for weeks or months working on projects, while she started resenting him.

Stop, Sarah ordered.

Tyler Prentiss wasn't in love with her. She didn't have to choose between him and everything else she cared about.

"Um, has Rosemary told Nathan about your sister?" she asked. They'd discussed it after Tyler had learned the truth, and he'd seemed deeply shaken by his mother's revelations.

"I'm not sure. Nathan hasn't brought it up, and Mom hasn't mentioned Kittie since that evening."

"It took courage to tell you. She could be worried about how Nathan will take it and wants to see how you handle it first."

"Possibly. Mostly I keep thinking how different our lives might have been if my sister had lived."

Sarah nodded. "It's hard not to ask 'what if.' I do the same thing about my mom. Like, if she'd stayed with us, what would be different? Maybe I wouldn't have grown up in Glimmer Creek, or I'd have siblings. Who knows? I might have become an architect instead of a cook," she said lightly.

"Then we still would have met."

His comment came close to suggesting that they'd been fated to meet, which didn't sound like Tyler. He was pragmatic, not whimsical.

Yet he'd helped open her eyes wider about her disastrous marriage. Forgiving herself would be a step forward.

"Will knowing about Kittie change how you see your childhood?" Sarah queried.

"In time, perhaps. I feel awful for Mom and haven't known what to say to her. It's as if nothing could be enough. I can't imagine how hard it would be to lose a child."

Her heart turned over. Tyler's expression was filled with regret and compassion. For once he wasn't holding back. But empathizing with his mother's grief didn't mean he'd changed his mind about having a family.

Besides, wouldn't it be selfish to want something that hindered his dream?

"It was a terrible secret to carry all these years." Sarah lifted a rack of jars from the canning kettle and set them on the counter to cool.

"Yeah." After a moment Tyler dropped his gaze to the new blueprints he'd unrolled on the table, and she knew he was ready to talk about something less personal. It was curious how she could understand that and still be so confused about him.

Maybe her only choice was to enjoy the time she had with him, accepting the broken heart that seemed inevitable.

"What are you showing me tonight?" she asked. "You've wanted me to keep an open mind until I've seen all the options."

"That's right." Tyler gestured to a spot on the top blueprint. "This is probably the last one. Yesterday you said it would be nice to preserve the original speakeasy staircase, so *this* plan incorporates that idea."

Sarah deliberately brushed his arm and shoulder as she leaned over the blueprint and felt him stiffen. "I like this plan the best."

"Uh, yeah." He sounded hoarse.

With a satisfied smile, she went back to her peppers and began pureeing more of them in the food processor.

"What are you making?" Tyler asked. He'd gotten up to watch. Unlike some people, he didn't hover at her elbow, staying far enough back that he didn't interfere.

"Sweet-hot pepper sauce. It's simple, but the family likes it on Mexican food or over cream cheese. Alone or mixed with mustard, it's a zippy sandwich spread. All sorts of uses."

"SO IT ISN'T a new recipe." Tyler's body was still burning at the not-so-innocent way Sarah had leaned against him.

"Just an old favorite. Have a taste." Sarah poured a spoonful of sauce over cream cheese on a cracker and handed it to him.

Tyler popped the morsel in his mouth. The sweet heat of the sauce was a perfect accompaniment to the cream cheese. "Mmm, that's fabulous."

"Thank you." She'd eaten a cracker herself and flicked her tongue over a trace of sauce on her upper lip.

He eyed her. Sarah wasn't the type to tease him too much without doing something about it.

As if reading his mind, she rose on her toes and kissed him. "Come upstairs with me," she whispered against his lips.

Tyler's heart began pounding so hard he thought it might burst through his chest.

"Okay."

Sarah led him to the stairs, and he saw her cat sitting on the top landing. The feline spotted him and scrambled away with a hiss.

"I don't think he likes me."

"Don't take it personally. I told you before, Theo doesn't like strangers."

A surge of longing went through Tyler. He wanted to stop being a stranger to the people he cared about, but especially to Sarah. She'd already uncovered parts of his soul that he hadn't known existed. Yet the thought scattered as he watched the gentle sway of her hips.

Her bedroom was simple and uncluttered, with a quilt on the bed in deep blues and greens and turquoise. He pulled her close for a kiss so long and deep that they were both gasping when it ended.

"You're good at that," she said.

"You are, too."

"I haven't had much practice lately. Except, you know, with you."

He grinned. "You've got natural talent. It's a quality I appreciate."

SARAH'S PULSE RACED. If anyone had told her making love with Tyler Prentiss would be both fun and sizzling, she would have said they were crazy. But here he was, proving she was wrong. It helped that he was totally hot and that his true smile, which she was seeing more and more often, was hell on a woman's equilibrium.

The phone rang as she stepped backward to remove her chef's apron. Tyler groaned when she grabbed the receiver and looked at the caller ID. It was Tessa's business line at Poppy Gold.

Sarah tossed the phone in her T-shirt drawer where it rang one more time, the sound muffled.

Tyler's smile widened. "Not urgent?"

"This is more urgent. I'll call back later." She sat on the bed and gave him a challenging look. "I did a striptease for you the last time, but you didn't even get your jeans off before the fireworks. It's my turn to see the show."

He looked embarrassed, but fair was fair. "Any chance of you inspiring me?" he asked.

"I have to think about it. You're prepared, right? Anything I've got is really old."

"Always. So, how about that inspiration?"

She debated for a moment, then took her blouse off. Most of the time she wore sensible undergarments, but that morning she'd indulged in silk and lace. Apparently seeing her in a skimpy, semitransparent bra was sufficiently inspiring— Tyler instantly began kicking away his shoes and removing the rest of his clothes. When his boxers came off, her mouth went dry. He really *was* impressive.

Quickly she shrugged out of the rest of her clothes, and he pulled her to him, hot skin to skin, every inch, her breasts tingling against the dark hair on his chest. Their legs tangled together as they rolled across her quilt, and her breath escaped in a hiss.

Moments like this could be all they ever had, and she wanted to savor every one.

CHAPTER EIGHTEEN

At 3:30 A.M. Sarah opened her eyes and stuck her tongue out at the digital clock. It was never light when she left for the shop, even at the summer solstice.

Getting out of bed was particularly unappealing with Tyler's arms wrapped snugly around her. Her body felt drugged with satisfaction.

Rise and shine, Sarah ordered.

She tried to ease away from Tyler without disturbing him, but his arms tightened.

"Where are you going?" he muttered groggily. "It's the middle of the night."

"I need to shower and get to work. Stay and sleep if you want."

"I'm not interested in sleeping any longer." He teased her nipples, sending tingles everywhere, so she elbowed his ribs.

"You're out of protection," she reminded him. They'd made love twice and would have a third time, except he only carried two condoms in his wallet. She remembered discussing a trip to the twenty-four-hour convenience store on the edge of town, but they must have fallen asleep before a decision was made.

"Right."

His fingers stopped their tantalizing dance, and Sarah got up, wishing she could stay. She'd slept better than she had in weeks. Getting a healthy amount of exercise might be partly responsible, but she'd also felt safer with Tyler sleeping next to her.

She got into the shower and washed her hair, arguing that it was normal to feel safer under the circumstances. But she hadn't seduced Tyler for any reason except wanting to have as much time as possible with him before he left.

The shower curtain opened, and he stepped into the tub, big as life and fully aroused.

"There isn't enough room for two," she advised, averting her eyes. One of them needed to exercise self-control. Not that getting pregnant with Tyler's baby would bother her, but he'd insist on doing the "right thing," which would go against what she'd decided…that she couldn't be the reason he lost out on the future he wanted.

"This is a big bathtub. I'm sure we can manage."

"I don't think it's a good idea. No protection, remember?"

Tyler gave her a devilish smile. "Trust me, I can do wonders with my hands."

Sarah already knew that, but he proceeded to prove it to her again…

"See?" he murmured when the world had stopped spinning.

She reached around and turned the water off. "And all it cost was a shower curtain and a few gallons of water on the bathroom floor."

"Sorry about that." He looked at the torn curtain. "I'll buy you another one. Get dressed while I mop up the flood."

It was even harder now to care about going to the sweet shop, but Sarah donned her usual jeans and T-shirt and French braided her damp hair. Downstairs, she sighed at the mess she'd left in her kitchen and began loading everything into the dishwasher.

TYLER USED THICK TOWELS to soak up the water in the bathroom, mentally designing a home with a shower large enough for two. Perhaps it could be lined in natural stone tile and set so deeply that aquatic-related gymnastics wouldn't cause a problem.

Damn, he felt good.

Sarah was a generous lover, but it wasn't just the mind-blowing sex that had cheered him. It was the spirit and laughter she brought to everything. How many people could deal with a stalker and continue being that way?

He walked downstairs and found Sarah making omelets. His stomach rumbled. "I left the wet towels in the bathtub, but I can bring them down if you want," he offered.

"I'll do it later." Her knife began flying over a cutting board.

"Did your cousin leave a message?" he asked, recalling the way Sarah had ignored the phone the night before.

"What? Oh, I checked and it wasn't urgent. She's making plans for Uncle Liam's birthday party in October. She plans ahead, just like me. I'll talk to her later."

Sarah handed him a cup of coffee.

"Are you having baby pangs or is this related to your baby-obsessed stalker?" he asked idly, looking down at a health magazine next to the phone.

"Excuse me?"

Tyler leafed through the publication. "This is devoted to the hospital's obstetrics department."

"Drat, that came the day the postman gave me all those packages, but I didn't think to give it to Zach. I saw him yesterday, by the way."

"Has he come to any conclusions?"

"Nope, other than there seems to be a baby theme." Sarah checked the omelets on the stove. "But it could just be a distraction. Complaints to the city and slashing my catering vehicle tires aren't baby-related. I just don't know why anyone would be angry about the shop or how it could be a case of mistaken identity." She turned and frowned. "Unless someone *else* is the target, and it's classic misdirection."

"That would be an extreme case." Tyler set the magazine down and rolled up the blueprints he'd shown her. "The food smells great."

"Dig in," she urged, putting the plates on the table.

Tyler hurriedly ate. Then he stood outside and watched as Sarah backed out of her garage. He knew her staff would be on pins and needles until she arrived; the entire community seemed to be on alert, watching after her. The thought was underscored when he saw a police car drive by.

Reluctant to be questioned about his presence outside her house, Tyler got into his rental and returned to Poppy Gold Inns. He let himself into the side door of the suite and listened. Everything seemed peaceful. In the living room, he found Nathan asleep on the couch, his body relaxed.

Tyler quietly went upstairs to his makeshift office, wanting to sketch what Sarah's building would look like after the remodel. Normally he used a computer-aided design system, but he could do them by hand when needed.

The sun was coming up when he heard a noise

from down the hall. A moment later, his mother appeared at the door.

"Good morning, son. When did you get in?"

"I'm not sure. Nothing happened while I was out?"

"All quiet." Rosemary walked over and looked at the two sketches he'd done, with watercolor washes to give them more depth and interest. "These are wonderful. You always had so much artistic ability. The one with Sarah is particularly lovely. You really captured her."

Tyler was embarrassed. Generally when he placed "people" in a drawing he used feature-less figures for perspective, but he hadn't been able to resist putting Sarah into the picture...the way he wanted her in his life.

It was true. He wanted her on any terms, for however long she'd let him stay.

Any terms?

A vision of Sarah holding a baby, smiling the way she'd smiled at the Forrester twins filled Tyler's brain. Having children with Sarah wouldn't be a compromise. It would be an adventure. It didn't mean he was crazy about the idea of changing dirty diapers, but he didn't love every-thing about architecture, either.

"Tyler? You have the strangest expression on your face. Is something wrong?"

Tyler stood and kissed his mother's forehead. "No. I'm just figuring some things out, that's all."

His mother nodded and left while he gazed at the sketch. Only a mother's pride would see it as particularly talented. When a computer-aided design program wasn't available, he was competent at sketching, nothing more. On the other hand, Sarah's personality shone through everything, even a prosaic drawing.

Sitting down again, he kept thinking about the ways he'd already changed since coming to Glimmer Creek. And because he'd changed, the direction for his life had to change. It was really quite simple.

Tyler smiled. He was going to stop thinking and look for the right moment to propose to Sarah. Then he'd know if there was any chance of them being together.

ON SATURDAY ROSEMARY was sitting out in the garden with a cup of tea and her book when Kurt rounded the corner of the house.

"I didn't expect to see you today," she said.

"Just taking a break. It puts Sarah on edge when I hover too much." He sat on the chair next to her and stretched out his legs. "Letting go is hard."

"I'm sure you'll get there."

"Yeah, but I'm not enjoying it. Especially with a stalker on the loose."

Rosemary shivered. "Let's talk about something else."

"Suits me. Yesterday you mentioned telling your sons about their sister, but you didn't say how they took it."

"Tyler seems all right. And I think Nathan was able to relate because he expected to get married and start a family last year until his fiancée broke off the engagement."

"Was it a bad breakup?"

Rosemary shook her head. "I don't think so. Pamela simply decided she couldn't handle being married to a soldier. But I think the desire to become a father helped Nathan understand how much Kittie's death affected Richard."

"Could be." Kurt smiled at her. "So, have you made up your mind about moving to Glimmer Creek?"

"Yes. I've told both my sons that I'm doing it. And can you believe it? I've already been invited to join the historical society, a quilter's group and the firehouse auxiliary. Your father and brother have called on us, too."

"We like to think we're friendly. Just so you know, there aren't many rentals in town. You may have to buy."

"That's what I've heard. But I ran into Leah

Benton the other day, and she told me I could stay in their garage apartment while I'm looking. Isn't that nice?"

Kurt bobbed his head. "That's my sister."

Rosemary tried to recall if Leah had mentioned being related to Kurt, but she'd met so many people lately and there were so many connections in Glimmer Creek, it was hard to keep everything straight.

"I didn't remember she was your sister. Sorting out your relatives is challenging," Rosemary admitted.

"Don't worry about it. Just assume everyone you meet is connected. You'll be right more often than not."

"I'll do that."

"Good. Mind if I take a nap while you read?"

"Be my guest."

Kurt crossed his arms over his chest and closed his eyes. Rosemary smiled. One of the nicest things about him was his ability to relax. She'd spent thirty-six years with a man wound tighter than a snare drum, which meant she'd rarely been able to loosen up herself. A faint flash of guilt went through her before she pushed the thought away.

Moving on didn't mean she was forgetting Richard or the love they'd shared. And a part of her would always hurt because he wasn't there.

But she had to make a new life for herself. While things wouldn't always be perfect in Glimmer Creek, the future looked interesting.

CHAPTER NINETEEN

"I WISH MY FATHER had talked to me the way your dad talks to you," Tyler told Sarah a couple of evenings later.

He leaned against a counter, watching her stir a pot on the stove.

"They say getting older makes people assess their lives and relationships. Maybe your father would have done that if he'd had more time."

Tyler wanted to believe that. He was finally seeing Richard Prentiss as simply a man, struggling with pride and grief and a haunting sense of failure because of something he couldn't control. Understanding didn't change anything, yet in a way it did make a difference.

"It's hard to say," Tyler said. "He had a lot of mixed-up ideas—more than I ever realized—but I feel sorry for him."

Sarah's eyes were warm with concern and Tyler ached, wanting to know if it meant she was in love with him or if she was just being compassionate.

He opened his mouth, then promptly closed

it. He'd discovered it was one thing to decide to propose and another to risk rejection.

How did a guy who kept everything to himself learn to open his heart to the one woman who'd made him trust her? He knew it was all right to let Sarah in, yet he was fighting a lifetime of self-protection.

"Do you think my mother would be upset if I ask about Dad and Kittie sometimes?" he asked, his voice husky.

"Ask if it bothers her. If she doesn't want to talk about them, she can say so. But I suspect she'd love to. Here, have a taste." Sarah held out a spoonful from the pot she was cooking, and Tyler looked at it suspiciously, remembering she'd been working with oversize green squash.

"What is it?"

"Zucchini relish. Come on, it's essentially pickle relish. I've been tinkering with the recipe to get it just right."

Tyler put the spoon in his mouth. As a rule he could take or leave pickle relish, but this stuff was delicious. "It's great, but I might not be the best judge."

"Oh?"

"It's hard for me to find fault with anything you do."

The pink brightened in Sarah's cheeks. "Smooth talker."

"Nah, that's my brother," Tyler said, remembering she'd said the same thing to Nathan. "When I say something, it's because I mean it."

Their gazes locked and her breathing quickened. The expression in her eyes almost looked like...hope? Or maybe that was more wishful thinking.

He was about to ask when the doorbell rang, making them both jump.

"I'll see who it is," Tyler told her. "You were going to finishing filling the jars with that relish, weren't you?" he added, knowing she'd object if she thought he wanted to answer the door to safeguard her. In this case it wasn't a problem, Zach Williams stood on the porch.

"Good evening, I need to speak with my cousin."

"She's cooking, naturally."

They headed for the kitchen where they found Sarah putting jars into a boiling water bath.

"Hi, Zach," she called over her shoulder. "Just give me a minute." Before long she turned and smiled. "What's up?"

Zach held up a sheet of paper. "I wanted to tell you about the latest packages received."

"I'm sure that's going to be a cheery list."

"Don't let it get to you. Whoever this is, they aren't rational."

She rolled her eyes. "Oh, yeah, that makes me feel a lot better."

Tyler didn't feel any better about it, either.

Sarah sat down at the kitchen table and read through the list. "More baby clothes. Receiving blankets. A photo album for baby's first year. Oh...*ick*...two home pregnancy tests, opened and used. With negative results." She shuddered.

"I sent an officer to personally deliver this to the state crime lab, Sarah," Zach explained. "We'll get to the bottom of what's happening. In the meantime, just hang tight and be careful."

SARAH WALKED HER COUSIN to the front door. For some reason the pregnancy tests bothered her even more than having her tires slashed. Pregnancy tests and broken baby rattles were deeply personal.

"Sarah?" Tyler prompted and she realized she'd been staring into space, lost in thought.

"Sorry. It's just so creepy."

"But you're certain your ex-husband isn't involved?"

"Zach is reasonably certain. Besides, the baby-related stuff feels more like something a woman would do."

"Nobody knows what goes on in a disturbed mind, Sarah."

She shivered and Tyler pulled her to him. "I suppose it would be crass to propose going upstairs to your bedroom for relaxation therapy," he said suggestively.

"It's tempting, but I've got more canning to do tonight."

Tyler didn't look too put out by her refusal, and she wondered dismally if the spark was gone. Then she glanced down at his jeans. Men had a hard time concealing their response and he was no exception. Electricity zinged to the apex of her legs and she gulped.

She hurried to the kitchen and took the jars of relish from the boiling water bath.

"I want to help. Where do I start?" Tyler asked, rolling up his sleeves.

Sarah turned off the stove, walked over and kissed him, deciding the remaining vegetables and fruit would have to wait another day. "With me. I changed my mind. Let's do that relaxation therapy thing. It sounds intriguing."

A laugh rumbled through his chest, and he cupped her bottom. "Yes, ma'am. I aim to please."

TWO DAYS LATER, Tyler was more sexually satisfied than he'd ever been…and climbing the walls with worry. They'd gotten *zero* news about who could be stalking Sarah, and it was wearing on everyone.

Actually, Sarah seemed to be holding up better than the rest of them.

Her father was morose and bad-tempered, the bakery staff was jumpy, Zach Williams seemed to have a permanent scowl on his face and Tyler's mother had called 911 twice because of raised voices in the front of the shop.

Tyler had been there when his mom apologized for one of the disruptions, but she'd sounded more defiant than repentant. Of course, that might be due to the thumbs-up he'd given her from behind Sarah's back.

Finally he dragged Sarah out for another drive, saying he needed to get a better feel for the SUV he'd rented.

"This was a good idea," she said, directing him through the back routes she favored. He liked them too, because it would be hard for anyone to follow them without being observed.

"Yeah, you're making me lazy," he drawled. "I could be working on ideas to show Luke Forrester, but I'm doing touristy stuff instead."

"Poor baby. Someone is making you have fun instead of working." Sarah pulled her knees up and rested her bare feet on the dashboard. "Jeez, why didn't you switch the sedan for a convertible? That would have been nice."

"Because people in Glimmer Creek seem to mostly own trucks and SUVs, and I wanted to fit in."

She grinned. "Fitting in isn't all it's cracked up to be."

They drove around a bend and saw a view of the foothills below, bathed in late afternoon sunlight, but a jarring ringtone sounded from the floor. Sarah scrunched her nose. "We must have gotten a cell signal back. Sometimes I hate modern technology."

She squirmed in the passenger seat, hiking her T-shirt up to her midriff while retrieving the phone from her purse. Tyler clenched the steering wheel, praying for control.

A minute later, Sarah sighed. "It was a voice mail from Zach. He got the report from the state crime lab and wants to see me. He'll be at the police station until six and will come by the house if doesn't hear from me before then."

"Let's go to the station," Tyler said immediately.

Sarah's mood was decidedly more solemn as she directed him back to Glimmer Creek.

The police chief was talking to a group of officers when they arrived at the station, and he gestured for them to wait in his office. A few minutes later he walked in and closed the door, though he plainly wasn't too pleased to see she had company. "You don't have to be here, Tyler."

"Yet here I am."

"Please skip the testosterone," Sarah interrupted, visibly tense. "What's in the report?"

Zach pulled out a file. "We finally got a decent fingerprint. It belongs to Nell Sheehan, your ex-husband's second wife. We got lucky. She was arrested for shoplifting years ago, so her prints are on file."

SARAH STARED. "YOU aren't serious. I've never even met the woman."

"That's what the crime lab found, and it's their opinion it matches the partial lifted when your tires were slashed. I've talked to the LA police. Ms. Sheehan wasn't home for questioning, but they spoke to your ex. He claims no knowledge of his wife's actions, stating that she's often away and that her behavior has been erratic since she learned she can't have children. That part seems to fit with the baby-related items, especially the negative pregnancy tests."

"But why would she care about *me*?" Sarah protested. "It isn't as if I want Douglas back. The guy is a manipulative creep."

Saying it was liberating. She wasn't trying to pretend any longer. She'd made a mistake, done her best to correct it and now was moving on. End of story. And even though Douglas was connected to her present troubles, she didn't feel the drugging fear she'd known while living with him.

Zach shrugged. "Who knows why these people do what they do? We're checking to see if anyone has seen her in Glimmer Creek, and my officers are on the lookout. This is her photo. Do you recognize her?"

Sarah looked at the picture. "Not really, but I've been living in a kitchen for the past four years. She could have been in the shop a dozen times. Is there anything else?"

"Not for the moment. Just be careful. The vandalism alone is a potential felony, depending on how the prosecutor decides to handle the charges."

Subdued, Sarah thanked her cousin and left the station with Tyler. "It doesn't make sense," she murmured.

"You think Douglas is manipulating his wife to harass you?"

"Except that doesn't make sense, either. I'm pretty sure he lost interest when my friends promised to cut off his testicles if he ever bothered me again. At heart he's a coward."

Tyler let out choked laugh. "I can see how that might have discouraged him." He put an arm around her waist. "Tell you what, let's be couch potatoes and watch *Bringing Up Baby*. Does Glimmer Creek have a video store?"

"Sure, but wouldn't you prefer a Gary Cooper film?"

"A little silliness would be better. The jail scene in *Bringing Up Baby* is always good for a smile. I could watch Katharine Hepburn scold that leopard a thousand times."

Sarah melted a little more. Tyler was right—silliness was exactly what they needed.

OVER THE NEXT few days, Tyler and Sarah only heard small snippets of news about the case from Zach Williams.

Apparently Nell Sheehan had stayed at Poppy Gold occasionally, though more often at nearby towns. At the shop, Aurelia had recognized her picture, saying Nell had been there on different occasions, mostly sitting and watching the customers and seeming sad. Aurelia was astonished she might be the vandal, and Tyler grew alarmed when he saw the expression on Sarah's face—she didn't need to feel sorry for the other woman, she needed to protect herself.

He'd talked Sarah into letting him use the apartment above the shop during the day to work on the hospital design, saying the speakeasy history made it more creatively inspiring. It put him close, even though the card table he hauled up the steep staircase was a dismal alternative to his drafting equipment.

The fact she'd let him do it gave him hope.

Tyler rolled his tight shoulders. He was actually getting a great deal of work done. He hadn't called the Forresters, but he liked the idea of becoming the lead architect for the new Glimmer Creek hospital. His early work on medical facilities had been very satisfying and the thought of going back to his roots was appealing.

The situation in Illinois remained a nagging concern, but he was mostly worried about Sarah.

Just then, Tyler heard heavy thumping as someone climbed the staircase—obviously *not* Sarah, who was so light of foot, she often took him by surprise.

It was Kurt Fullerton.

"Anything new?" Tyler asked immediately.

"Nothing, but my daughter is still telling Zach to be gentle with the Sheehan woman when she's caught."

Tyler frowned. He and Kurt had united over the concern that Sarah would be too sympathetic toward Nell Sheehan to properly protect herself. Sarah's soft heart was one of the things he loved about her, but Nell was a threat that couldn't be ignored.

"Somebody is with her most of the time. That's some comfort."

Kurt glared. "Yeah, right, *you're* with her all

night. Tell me, is it just sex, or are you serious about my daughter?"

Phew. Tyler had known that a question about his intentions was inevitable, but he hadn't expected it to be so blunt. He looked Kurt square in the eyes. "I couldn't be more serious."

A series of emotions chased across the other man's face. "Then don't hurt her."

"I'd never knowingly cause Sarah pain. If she'll have me, I'll do whatever I can to make her happy."

Kurt sighed. "I believe you. But I'd better get going, or else she'll be up here asking why we're yakking when we have work to do."

When Tyler was alone again, he bent determinedly over the design he was working on. He always wanted to be the best architect possible on a job, but the hospital plan held a special importance.

After all, it could be the place where Sarah gave birth to their children.

SARAH HUMMED AS she worked on a new recipe in the candy kitchen—a "jelly" layer to put on top of peanut butter fudge. Her first attempt was all right but too mild. Raspberry instead of strawberry, she decided.

She began measuring ingredients for raspberry fudge. This time it had the bold fruit flavor she'd been hoping for, and she poured it over a waiting batch of peanut butter fudge. But before she could scrape the last bits out, she heard an agitated hum of conversation from the main kitchen.

Sarah hurried out. "What's going on?"

"Aurelia spotted that woman out front. It's bizarre—she's wearing a green sundress, just like the one you wore to the Fourth of July barbecue," Gabby said excitedly. "Rosemary is calling the police."

Oh, God. Gabe McKinley listened to the police scanner over at Poppy Gold, which meant an army would be descending.

Sarah hurried to the front. "Where is she, Aurelia?"

"She just left. I'm sorry, I think she noticed me watching her. I told 911 that it looked as if she was headed toward Poppy Gold."

Sarah raced out the door over Aurelia's frantic protest. She *had* to know why Nell was focusing her misery on a stranger. Down the block, there was a feminine figure in green and Sarah followed, catching up near the Poppy Gold town square park.

"Wait, Nell," she called. "We need to talk."

Nell Sheehan turned slowly. She was blonde and pretty, with eyes so haunted that Sarah drew a sharp breath. In a way, she might have been looking at herself when she was married to Douglas.

"Stay away," Nell cried. "You're the one who stole everything from me."

Sarah didn't go closer. While it was unlikely that Nell could be hiding a gun under that sundress, she couldn't be sure about other weapons. "I don't know what you mean, Nell."

"You refused to have kids, but you also didn't want to bother with birth control, so you made Doug get a vasectomy. Then you walked out and nearly destroyed him. He was afraid to tell me when we got married. He tried to have it reversed, but nothing has worked and now it's too late. I have endometriosis, and the doctor says it's progressed too far for a baby."

More damage from Douglas's lies?

A weary sorrow swept through Sarah. "If Douglas had a vasectomy, I didn't know about it," she said quietly. "I tried to get pregnant. When it didn't happen, I went to a fertility clinic. I still have the paperwork showing there was no medical reason I couldn't conceive. But Doug refused to be checked…which makes sense if he didn't want me to know he'd had a vasectomy."

"No, no, *no*. That can't be," Nell said frantically. "He said the only thing you cared about was starting your bakery. I mean, he wanted to wait a while for children after we got married, but when I found out about the endometriosis, he told me the truth and went to New York to have the procedure reversed. He's had two other surgeries since then, but none of them have worked."

"The surgeries were always out of town, never with you there?" Sarah asked.

A small sob came from Nell. "H-he said it was better that way. Easier on us both."

"Douglas could always make things sound plausible. I started trying to get pregnant when he accused me of having an affair. I thought it would prove that I wasn't looking at other men."

"A-affair?" Nell's face went even whiter, if possible.

"That's right. I was never unfaithful, but he'd call me over and over when he was at work or on a business trip to make sure I was home. Except it would just be silence when I answered."

"And the number is unavailable, so you don't know who it is," Nell whispered as if in a trance. "He says it isn't him. He says you're imagining things. That everything is just in your head."

Sarah burned with anger. Apparently her ex hadn't changed his old ways. "Doug is a liar and a womanizer and spent most of our marriage terrorizing me. I *was* the one who left, but it was because I caught him with another woman."

With a moan, Nell sank to the ground, arms wrapped around her stomach, rocking back and forth. "I believed him, I believed him," she kept saying over and over. "How could I believe him?"

Sarah had been so focused on Nell, she hadn't seen Tyler, her father, Zach, and a dozen other people arrive.

She put up a hand to stop her cousin from grabbing Nell, but it wasn't necessary. Her fragile condition was obvious. So much pain, all because of an insecure, horrible man.

Hopefully Nell would get the help she needed… and a divorce.

"People are here who want to help you, Nell," she said gently. "Please let them."

Nell looked up. "I'm so sorry. I wanted to believe Doug, and he kept talking about how it was your fault I couldn't have the babies I wanted. I wanted you to pay for what I'd lost. *I'm sorry.*"

"I know, but go with Zach now. He wants to help."

Seeming docile and almost childlike, Nell let Zach put her in the squad car that had just pulled up.

Kurt marched over. "Sarah, you scared the hell out of me. I know you're an adult now, but don't ever—" He released a sigh. "Oh, forget it." He pulled her into a bear hug and whispered, "I love you" in her ear.

Gabe stepped forward, as well, clearly intending to scold her, but Tessa was there and she grabbed his elbow. Though she was half her husband's size, he froze and locked gazes with her. Sarah almost laughed—in a battle of wills, husband and wife were equally matched.

"Let's get out here," she told Tyler.

Undoubtedly Zach would want her to sign a statement, but right now she wanted to forget for a while.

TYLER'S RENTAL SUV was closest, so they headed to the parking area near the John Muir Cottage. He drove out of Glimmer Creek until he found a small wayside with a historic marker.

He parked in the shade and glanced at Sarah. He'd been terrified for her, yet a part of him understood why she'd taken such a risk. She was loving, bright and filled with compassion. Her compassion even extended to someone who'd terrorized her.

"Don't ask me to justify what I did," Sarah said, lifting her chin.

"That isn't what I was thinking."

"Hmm." She gave him an appraising look, then wiggled out of her chef's apron and tossed it into the back seat. "I feel like I've been set free. You wanna make out?"

He grinned, both amused and aroused. Sarah was like an uncorked bottle of champagne, intoxicating to a man who'd lived in a self-imposed emotional prison his entire life.

"I always want to make out with you, but I'd like to talk first."

She made a face. "No lectures, okay?"

"How about me saying how wonderful you are?"

"That's okay."

"And that you're also brave, impulsive and totally breathtaking."

SARAH DIDN'T HAVE a huge amount of experience with relationships and breakups, yet she was starting to wonder if there was a "but" coming.

But I'm afraid you've gotten too serious about me.

But I'm only in Glimmer Creek for a short time.

But...

"Uh...thanks," she said, determined not to say anything stupid or juvenile. "What else do you want to talk about?"

Tyler looked distinctly apprehensive. "Okay, this is the hard part." He took her hand. "I'm crazy in love with you, Sarah. Will you marry me and be the mother of my children?"

Her eyes widened. "You're proposing?"

"Yes."

She got dizzy. In a fantasy world, the hero proposed and everyone was happy, but this wasn't a fantasy. "I love you, too. But I…I can't accept."

Tyler's breath hissed out. "Is it the ice man thing?"

"*No.* Well, it was a problem at first. Not that you're an ice man," she said hastily. "You're a challenge, but I'm learning how to get around your barriers."

"Then why? God, Sarah, I swear I will do whatever it takes to be a good husband."

She believed him. But that was the problem; she couldn't be the reason he didn't achieve everything he'd ever wanted.

"Tyler, you're an amazing man," she said carefully, "but you said yourself that you don't have room in your life for a wife and family. You've got a dream, and I can't be the one who threatens it. Right now you're probably wondering if you even *have* a career because of the mess in Illinois, but it won't be long before clients are begging you to design their buildings. You'll be more in demand than ever."

Tyler hiked an eyebrow. "This has nothing to do with Illinois. As for threatening my dream? I've never been so inspired. Ideas are pouring out faster than I can get them down on paper."

"That could have happened anywhere."

"Sarah, listen to me," he said intently. "Deep down I've known there was always something missing in my projects. Now I know what it was. How can I make people's hearts beat faster if my own heart isn't in my designs? It was lost and you found it. And since my heart and soul will always be in Glimmer Creek with you, I'll never become the architect I've wanted to be unless I'm here, too."

Sarah gulped at the raw sincerity in Tyler's face. Her hand fumbled at the door handle and she got out, feeling as if she couldn't breathe.

He was offering her everything. He'd even mentioned children.

The other door opened and Tyler rounded the front of the SUV. "Are you all right?"

"I'm not sure." Sarah's head was still spinning, so she latched on to the first thought that came to her. "You mentioned having kids, but it wasn't very long ago that you gave me a very logical, thought-out explanation for why you *didn't* want a family."

TYLER WINCED.

He suspected countless men had spouted their reasons for not wanting a family, only to discover it was complete nonsense when they met the love of their life.

"Can I plead idiocy?" he asked. "I wouldn't blame you for doubting my sincerity after seeing me with the Forrester twins. But loving you has made me understand why people want children. Not as copies of ourselves, but as wonderful acts of creation we can teach and learn from. And I do mean *learn*. Beth and Annie cut through all the nonsense and wanted to know if I was going to marry you. That was pretty smart of them."

"Kids are artless and say the first thing that occurs to them. It doesn't mean they're sharing a great insight."

Tyler thought about it, then shook his head. "They knew. I think I've always been uneasy with children because they see what I've tried to keep hidden. The way you see me, except now I don't mind. If you're willing to help, I'll do my best to be a good, loving father. I'll even change stinky diapers, though I don't expect to enjoy that part."

The corners of Sarah's mouth twitched. "Stinky diapers aren't an aspect of parenting that very many people enjoy."

Tyler stroked her face, loving her more than ever.

"Trust me," he pleaded. "I'm going to get certified in California and open an architectural office right here in Glimmer Creek. And I'm going to stop traveling so much. When I have to be at a job site, I hope you and our children can go with me, at least part of the time. The only thing I'd ask is that we both take days away from our work and spend them together as a family."

SARAH WAS SILENT for a long minute, wanting to fling her arms around Tyler and never let him go.

Somehow she'd known from that very first wonderful smile that she was going to fall for him. Not that a marriage to Tyler would be easy. She'd have to keep knocking down the barriers he'd built to protect himself, but she could do that. And when she thought about the ways he'd opened himself already, she knew it would be all right.

Some of it she would simply have to take on faith.

But if he thought she was going to just sit idly by and let some commission in Illinois take its time deciding his future, he'd better think again.

"All right, I'll marry you," she said, then stuck her chin in the air. "But we're going to Illinois and making the commission clear your professional name. Rosemary can run things at the sweet shop, and my father can keep an eye on Nathan and make sure he gets to his appointments and does his therapy. Dad will love it— he's a natural mother hen. Those are my terms. Take it or leave it. This time, we're all taking care of *you*."

Tyler grinned and tugged her close. "So the

princess rescues the prince, and everybody lives happily ever after."

"With a few arguments along the way."

"That's okay. We'll have fun making up. *I love you*."

He kissed her and Sarah's last doubts fled. After all, love was the most powerful force in the universe.

The following summer...

Sarah watched her husband grin as he slid into home plate.

"Safe," cried the umpire.

"I tagged him out by a mile," Gabe yelled.

"I said he's safe. Are you arguing with me, McKinley?" Great-Uncle Milt demanded, taking off his umpire's mask.

"Maybe you couldn't see well enough from your angle."

"The call *stands*."

Tyler was still lying on the ground and his grin turned into a hearty laugh. He laughed a lot these days.

Nathan had fully recovered and was back on duty. Tyler's architectural career was also recovering. The commission had absolved him of any responsibility for the building collapse in Illinois, and Milo Corbin had settled out of court on the slander suit. Practically everyone involved was doing court-ordered community service or had been fired. Blame for the collapse had even extended to the county's building office, which had ignored the warning Tyler had sent prior to the start of construction.

Right now he was busy leading the design team for the Glimmer Creek hospital, and had delighted Carlie and Luke with the plan for their new house.

Like Gabe, Tyler was finding his place in the family, along with his mother. Rosemary had become "Aunt Rosie" to kids all over Glimmer Creek. She reveled in it, but was looking forward to her first grandchild even more.

Sarah patted her gently rounded tummy. In another few months Rosemary would be Grandma Rosie.

She locked gazes with her husband as he got up and dusted off his legs. He winked, and she wondered how he'd ever seen himself as an ice man. They still had rough periods when he disappeared into himself, but they dealt with it one day at a time.

It was all right. Perfection would be boring, and she didn't intend for their life to *ever* get boring.

* * * * *

*If you enjoyed this story, be sure to check out
Juliana Morris's earlier books in the
POPPY GOLD STORIES miniseries.*

*Watch Gabe and Tessa spar in
UNDERCOVER IN GLIMMER CREEK
and see Carlie and Luke create their family in
CHRISTMAS WITH CARLIE.*

Available from Harlequin Superromance.

Get 2 Free Books,
Plus 2 Free Gifts —
just for trying the Reader Service!

Get 2 Free Books,
Plus 2 Free Gifts—
just for trying the Reader Service!